LIAR

Olivia Lockhart

For every person brave enough to fall

ONE

AMBER

T he balls of my feet throbbed as I peered out of the staff room window which overlooked the small car park. It didn't seem to matter how much I spent on shoes that claimed to be cushioned, featherlight, soft as air – nothing rid my feet of that tired ache at the end of every shift. A weary, drawn out sigh escaped my lips, the steam from my lemon and ginger tea warming my face as the mug neared my mouth.

The siblings I'd consoled for the past hour, now sobbed in a tight hug next to their respective cars; it had been a tough day for them. I could only hope that my presence, the centre here, had maybe eased the trauma a little when their mother had passed away earlier this afternoon.

Oak Tree Hospice, named for the imposing, beautiful trees that surrounded the building, was a serene and peaceful sanctuary, as odd as that sounds for a place where people came to die. Calmness, dignity, and respect seemed to have been absorbed into the walls. The team here did everything possible to ensure people at their end-of-life journey were comfortable and surrounded by the friends and family they loved.

Physically, this job exhausted me, and mentally, it drained me. But spiritually and emotionally, there was no better reward. It was easier to fall asleep at night, satisfied that you'd made a difference to a person's day, one of their most painful and difficult days.

"Parcel for you, Amber," called Ellie as she entered the staff room, kicked her shoes off, and flopped down onto one of the worn, but cosy, red sofas. Her long, black hair trailed over the cushions as she closed her dark eyes.

I grabbed the package from her outstretched hand with a smile as I opened the card which had been taped on top:

To Amber,
Thank you for all you did for Mum.
Her struggle is over and that gives us peace.
Jack & Roberta Parker

I didn't do my job for the thanks, but they were heartily appreciated, nevertheless. I opened the gift-wrap and found a beautiful deep-green scarf; delicate leaves embroidered around the edges. Green was my favourite colour, I loved to wear it. Compliments hadn't been in abundance when I was young, but I had vivid memories of a kind teacher telling me how my jade party-dress brought out the green flecks in my otherwise blue eyes.

"It's from the Parkers. That's so kind." I said, as I pinned the card to our staff notice board.

"Told you he fancied you," Ellie smirked.

"Ellie!" I snapped. "I'm sure that's not what was on his mind as his mum was dying."

"Shouldn't you have finished an hour ago?" she asked, her forehead wrinkled up in concern.

"Yeah, I just wanted to make sure they were OK." I motioned my head towards the window as the two cars drove away, then took a seat, squashed at the end of the sofa next to Ellie's feet, as I finished my tea.

"You have a whole weekend off, lucky thing. Please tell me you have shenanigans planned?"

I put my now empty mug down on the coffee table and began to rub her feet; it had been a tough shift for us all. "Not really. The house needs a good clean, and then I'm volunteering at The Daffodil Centre on Sunday. The kids there are making Easter baskets, to sell towards the fundraising."

She wriggled her toes at me as she opened her eyes, a tired smile on her plump lips. "One day, Amber, you need to focus on you."

"One day..."

I surveyed the dark circles under my eyes as I brushed my teeth; they were more prominent than they should have been for someone aged twenty-five. I was so tired at the end of the day that skincare wasn't top of my list - bed, book, and a herbal tea, however, were far more inviting. My blonde hair sat just below my shoulders: practical, easy, and in need of a trim. The finer things in life didn't interest me; I'd much rather be the one helping, reaching out. It gave me an inner glow of warmth and security

I'd never met my father, and my mother had passed away from cancer when I was eighteen. That was a big factor in my choice of career, as all through nursing school, I knew it was palliative care I wanted to aim for. Mum's life insurance had paid off the mortgage on our small, two-bedroomed house, and I'd remained here. I was fulfilled with this life, that's what people didn't seem to understand.

I'd confided in Ellie a couple of months back, after a rare beer, that she'd foisted on me in a moment of weakness, that I was still a virgin. She was mortified. Boys, men, guys... I heard the way the other nurses went on and on about them, I just wasn't bothered. I didn't seem to have any urges like they did, no aches in my loins, dirty thoughts, feelings of arousal. It just didn't seem to happen to me, and I wasn't bothered. I sometimes wondered if I was invisible to men anyway, as regardless of my own foibles, nobody had ever pursued me in a romantic sense.

I could see how people were attractive to others, though, I appreciated beauty and kindness, but never had I felt the urge to kiss someone, to ask someone out, to be with someone. Ellie had asked if I was asexual, but I had no idea. It didn't enter my mind until others asked, which they did more frequently than I'd like. It seemed at times like the entire world, save for me, was permanently horny and on the lookout for a mate. I simply didn't need or want anyone to 'complete' me.

I placed my empty cup on my uncluttered bedside table, next to my half-finished book, then pulled my satin eye mask down as I settled under soft blankets and thanked the universe for the day.

I lay in the meadow, rays of golden sunshine warm upon my skin as I stretched my arms up above my head, the satisfaction of the stretch bringing a sigh to my lips. I tugged at the hem of the blue sun dress I wore, anxious it had ridden too high up my thighs. The grass tickled at my skin, and it made me want to laugh with joy, like a toddler let out to play.

"You look so beautiful in that dress," he said. "The exact same shade of blue as the sky."

I glanced to my left and smiled as I noticed the remnants of a picnic behind him, all my favourite things half nibbled across the tartan blanket – cheese, crackers, grapes, strawberries, scones with jam and cream, freshly squeezed fruit juice.

I bit my lip as he leant down towards me, and his blue eyes twinkled with warmth. His mouth was so close I could smell the fresh juice on his lips, and I was entranced. His bright, blond hair fell forwards over his forehead. He was stunning.

I glanced from side to side, confusion plaguing me as I awoke. I was still in my room, of course, and everything was normal, but I could smell the strawberries, it was surreal. I ran my hands down my arms, a frown formed as I felt my warm skin, as though it had been bathed in sunlight.

Sleepily, I dragged my hands down my face in an attempt to shake the grogginess away. Of course, my arms were warm, I'd been asleep under cosy blankets. What was that dream, though? I never usually had vivid dreams like that.

As I twisted my legs around to get out of the bed, my thighs pressed together, and my breath caught for the slightest moment. That felt nice. *Why* did it feel nice? I squeezed them together and felt a warm, lush sensation in my lower stomach, and I wasn't altogether sure I liked it. I opened the window wide, hoping the breeze would blow the memories of that dream away. Everything unsettled me as I hopped into the shower, setting it to cold as I focused on my tasks for the day.

The house was blitzed, spick and span with no clutter in sight. The cleaning spree had been cathartic, and thoughts of boys and picnics had been dusted away; a busy mind was a healthy mind as my mother had always told me.

I ambled into my simple but charming garden, a haven for bees and wildlife with its wildflowers, compost patches, and bird feeders. It had been my only splurge with the life insurance money; I'd had a large, natural lawn laid, whilst the borders nurtured six stunning cherry blossom trees. My bedroom faced the garden and when the trees were in bloom, the blossom would sweep in and scatter across my bed like a floral, pink snowdrift. I could lay there for infinity as it floated into my room, dancing on the breeze.

The season was too early for blossom, but I thought of the trees as year-round friends, silly as that may seem. I leant back against one of them as I bit into a crisp, sharp apple and opened a book. I loved to read but finding the right choice was problematic – romance didn't interest me, crime unsettled me, and high fantasy was too unfeasible. The only genre I seemed able to read was that aimed at a teenage audience. Make believe, targeted at people of an age with no sense of belonging, trying to find their place in the world and all the struggles that come with that. I worked my way through so many of these books, and this was an especially intriguing one. The young girl, about to finish high school, couldn't work out why nothing felt right, why she had strange voices in her head. Feelings and senses far outside of those her friends had. I was eager to know what would happen, how the plot would play out, but right now a snooze under this tree sounded like perfection.

His arms felt like heaven around me. He pulled back, a beautiful smile on his lips. He raised his hand above my head and slowly, seductively, the pink cherry blossom petals fell from his fingers, fluttering in front of me like a cacophony of beauty.

Even though his hand dropped down and took hold of my own, the soft shower of petals continued. He broke through the pink flurry, his thumb rubbing my cheek as his lips moved toward mine, that hair flopped forwards again and hid his bright, blue eyes, just for a second.

Those eyes, it was as though they sang to me, a tune that would guide me home...

I gasped for breath as I sat bolt upright, swiping at my face as I realised an errant leaf had blown onto it that now tickled at my nose. What was going on with these dreams? I blamed Ellie and her talk about shenanigans; she was always chasing after the latest, hottest guy, and had a thing about blonds. He would be just her type.

As I stretched my neck from side to side, I noticed the blue skies had been replaced by dark clouds. Weighty droplets began to fall onto me, but the sensation felt good, it made me feel alive. I tucked my book inside my hoody to keep it safe and then I let the rain drench me. Enjoying the moment, the feel, the power of nature.

Thankfully, the dreams of Blue Eyes, as I named him, seemed to be a one day only occurrence. The rest of the weekend was entirely normal, and I felt a great sense of satisfaction at what I achieved. The fundraising on Sunday had been very positive, so many kids in the city had awful starts in life, and organisations like The Daffodil Club helped keep them on the straight and narrow, giving them a purpose other than loitering around the streets whilst causing trouble for the locals. It was a great way to instil a sense of community in them; community was so important to me. I may have lived alone, but I thought of myself as a cog in a wider machine, we all had to work together to make the place we inhabited healthy and happy. The state of the world destroyed me at times. I couldn't bear to watch the news, I would be in painful tears at the cruelty, the waste, the destruction. It angered me that I was helpless to resolve these things, but at least, in my little corner of the world, I could try.

Work was rewarding but heart breaking, every day, relentless yet unique. People... mothers, fathers, sisters, brothers, sons, daughters... came to us in immense pain, needing our help, often family having cared for them until exhausted and drained. There wasn't the opportunity for us to have a bad day, a lazy day, give less than one hundred percent. Occasionally, whilst waiting for a doctor to sign off medication or hoping for the arrival of a loved one stuck in traffic, I'd catch myself beseeching the universe to speed or slow time, as if I could feel clock hands moving like a scythe over the room. All we could do was ease and comfort, and I put my all into each and every day.

Death wasn't the end of the job; relatives would often need to talk, adjust, and I went further than I should to try and help them. One of the most common reactions I saw, but which was seldom discussed, was relief. How could anyone admit the relief they felt as their loved one passed? Yet compared to the horror of their suffering hour after hour, day after day, of course it was a relief. I'd spent so many of my days off in attendance at funerals, wanting to complete that circle of care I tried to provide. And afterwards, the hospice beds would be full again, and a new circle began.

The hours were long, the pay mediocre, but I couldn't imagine myself doing anything else. I'd never had problems with my focus, no matter how long the shift, this had always been my vocation. But I wondered now, if I was succumbing to a bug or virus, because my head was all over the place.

On Wednesday afternoon I was assigned to a fifty-year-old man in the final days of a stage four, pancreatic tumour. Too young to leave his family, too brave to admit the pain and fear he felt. His wife and mother were taking fifteen minutes to sit under the oak trees outside and compose themselves. We all knew the final few hours were here. His name was Tom, and I held his hand as he dozed in and out of consciousness. I really didn't want him to feel alone.

As I gazed out of the window sunshine flickered through the boughs of the great trees. I closed my eyes, wanting to be at peace in this scene, in the moment.

"You're safe. I'm here for you," a soft voice whispered. My eyes shot open in bewilderment; it was exactly the type of phrase I would use. But *I* hadn't said it. The words almost sounded as though they came from the trees, a ridiculous notion but it felt true.

I looked down at Tom, and although his eyes were still closed, I saw a faint smile on his lips. His tongue flicked out and licked at his parched skin and I pressed a cup of water to his mouth. He gratefully sipped, absorbing mere drops to ease his dryness.

"You heard it, too, didn't you?" he croaked.

"Heard what, Tom?" I spoke softly, as I stroked the hair across his temple.

"My welcome party." He tried to laugh, but the effort brought about a painful spasm of coughs. I rubbed his back and offered more water until he settled back into a steady sleep.

My eyes were drawn back to the window, but now the trees were still, there were no longer whispers or voices. Maybe the stress of this job had finally got to me.

TWO

AMBER

The tasks of nursing revalidation and annual appraisal were due, and today was the day to work through the red tape with Oak Tree's manager, an imposing woman named June. If you conjured up the image of a stereotypical, old fashioned matronly type, that would be June. She took no prisoners; nobody would dare put a foot out of place under her leadership. She seemed to bulge out of her uniform, which she insisted on donning despite the fact she hadn't worked a clinical shift in years. Underneath the harsh bun that held back her grey hair, she had a heart of gold.

"Amber, good to see you," she said with a nod towards the chair opposite her. "How are things?"

"All good. Did you get my email about the syringe pumps?"

"I did, it's with finance. Don't hold your breath, they seem to trim that budget every year." June began to work through the evaluation paperwork with me, it was just a tick box exercise at this point. If she'd had any form of problem with me, or anyone, she would have said straight away; she wasn't the type to hold her tongue.

"All done, just sign here please." She pushed the paperwork over the desk towards me a couple of hours later. "Just one other thing, though, before you go..." I signed my name with a satisfied flourish as I glanced at her, intrigued as to what she needed. "That request last year for an additional bereavement counsellor that was refused, if you recall? Well, they had a U-turn for some reason. I'll email you the details, he'll be here on Monday. Maybe once he's trained up you could go home on time once in a while?" She watched me as she spoke, her hand rubbing at her chin.

"Maybe," I said, non-committedly, as I headed out of her office and straight back to my own to check out this email.

I scrolled past the spam, the annual leave requests, the multiple reminders about the night out planned for pay day, and double clicked the message I'd been hunting for. Ben Hagan, our new bereavement counsellor, he would be the only man in the team. I hoped he happily married and unavailable or there would be a clamour of single nurses vying for his attention. Whatever his age or appearance, he would be a welcome addition; this place got busier each month and we needed an extra pair of hands. I loathed the moments I had to leave grieving families when they still needed to talk and process what had happened, but when there were other patients in need of me, there was no choice. An additional bereavement counsellor would bridge that gap and enable me to take the extra time necessary.

I walked into absolute chaos on Monday morning, when three new admissions arrived at the same time. Unfortunately, two of our housekeepers hadn't turned up thanks to an outbreak of norovirus, which I prayed wouldn't spread any further amongst the staff.

With sleeves rolled up, I began to clean and disinfect room seven as I shouted for other nurses to get to work on rooms nine and ten. At least this work didn't require too much mental effort from me as my mind meandered back to those dreams, in wonder at how vivid they'd been. The memories weren't fading; I could remember them so clearly, even down to the smell of the strawberries, the sensations of warm sun on my skin.

I yanked at the bed sheets in frustration, wanting to get them into the laundry cart so I could dress the bed with clean linen. As I tugged at a particularly stubborn corner, I felt something heavy shift in the bed. I sucked in a deep breath and my eyes screwed shut as cold, pungent urine splashed down my black tunic; the bedpan clattered on the floor, spinning before it settled.

My career had never been glamorous, but I was mortified. The stench seemed to soak into me as the wetness seeped through to my bra. I stood with my arms raised in shock as it dripped down onto the floor that I'd mopped mere minutes ago.

"Erm... Miss Carmichael?"

I twisted around as I heard the man's voice and found myself eye to eye with... him.

My dreams replayed through my mind, somehow in slow motion and double speed all at once. Those blue eyes from the meadow, that blond hair flopped over his forehead just like under the blossom. His lips moved in speech. Were they the same lips that had smelled so sweet at the picnic? Or was I just over tired and emotional?

"Miss Carmichael?" he repeated.

A rush of heat spread from my chest to my forehead as I looked up at him. A little over six feet tall, broad shouldered, his smile, although bewildered right now, was completely charming and caused dimples to form in his cheeks. The blond hair that fell over his forehead curled softly at the ends, as if to showcase the handsomeness of his face. He was so like Blue Eyes from my dream, but I knew that was impossible.

My heart hammered in my chest as I looked down at my wet clothes, anything to break the intensity of his gaze. I wanted to laugh at the incredulity of meeting a person, regardless of if they had or hadn't been in my dreams – whilst soaked through and smelling foul.

I held my hand out, then immediately snatched it back, mortified as drops of dubious liquid splashed onto the floor.

"Amber Carmichael," I said hurriedly. "Can I help you? Are you looking for a patient?"

"I'm Ben Hagan, the new counsellor. Reception told me to look for you." A nervous smile flashed across his mouth and his brow froze in a furrow.

"Of course, Ben, sorry." I coughed and headed over to the sink to wash my hands as I attempted to still my racing mind. "I need to change but you can wait in my office, if that's OK?"

I didn't wait for an answer as I bustled out of the room, holding the door open behind me. I could feel the heat take over my face and I was so frustrated. I needed to get out of this soiled tunic, into something clean, and give myself a good talking to for a couple of minutes. He had blond hair and blue eyes, but that didn't mean he was the man from my dreams.

After showing Ben into my small office, I jogged to the laundry room and grabbed a clean uniform. Washed and fresh, I took a moment to compose my thoughts. This was just coincidence, surely? Those dreams had only even happened because of Ellie going on about her latest beau, no wonder my poor brain conjured up these scenarios. He was just another member of the team and I needed to be professional.

I glanced through my office window as I approached; Ben

had his back to me as he browsed the professional certificates on my office wall. I opened the door forcefully, not wanting to sneak up on him.

"Hope I smell a bit better now." I smiled in apology as I spoke and headed over to my coffee machine which sat on a filing cabinet underneath the window. "Coffee?"

"That's the same model I have at home," he said, nodding towards the machine as I opened the top, ready to add water. "Don't suppose you've got the Odacio pods, do you?"

I twisted the pod holder open to reveal a stack of blue foiled domes. "They're my favourite, how weird! I take it that's a yes, then?"

"Yes," he smiled and ran a hand through his hair. "I would have applied here earlier if I'd known the coffee was this good."

"Ahh, it's not quite so nice in the staff room, I brought this from home, keeps me sane. Just shout any time you need some Odacio-flavoured sanity. I'm more of a tea person, but these are good."

We faced each other across my desk, mugs of dark coffee steaming away as I pulled out the stack of induction paperwork that we needed to work through.

"Have we met somewhere before?" he asked, as thoughtful lines settled between his brows.

"I don't think so." I glanced at his date of birth on the forms and noted he was only six months older than me. "Where did you go to school?"

"Oh, I moved to the area a couple of months ago so it wouldn't be from school. Maybe I've just spotted you around town; you seem familiar."

I didn't want to admit that he was familiar to me too, for juvenile dream-like reasons, so, instead, I began to work my way through the lists of policies and procedures. A loud knock sounded at the door and my pen jarred across the paper.

"Amber, sorry to interrupt," Ellie began, her eyes widened

as she noticed Ben. "Mr Lewis passed over an hour ago, his wife isn't willing to leave him."

"I'll come and talk to her," I said, before turning to Ben. "Best way to learn all this is to come and do it. Let's go and see how Mrs Lewis is doing."

Ben followed me down the corridor to room four, which Mr Lewis had been resident in for three days. For him, it had been lung cancer. It broke my heart to see how bitterly a person could regret their years of poisoning their own lungs once it got to their final act. Mrs Lewis held her husband's hand and whispered to him through tears. Persuading loved ones to leave the room for that final time was often the hardest part of this job. We tried to give as much time and space as we could but there had to be limits. Sadly, there were always more patients waiting.

"Mrs Lewis," I said as I knocked, and cautiously entered the room, "it's Amber. I'm so sorry, is there anything I can do for you? Anyone I can call?"

She smiled kindly up at me as she replied, "He looks peaceful now, his face, the tension is gone. I don't want to leave him though, not yet."

Before I could reply, Ben had pulled up a chair next to her, his hands wrapped around hers. "I'm Ben, it's my first day working with Amber here." He motioned towards me as he spoke. "Why don't you tell me how you met your husband?"

My breath caught in my throat with doubt. She'd just lost her husband and he wanted her to talk about how they met? Yet within ten minutes, Mrs Lewis was hugging Ben as she headed to the relatives' room for a cup of strong, sweet tea. She'd laughed, she'd cried, she'd confided in him – he had achieved in ten minutes what I'd seen more experienced coun-sellors not manage in hours.

"Wow," I said, "you were incredible with her, thank you."

"I'm just good at reading people; I sense what they need.

I'm really, really looking forward to working here with you, Amber."

It was the strangest sensation as a prickly heat flushed up my neck and across my cheeks, I was painfully aware as it spread throughout my skin. Was all of this down to some romantic dreams?

"Likewise," I coughed awkwardly. "I need to make arrangements for Mr Lewis, are you OK to work through that induction paperwork for now?"

"Of course." He smiled and it was as though pure goodness shone out of him. I could sense a kindness, as though serenity flowed within him. My heart raced with anticipation as I scurried away to the nurses' station. I needed to keep busy, not be distracted by him.

It didn't help in any way, shape, or form that the hot new counsellor seemed to be everyone's favourite topic of conversation. I found myself in the role of grumpy nurse, barking orders and tasks just so that I didn't have to listen to the tedious discussions about his dreamy eyes or his toned physique. There was one thing none of them had noticed, though - the way his hair shone golden at the ends as it curled.

Over the next few days, Ben wholeheartedly integrated himself into our work family. The patients loved him, the staff adored him, he was punctual, courteous, compassionate, energetic, everything we could ever have wanted. On a couple of occasions, I caught myself gazing at him and berated myself as I hunted down more work to keep my thoughts from wandering.

I pinned my team's rota onto the staff noticeboard, next to the counsellor's rota, as always. It immediately became apparent that Ben and I were scheduled for the same two days off: Wednesday and Thursday. As my eyes scanned between the slips of paper, a soft sensation surrounded me. The hairs on my arms stood up as if the air were frigid, yet my skin flushed red as though caught in rays of heat. My stomach fluttered and twisted in a way I hadn't felt before and I knew... I knew before the sound waves entered my ear that Ben was talking.

"Spring is my favourite season," he said, low and melodic. "Why don't you come to Queen's Gardens with me on Wednesday? They're magical at the moment, you can almost see the plants bloom to life."

He wasn't touching me, but my skin seemed to think he was. I could feel soft strokes move up my arms, a tickle across my neck which although so delicate, seemed to set me on fire. I turned around to face him, my eyes level with his lips as I looked up into those sky-blue eyes.

"Erm, I'm not sure I should," I stammered. "With us working together and everything, I'm not sure it's allowed."

"Amber, it's allowed," he said, his eyes never leaving mine. They bore into me, as though he was learning everything about me even though I didn't speak.

"OK," I squeaked, my lips dry as my throat sank into an awkward gulp.

"Have you got your phone?" he asked with a smile. Not a confident, cocky smile, not the smile of a man who just got what he wanted. It was a smile of relief, of joy, and warmth.

I pulled my phone from my pocket, he took it and held it to my face as the screen unlocked before adding his number to my contacts. "I know my number will be on my staff file, but I wanted you to have it on a personal level. You can call or text me anytime."

"Thanks..." I was struck dumb. I yearned to say something witty or meaningful, cute even, but I just stood like a foolish kid while his eyes roamed over my face, as if searching, but for what? I didn't know.

"Wednesday then?"

I nodded slowly, drawing my lips together as tension vibrated through my whole body. "Yep, Wednesday."

"That green scarf looked beautiful on you this morning, by the way. Really brings the green flecks out in your eyes."

Ben smiled as he left the staff room. I gawped after him, like a fish out of water. Had I seriously just agreed to go out with him on Wednesday?

THREE
AMBER

I didn't mention my Wednesday plans to a single soul. I wasn't even sure what it was myself, so how could I explain it to friends? Was it a date? Was it a guy new to the area after some company? Did he just want to teach me about plants in springtime? How was I supposed to know? How did people navigate these situations each and every day?

I'd never been on a date in my life, and that didn't bother me. If I sat and thought about it all, I did feel invisible, but it was a strange relief. I saw the way women got whistled at, cat-called, approached in bars and so on, and it would be misery for me, I'd hate it. All through school, college, and work, men had never noticed me, and I was happy about that fact.

Yet, when Ben looked at me, it was as though he peered inside my head. The sensation made me anxious and edgy, but it also summoned a feeling and longing that I struggled to describe. As if I were on the edge of change, a hum spread throughout me, with the potential to grow and overtake me, if I were to let it.

We'd exchanged a few text messages, just to confirm when and where to meet, but other than that, I felt awkward contacting Ben, in case I interrupted or annoyed him. I was torn between being too much, yet somehow not enough, and I began to feel annoyed at myself with how much mental energy I put into overthinking this, energy which could be so much better placed.

The spring sun rose high into the sky on Wednesday morning, spreading warmth and light throughout a perfect blue sky which housed the fluffiest of clouds. I remembered Ben's comment about the green flecks in my blue eyes, something that people very rarely noticed, and so dressed in a long, forest green maxi dress with a simple cream cardigan to keep the spring chill away.

As I waited at the entrance to Queen's Gardens, so named after a visit from Queen Victoria long ago, I took deep breaths of the fragrant air. This was just a walk with a colleague, nothing to be scared about. There was no need for the anxiety that crept around my mind right now.

"Hey." He spoke softly as I pivoted around in the direction of his voice. "Sorry, I didn't want to creep up on you." The top of his nose crinkled up as he smiled, and his blue eyes radiated a sense of calm.

"You didn't. Beautiful day, isn't it?" I squinted at the bright sun as I took in his linen shirt and dark jeans. A section of blond hair had curled around his ear, and just for a moment, I wanted to reach out and free it.

"Ahh, the joys of being British, got to talk about the weather," he joked, as his eyes shimmered in a trick of the sunlight and distracted me from my thoughts. "One more thing we need if we are to truly embrace the Britishness is, of course, tea."

He moved his arm towards me, and I noticed that he carried a cardboard cup carrier. He nodded his head towards the tall cup nearest to me.

"I had to take a guess, but I thought you looked like a

honey citrus girl." He blushed ever so subtly as I took the cup and raised it to my face, inhaling the luscious scent.

"It's one of my absolute favourites, thank you, that's so kind."

"You're welcome. Shall we?" He gestured towards the imposing iron gates which guarded the main entrance, then he pushed the cardboard carrier into a recycling bin and took a sip of his own drink.

We strolled around the gardens over the next hour at a leisurely pace. Ben had been right when he said spring was stunning. He pointed out so many plants and shrubs, showing me the buds in bloom, the subtle changes the incoming season wrought upon the foliage.

"We could have brought a picnic," he said.

A flush spread up my cheeks and I made muffled noises as I threw my now empty cup into a bin.

"What's wrong?" he laughed as he asked. "You don't have to feel embarrassed around me."

"I'm fine, it's nothing. I just... I had a dream about a picnic, so it was weird you suggested it, that's all."

"Oh, really? What kind of dream?" He winked as he asked me.

"Not like that!" I laughed and budged into him with my hip as he guided us towards a wooden bench which over-looked the large lake.

He turned to me as we sat, his eyes large and clear, and something about them seemed to call to me.

"Amber, I don't want you to feel on edge with me. There's no need, I'm not going to hurt you."

My lips pursed together as I listened to his words. "I'm not sure what you mean. We're just having a walk together; I didn't think you were going to hurt me."

He ran a hand through his hair, and I couldn't help but notice his foot tapping against the ground. "I was hoping it might be more than a walk. From the first day I met you at Oak Tree, I've felt drawn to you. I want to get to know you better. I want to let you know me."

I looked down at the grass, buying for time. I definitely wasn't invisible to Ben, and I didn't know what to make of that, how to respond to him. As much as part of me longed to be hidden again, another part resonated with his words. I did feel drawn to him; he'd described it perfectly. But what if I just reacted that way because he was the first person to give me attention like this? I didn't want to make myself, or him, look a fool.

"I'm just..." I bit my lip as I tried to think of the correct words. "I'm not a relationship person, but, if you can deal with my hesitancy, I would like us to get to know each other better."

He cupped my hand in his, a couple of his fingers loosely wrapped around my own. "I can definitely cope with that." He smiled and just for the blink of an eye, reality seemed to shimmer around softened edges. His hand was warm, but I felt a heat above it that tingled as it snaked up my arm.

He surveyed me; his gaze intense as the heat reached my elbow. I yanked my arm away from him with a jerk, as if a bee had stung me.

"You won't feel that way, I'm not like all the other women you will have known. I mean, look at you... you're gorgeous. I'm a sorry excuse for a girl, and then things will be weird at work and—"

"Shh," he whispered, and it was as though my brain responded to him on auto pilot. My words stopped as I listened. "You are beautiful, Amber. I wish you could see what I see."

"What do you see?" I asked, still entranced in the blue of his eyes as they reflected the shimmer of the sun.

"I see someone who is clever, brave, kind, and selfless. A

girl who doesn't know how rare those qualities are when put together. She's beautiful, and it's a natural, timeless beauty that doesn't need to be amplified or shouted about." He ran his finger down my cheek before his head twisted away and he looked to the ground. "Sorry, that was too much. I didn't mean to overstep."

"That's the nicest thing anyone ever said to me," I sighed, in love with the effect his words had on me but truly confused about where they came from.

"It's all true." He stood and offered his hand to me. "Shall I walk you back to your car before I make even more of a fool of myself?"

I giggled as I stood up, a proper girly giggle, very unlike me.

We chatted as we walked and something felt vaguely different, shifted, but I couldn't pinpoint it. It was as if the sharp edges of myself had had their corners curved by his touch, his words. All too soon we arrived back at the car park, and I surprised myself as I wished this didn't have to end quite so soon.

"So," he said, an easy smile on his lips, "I don't know how often the rota will allow us the same day off, but, seeing as we're both off tomorrow..." he paused and gulped, then his words shot out in an urgent flurry, tripping over themselves, "would you like to come round to my place for dinner? I understand if not, don't worry. Or we could meet in a restaurant if you don't feel comfortable at mine?"

"I'd love to come round. I never feel at ease in restaurants, and I hate the way they always ask you if everything is OK with your meal, just as you have a mouthful of food and you're forced to gesture yes or no."

His face lit up with a charming smile, a smile that I was sure would have anyone doing his bidding, but, for some reason, he'd saved it for me.

"Tomorrow, then," he said. "I'm vegetarian by the way, are you happy with one of my finest plant-based creations?"

The strangest, warmest feeling spread across my chest as I replied. "I'm vegetarian too, even better."

He leaned forward and pecked me on the cheek, and time seemed to slow, as if we were travelling through thick treacle. "I know you are, my love." The words echoed around my head, but they weren't from Ben; his lips were still pressed to my cheek and no sounds had escaped his mouth. Had I imagined his voice?

He waved with a coy smile as he headed towards his own car. I touched my cheek where he'd kissed it as I fastened my seat belt. What was this? It made me uncomfortable, awkward, edgy... but I didn't want it to stop.

It turned out Ben's flat was only a gentle stroll from my house, so I meandered there in the late afternoon sun. I'd barely slept last night as I replayed the walk in the park and agonised over everything I'd said and done. Had I been too eager? It certainly felt that way and I didn't want Ben to think I was desperate and lonely, throwing myself at him.

I didn't have an overflowing wardrobe; I'd briefly considered asking Ellie for help but didn't want to confess my plans. I couldn't face the gauntlet of gossip at work. That staff room was like a gossip rag on publication day each Monday morning.

In the end I'd settled on simplicity: Jeans, wedge sandals and a fitted, flannel shirt. I never wore my hair down as it just wasn't practical for work, but today I let it hang loose and fall around my shoulders.

A heaviness settled on my stomach as I rang the bell next

to the small label - *B. Hagan, Flat One*. The others had curled edges and grubby fingerprints, but his looked pristine.

The door opened a minute later, and Ben's smile shone through as I took in the newfound familiarity of his face. His dimples seemed even deeper today, and his hair was fluffy, as though he'd not long since got out of the shower. I could smell oranges, and a peppery citrus tang reached out to me from his skin.

"Amber," he sighed as he spoke, a happy and contented noise. I felt my nose wrinkle in confusion. Why was he so happy to see me? I couldn't comprehend.

I thought back to all the TV shows and movies I'd seen, the nearest to dating I'd been, thinking how people always brought flowers, or a bottle of wine. I was such a klutz.

"I'm so sorry I'm empty handed. I should've brought wine or dessert. I didn't think." My mouth dried out as I waited for his response.

"I didn't need, or want, you to bring anything except yourself." He moved to the side and motioned me inside. "Besides, I don't drink."

"Neither do I," I replied, biting on my lip as I followed him into the ground floor flat. Why did he make me feel all girly and vulnerable; I never got like this.

"Welcome to my humble abode," he said, gesturing around the living room before closing the front door behind us. My shoulders relaxed as I surveyed Ben's flat, a light and airy space with beautiful, classical artwork adorning the walls. The furnishings were simple, yet homey and inviting. There wasn't a television in sight, but my eyes were drawn to an imposing bookcase, where hundreds of books were organised by colour. It was like a literary rainbow, and I adored it.

I took the deepest breath as a feeling asserted itself within me, something I wasn't accustomed to, and my eyes closed of their own accord as I focused on the oxygen that flowed throughout my body. Blowing out a warm breath, I opened my eyes, straight into his. My breath caught as that ache within me grew, firmly centred in the very pit of my stomach. It was a dull throb that I wasn't accustomed to, yet demanded satisfaction, needing to be answered.

"You never wear your hair down," he said, his voice soft as he ran his finger down the fine, honey blonde strands. "It suits you."

I gulped, my mouth open slightly, yet no words formed in my throat. I was sure he must be able to hear my heartbeat as it pounded within me.

Ben's head tilted a little to the left as he watched me, the silence between us deafening. Then he raised his hand slowly, as if I were a wounded animal. I sucked all my breath in as he touched my cheek, his fingers softly caressing.

"I missed you."

I heard the voice, yet once again, I hadn't seen his lips move, just as had happened yesterday. That made no sense, though. I seemed to be carried away in this, in us, in whatever I was imagining this to be. I'd never kissed anyone before, yet an internal pull begged me to kiss Ben. My voice followed ahead of my mind as I heard my words in the air, "I don't know what to do."

His hand swam from my cheek to the back of my head as he pressed his forehead against mine. This close, his eyes merged into one and I felt dizzy as I tried to focus. I let my eyelids flutter closed and then I felt warmth as his lips neared mine.

A softness landed upon my mouth with grace, as if a delicate cotton sheet was held against me. Then, that cotton became the softest down in the world as his mouth pushed against mine. His full bottom lip mirrored my own, his deep cupids bow allowing the tiniest sliver of air to pass into our mouths. We didn't move, it was as though the world stopped

– this wasn't like a French-kiss from a movie where he pushed me against the wall, and we clawed at each other frantically – we simply sank into each other.

It was a timeless moment with no pressure or expectation as we breathed each other in. An image flashed through my mind of a long table under a moonlit sky, a family gathered together. Orange trees blossomed above and filled the air with their scent, their health and richness flowing into the land, into the people - us. Hallow, like family, why did that word float amongst my thoughts?

Then Ben pulled away, his eyes full of hope, yet also fear as they anxiously scanned my face. "Sorry, I didn't mean to..."

"I wanted you to," I reassured him, as I slid my hand into his.

He led me to the dining table and the tight tension of the last few minutes ebbed away. The food he'd prepared smelled luscious. Somehow, he'd chosen my favourites – a vegetable moussaka with the freshest aubergine, alongside light focaccia drizzled with rich olive oil.

We chatted familiarly as we ate, and I told him more about the city while he made me laugh out loud with tales of his escapades at university. I couldn't deny the pull towards him that bloomed within me, but concern accompanied it. Was this entrancement part of an act, a ploy he used to seduce women? I didn't want to be one of those women, part of a list.

"Crème Anglaise?" he asked, as he held a white, porcelain jug over my bowl.

I nodded, still smiling shyly, and motioned for him to stop as the vanilla scented custard flowed over the sweet pastry dessert he'd prepared.

"Ben," I began, "I don't know what this is." I motioned between us. "I'm not the type of girl you should be pursuing."

"I'm not interested in 'girls'," he replied, as a slow breath escaped his lips. "I'm very set on what I want."

"Me?" I felt like an absolute idiot for asking, but I needed to know.

He nodded. "You feel a connection between us, don't you?"

I drew in a deep breath once more and the scent of him flew back into me with an ache. An ache that I sensed wouldn't settle until it was satiated.

"I do, but Ben, I'm..." I gulped as I let my dessert fork clatter to my plate. "I'm a virgin. I don't do this. I don't know what I'm even doing here. I will not be enough for you."

He placed his own fork down and took hold of my hand. Instantaneously, a heat flourished up my arm, warming every muscle, tendon, and vein. "Why do you think that's something to be ashamed of?" he asked. "I think it's perfection in itself. I know what crosses your mind, that I'm out to seduce you, that you are one in a long line. But nothing could be further from the truth."

I sucked my bottom lip as I surveyed him across the table. That ache between my thighs had returned; I felt damp and full of angst and wanting. I had nothing to say, and if he'd asked, I would have lain back and let his hypnotic words wash over me.

He continued to speak. "I've only made love to one person. One person, Amber. And I truly, truly loved her with everything I had and would ever be. But she was taken from me."

His eyes cast down towards the table, heavy with regret, and I instinctively reached out for him, my fingers cupping his chin. "I'm so sorry. I guess that makes sense why you became a bereavement counsellor?"

"Not everything is lost forever, though. Some things are reborn." His words were melodic, and I felt that pull towards him grasp me tighter. "Amber... We can't rush this. Let me walk you home."

A shiver ran throughout me as forces shifted within the room. "There's no need. It's only ten minutes away."

"There's two needs," he smiled, as he responded. "First, I love being outside under the stars. Second, I need to know you're home safe."

The world was silent as we walked, a faint spring frost had stilled the streets. Ben's fingers wrapped around mine as our breath mingled and intertwined ahead of us. The night sky was so clear, and it seemed as if every individual star twinkled with a brighter light than normal as it guided us on our journey.

I slowed as we approached my house and Ben smiled at me, sweeping his hand through my hair again to move it back from my face. "Can I show you something?" he asked as he moved behind me, one arm wrapped around my stomach. His chin rested on my shoulder, and I felt him take a deep breath. "See that star, the brightest one?"

He took my hand and pointed it towards a glittering, sparkling speck in the dark sky. I nodded. "I see it."

"That's Arcturus. From here, it's almost always visible in the night sky. It's my favourite, I don't like fleeting things, passing trends. Things that last, things with meaning, they're what matter." He kissed the top of my head with the softness of silk, and turned me around. "Sleep well, I'll see you at work."

"Goodnight, Ben." I moved out of the warmth of his body and immediately longed to be with him again. The front door always swelled as the seasons progressed, as if the wood soaked in the changes. I tried to look graceful as I pushed against it with my shoulder, blowing my hair out of my eyes.

Ensconced back inside my home, I closed the curtains, leaving just the tiniest gap, as I watched him walk away. The warmth in the centre of my chest still burned, and as much as I didn't like the anxiousness, I also longed for that heat to spread and grow.

The sweetest dreams found me that night, dreams of running through orange groves in the evening sun as the warm rays and delicious smells soaked over me. A time of innocence and love that should have continued longer than it did.

FOUR

ANWIR

I slammed the door as they scurried out, tails between their legs. I felt the resistance as it caught one of them and knocked them onto their knees, but I didn't care. They were an annoyance, an absolute waste of my time. My hands balled up into tight fists as though every muscle in my body was coiled, brimming over with lactic acid as they waited to move in the ways they longed to, but the physical cramps were nothing compared to the pressure inside my mind.

Nobody understood the duress I was under, what it was like to suffocate with this burden, this stigma, all caused by *him*. The lesser ones were supposed to help me find her, but they'd done little except waste my time with false sightings and stupidity. How could it be so hard? The human plane grew sicker and more twisted by the day; surely spotting pure good wasn't that fucking hard?

One more moment in this room and I was sure I'd begin to tear my hair out; the air was stifling and rotten with the decay of the others who lived here – my terror, my demonic family. They nauseated me; they were nothing more than shared history. I'd wipe them out if I could. Anything that tied me to *him* needed to be drained and purged. The house was practically in ruins, mould grew along the damp stone and the dirt floor concealed years of grime. There was nothing of comfort here, nothing to love, nothing to miss. Just tattered furniture, bad memories, and an utter void of dreams.

Of all the terrors to be born into, why did it have to be this one? The one with the failure at its head, the biggest fuck-up of them all. The fact I shared his blood sent waves of repulsion from me every time I tried to move on in life. I was sick of it, all of it, and with nothing good in my life, I had nothing to lose. And that's why I was going to fix this, end *her*.

After a brisk walk, I relaxed back in a curved seat, hidden at the back of my favourite bar. The sky was grubby and milky, no clear view of the stars, pretty much the norm in this plane. I added to those clouds as I blew out hot air from my lungs, watching as it billowed and pulsed into steam within the coldness. I glanced down at the woman's head as she unfastened my trousers and put her mouth to work. Maybe not everything about this plane was that bad, at least we didn't suffer the ridiculous emotions of shame and guilt just for enjoying our bodies and their natural needs.

I closed my eyes as she continued, the sensation a welcome distraction from the epic failure that was my life – thanks to my father. How was it he had died before I was born, yet had still cursed my entire existence?

My nails scraped at her scalp as she moved up and down me, a perverse part of my brain wondering how much of her DNA would collect underneath them. I pressed her down, hard onto me. In no way caring of her discomfort, this was a simple transaction in physical pleasure.

Just as I touched the back of her throat and relished in the resulting gag, it happened. One tiny, solitary flare of dusky orange rose above the human plane, most people would barely register it, but I knew instantly: I knew it was her. The precursor to everything else that was to come. She was awakening and I would end her before the process was complete. I'd finish what that cowardly shit had been unable to, fix this fucked-up destiny, end whatever pathetic prophecy still floated around the insides of this doomed existence.

As I sprang to my feet, the woman fell backwards to the floor. I didn't spare her a thought as I straightened my clothes and sprinted home, determined not to allow my thoughts to gather too densely.

Locked in the bathroom I rubbed my elbow across the dirt that coated the tarnished mirror on the wall, briefly appraising my appearance in the smears; a face only a mother could love. Except here, even the love of a mother wasn't guaranteed.

I focused intently as I pulled on the threads that connected my realm to theirs, and the shift began.

The pressure of the transition dropped me to my knees as bones bent and cracked, preparing themselves for the vessel they would inhabit. My soul screamed as it slid into one of those weak, human shells of indifference. I closed my eyes against the force for fear they would implode with the strain. I'd always hated this journey; hence I usually sent the lesser ones, but now I'd seen the signs of her, it needed to be me, it *had* to be me. My hands tensed against my skull, trying to alleviate the warring forces as I bawled to the point where I could take no more. A silence and a stillness encapsulated me. Serenity flowed briefly... briefly...

The only way we could inhabit a human body was to catch in it that fleeting instant that flickered between life and death. Fortunately, the human realm was so packed that there would be always someone on their final, gasping breath. I simply slipped in as they departed, none the wiser. It did mean that the host body was a lucky dip, and those of us who travelled to the human realm were adapt at amateur dramatics as we blended in with whatever scenario we found ourselves a part of. We were unable to hurt a human to get to their realm, but once in it, so long as you stayed under the radar, a whole world of joys opened up.

My eyes slammed open as the stench assaulted my nostrils. Trees, mammals, insects, life, oxygen... it flowed into me, and I struggled not to retch at the obscurity of it all. I felt squashed, condensed, weak and pitiful, too soft and rounded.

The air was pure, the toxic taints of my plane left far behind, and although these human lungs were able to handle that purity, I still felt the panic wash over me as I acclimatised. I squatted to the ground, my head in my hands as I controlled my breaths, composed my mind. It had been so long since I'd taken a body on this plane, I'd forgotten how vile the process and finished product was.

A shiver ran through me as I straightened and looked around. I seemed to have shifted from one bathroom to another, although my own would be unrecognisable as such when compared to this. A bright, lit mirror hung in front of me above a tall, porcelain white sink which I grasped onto with whitened knuckles. As I glanced at my new reflection, I was taken aback. Although we had no choice about the dying body we flew into, they were normally old or sick, and we'd be classed as one of those miraculous recoveries from injuries, or an awakening from a coma. This time I appeared to have found a specimen in the prime of his life. A male body, always my preference, tall, strong, maybe thirty years old, his thick, dark hair swept to one side above intense, brown eyes. He had white teeth, full lips, arched cheekbones... from my previous interactions on this plane, I knew he would be desirable. I, however, planned to be out of the body within a couple of weeks, at which point it would die, as it should have done this evening, and be of no concern to me anymore.

I patted down his pockets, now my pockets, and found a wallet and a phone. The wallet contained a lot of plastic, but it was only the name I desired. It was a habit I had. I liked to know the names of the bodies I took possession of; I collected them like trinkets, mementos, and this one was called Mason Donoghue according to the multiple cards I pulled out. Stupid name for a stupid race, and I couldn't be bothered with them. She was my one reason to be here, and I wouldn't forget that. I wouldn't be like *him*.

Just as I wondered what had killed a young, apparently healthy man, I glanced down to the glass shelf under the mirror and noticed the fine, white powder that seemed to glitter for my attention. Two straight, horizontal lines lay across the shelf, whilst abandoned next to them was a rolled-up bank note, the end of it dusted with the same substance. While I was here, and this body was technically dead anyway, there seemed little harm in partaking.

Blowing out a long breath as the drug settled into my bloodstream on its hazy, happy journey, I smiled at my new reflection. Was it possible I'd hit the jackpot with this possession? Were things finally going my way? Surely it was owed to me after all these years of utter misery?

I strolled out of the bathroom, caution abound despite my brain being lit up with endorphins, having no idea what I might walk into at this moment. I was in an apartment, and it was luxurious in ways I'd never seen. The living area was encapsulated within long glass windows that looked down upon a city below. A city that hummed and throbbed with filth, greed, jealousy, and lust. How was ours the plane with the twisted, perverse reputation when this one was so fucked-up? The apartment had all the trappings that should provide comfort: large sofas, gadgets of every imagining, and oversized pieces of art which lined the light walls. Yet, it felt no more homely than the shithole I'd just left. Filling a space full of expensive crap did not make a home, another thing the humans didn't seem to grasp.

Now, all I needed to do was watch for the signs, blend in, seek out her aura, her scent... and then wipe her from existence. I was undecided of the best way to do this. Should I follow from a distance, ingratiate myself into her life? So many options. It was vital that nothing distracted me from my focus and not just because of that cursed prophecy. I held little belief in its words, but I wanted to prove that I was not my father, and I would not let the angel get away. Not on my watch.

"Mason?" A sultry, welcoming voice called out. I twisted around in the direction I sensed it came from. "When are you coming back to bed? We're bored."

A smirk slid up one side of his mouth, *my* mouth, as I headed towards the voice into a large room in which more windows displayed the city view below. That view was the least of my thoughts as my eyes strayed to the oversized bed and the two women curled up together within it, who, when they saw me, beckoned me with open arms.

Screw distractions, I'd hit gold with this possession, and what was one night in the grand scheme of things?

FIVE

AMBER

My nerves were shot by the time I arrived at work, and I couldn't decide if it was due to excitement or dread. Ben was working today, I wanted to see him, but, at the same time, I was petrified to see him. How did people cope with these feelings and emotions running through them all the time? I was exhausted.

The hospice was full once again and Ben spent most of the day with a family who had lost their youngest daughter to cervical cancer. So much death passed through this place, and we had our ways to deal with it, cushioned by the fact we did everything in our power to make each passing as comfortable as we could for both the patient and those left behind. There was a stark difference, though, between losing a patient who'd lived a full life, to losing one whose life had barely begun.

The mood throughout all the staff was sombre as the shift finished and the night team came on duty. I watched her parents and sister leave the building; the pain radiated from them in waves. It was as though their pain crashed into me, physically hurting me. I clutched my stomach as a tide of nausea rolled over me and caused me to close my eyes as I snapped the blind down. All I could see was devastation, and the hopelessness sent me into a spin which caused my breath to shake and my hands to tremble.

Arms wrapped around me, firm, and grounding. Somehow, I knew they were Ben's. I turned and buried my head into his chest as my tears fell, frantic and unbidden, hot, angry, consumed with sorrow and fury and loss all mingled into this horrific tangle that burned at me, tore at my soul. How could life be this unkind, this cruel? When there was so much bad in the world, but young innocents like her were taken mercilessly, leaving never-ending pain for her family.

His scent was like a security blanket around me. I lost track of how long he stood steadfast with me as my tears soaked through his shirt. Slowly, he loosened his grip and I backed away, inch by inch as I looked up at him. "I'm sorry," I said, my voice weakened by emotion.

"Don't say sorry. I understand."

I sniffed and pulled a tissue from the box on my desk. "How are you? That must have been a tough day for you, too?"

He tilted his head to one side as he observed me, and narrowed his eyes. "Yep, but days like these... They just remind me that we have to enjoy life; we have to make the most of our time." He reached out and took my hand. "Please can I see you tonight? We shouldn't waste time, it's so precious. We could be special; I know we could."

"I'd be rubbish company—"

Ben placed a soft finger across my lips to silence my objections. "As if you could ever be. Come with me, let's go watch a movie, stuff ourselves with popcorn, escape reality for a couple of hours?"

He squeezed my hand, and that heat began to surge upwards once more. I struggled to understand the sensation. I'd heard people talk about a warm feeling but having never known anyone romantically, I had nothing to judge this against. It seemed like it was too hot, as if it would burn me. I was drawn to the feeling, yet hesitant of it all at once. I nodded in agreement and let him lead me from the building. It didn't occur to me to worry that people might see us holding hands, I just needed to be away from here and his presence soothed me. In my mind, it was as though his aura spread itself over mine like a protective gauze, still allowing me to breathe as it softened the harsher emotions.

The short car journey passed in silence, but not an awkward silence that needed to be filled, just a silence of understanding, of ease. I wiped the last stray tears from my cheeks as I added the young woman, Rebecca, to the list of those in my mind that I would never forget, but could also not dwell on, not if I were to continue to help others.

I breathed a sigh of relief as Ben turned into the car park outside a small boutique cinema. I was so glad he'd chosen this place and not the big multiplex in town. This was far more comfortable; small, intimate, quiet, very us. Was I really considering 'us'? He took hold of my hand again as we headed inside.

"Sweet or Salty?" he asked, as he motioned towards the popcorn stand.

It was a simple question that shouldn't have caused my mind such a problem, but I wanted to answer the right way, to please him. I cursed myself for being so silly. This debate in my thoughts had only been going on for a few seconds but he watched me with an intensity. "Erm... could we get a mix?" I blurted out.

Ben nodded and I turned my phone off as he bought the popcorn and tickets before we headed into the auditorium: screen two. The cinema had cosy, velvet sofas for two, separated from the others for privacy. He checked the tickets and led us to dark, purple seats on the left-hand side, about halfway up. There were only a handful of people in here and I was glad; I didn't want to be surrounded while I felt emotionally vulnerable. I struggled in crowds at the best of times.

"I didn't even ask what the movie is," I said, as I turned to him. I was trying very hard to stay distant, not get attached, but there was something undeniable about him. As he turned his face towards mine, I felt sucked into his gaze. I couldn't pull myself away, nor did I want to. Then, as the corners of his mouth rose into a beautiful smile, I couldn't help but mirror it. My cheeks burned as his full attention was on me and all I could do was smile back like a fool.

"It's the new one with The Rock, it's meant to be funny," he replied. His eyes flicked to my lips. "Didn't think you'd want something too serious."

"Perfect choice." He looked at my mouth as I spoke, and I ran my tongue over my bottom lip nervously, in case there was something there. "Are you OK?"

He nodded at me, his smile gone, a focused frown set on his forehead. "I want to kiss you every time I see you, Amber..."

Just then the lights dimmed, plunging us into blackness as the projector at the head of the room began to whirr. I felt his breath at my mouth as he leaned towards me and before I could allow my mind to overthink, I mirrored him.

This time I kept my eyes open, able to see the blueness of his eyes, even in the dimmed room. Neither of us moved as our lips grazed, our breath mingled into each other. My chest felt alive, as if I were going to flutter up to the celling with the joy of this sensation. That heat flowed through me again and I had to now admit that I wanted it, I wanted more of him. Maybe I'd end up heartbroken or looking like an absolute fool, but surely it would be worth it for more of this? I ran my fingers up into his hair and he sighed as his lips moved against mine, pressing tiny kisses from side to side, up and down, growing slowly firmer. He pressed his lips to the tip of my nose, and I couldn't help the giggle that escaped my mouth at the cuteness of the action.

A cough sounded out from behind us, loud and over exaggerated. Ben and I laughed quietly as we sank down into the plump cushions, our fingers entangled, bodies leant against each other as we settled to watch the movie. Even the popcorn was forgotten. Nothing could be as good as this.

After the movie, Ben drove us back to his. We were both quiet but again, I felt no awkwardness alongside it. Just a warmness, an anticipation. "Are you hungry?" he asked, as he took my coat and hung it on a tall stand alongside his own.

"Honestly, another hug would be better than food," I said, keen to feel his warmth once more. He crossed to me, a tender smile on his face as his arms wrapped around me. We were so still that time flowed over us as if we were elsewhere. The thoughts in my head that hurt seemed to soften, as if aeons of sand blew over them, rounding their sharp edges down.

Finally, I felt my breath flow free; my heart had slowed, my spirit calmed. I rubbed my hand up Ben's back and stroked my fingers tentatively into his blond hair, which curled loosely at the ends.

"Do you like to dance?" he whispered into my ear, as he walked us towards the patio doors and opened them wide.

"I've only ever danced alone." A glut of embarrassment hit me.

"Amber..." He rubbed my arms as we stepped into the darkness outside. "I told you, don't be ashamed of who you are, be proud. There's a reason for everything, I promise."

He pulled his phone from his pocket and swiped at an

app; two deep lines appeared between his eyebrows as he focused. Sorry," he mumbled, "not used to this contraption yet."

Then a beautiful melody began to play and I recognised it instantly. One of my favourite pieces of music, Chopin's Nocturne Op.9 No.2, I had no idea if he knew it was a favourite or if this was just a delightful coincidence. All thoughts drifted from me at that point as we began to dance.

My very first dance with a man, with anyone, to be honest. I'd always been far too shy to dance in public. It was a clear night and a multitude of stars twinkled above us as I glanced up. Ben stroked the side of my face with a soft fingertip and then pulled me closer to him, my face nestled into his neck as he stroked my skin. We began to sway in small circles to the music, lost in the moment, in the feeling. The cold air was kept at bay by that heat which now ran unbidden through all my limbs. It still scared me, but I wanted to explore it more, so we danced. Slowly, sensually - as much as I knew, anyway – absorbed in the moment and each other.

Time had blurred, the music had faded away. I felt Ben's breath, hot against my ear as he whispered, "May I kiss you again?"

I lifted my head from his shoulder and smiled at him shyly, then I nodded. The flutter in my stomach began to vibrate as it spread up and into my chest. He pulled my hands to his, holding them tightly within his own as he leaned forwards and kissed me.

His lips glanced against mine and I could only think of the star, Arcturus, that he'd pointed out to me. I focused on it, his lips soft and slow, whilst the star simply twinkled its light towards me. I gasped and he took the encouragement. His touch became firmer, his hands gripped me, held me to him. As the moment progressed, it was as if I were flying towards the star, faster with each movement of his mouth.

He walked us inside, closing the door with one hand as his other rested on my hip, his lips not stopping for a moment as he pressed soft kiss after kiss to my own, leaving me longing for more.

"Is this OK?" he asked.

"Yes..." I was shocked by how breathless I was. Our fingers were tangled like tree roots and the strangest realisation hit me, they looked too long; I couldn't understand it. I loosened my own from his and held them up in front of me, my face scrunched up in confusion.

He clasped his hands back around mine quickly, focusing my eyes on him. "Try not to worry, just trust in this."

"I..." I sighed, allowing myself to sink into his eyes once more. "I have no reference point for this, Ben. Is this normal? I don't know what I'm doing."

"Don't overthink." He leant forwards and resumed the kiss. I sucked a deep breath in as he traced the edge of his tongue against my teeth. I moved against him and now... now it felt like we were in one of those movie moments. He pressed me back against the sofa, then his hand trailed up into my hair and clasped it greedily.

The heat began to burn at my joints, in every description of passion I'd ever read or heard; this hadn't been mentioned and it concerned me, distracted me. I had an ache within me as I wanted more of him, yet this sensation hurt, a hot pain that flashed through me.

"I missed you..." He sighed the words into my mouth as our tongues pressed together in heat. I didn't understand what he meant. He'd only known me a short time, how could he miss me? The kiss was taking me over and any drive in me was not from my mind right now. My stomach somersaulted, my toes curled up, and my fingers begged to be let loose on him.

I slid down on the sofa and he manoeuvred above me, holding himself up on strong arms, his mouth never leaving mine. He bit gently on my bottom lip and as his teeth nibbled, I mindlessly moaned his name. Utter mortification hit me like a sledgehammer, but his name on my lips seemed to draw something out of him.

"Mireille..." he moaned in return as he pressed his whole body against me, an obvious erection hard against my thigh. I froze at the name, a name that wasn't mine. Was I so naïve? I sat up, missing his head by millimetres as I pushed him away.

"What the..." I stood, running my hand through my hair as he coughed and took a deep breath. "Get me confused with someone else? I knew this was too good to be true."

"Stop, you don't understand..." He scrambled up and reached for my hand, but I snatched it away.

"Am I just a joke to you? Was it a bet to see if you could seduce the dull virgin from work?" I snapped, as tears burned bright behind my eyes.

"Of course not, don't say that! It will all make sense if you just trust me... Please?"

I didn't speak for a long minute as my eyes darted all over him, then around the room, searching for signs of another woman, or of this encounter being in pity. He took hold of my hands and I looked down at the floor as feelings of inadequacy and stupidity flooded over me in droves.

"Who is Mireille?" I asked in a subdued tone, as I tried to fight back the tears that stung in my throat.

Ben sighed as his thumbs rubbed over the backs of my hands. "The woman I lost..."

"I'm sorry that you lost her, but I can't replace someone. I'm not her, I can't be her."

His eyes bore into mine as I looked up, and he raised a hand and stroked my cheek. "What if I told you that you were her?"

I stepped back in frustration. "I don't believe in all that reincarnation stuff. Why are you doing this?"

"I'm sorry, I've rushed in. Stay, Amber. Stay for some food?"

I shook my head as I backed towards the coat stand and lifted my jacket down with fumbling fingers. "I'm going home. I don't think you know what you want, and I don't want to be part of that."

"Amber, please, don't go."

"I'll see you at work... Bye, Ben."

I rushed out of the building as those tears began to flow, hot and acrid against my face. Consumed with thoughts of how stupid I'd been, how much simpler time was when I didn't feel attraction. Because even now, after just a few kisses and hours together, there was an echo within the hollow of my heart, and I didn't know what to do with the coldness that resided within it.

Six

Possessing a human like this was different every time, as you never quite knew the fight their mind would put against you. This guy, Mason, his body was strong, hence the pain as I'd inhabited it, but his mind was weak. I had access to his memories, his skills, the things that made him 'him'. Some humans managed to partition themselves off, block these elements, but not Mason.

He had a strange set of values, success for him seemed to be work himself into the ground all week, purchase luxurious items he didn't need, then drink himself into a stupor all weekend whilst sleeping with as many different girls as possible. This lifestyle did have its benefits for me, though, in the forms of a penthouse apartment that I could use as a base while I sought her out, and access to all those sexual encounters. Whilst I didn't want to be distracted, it would be ridiculous to waste the opportunity to try out this way of life.

I'd been at Mason's job all week, putting in the bare minimum effort, the only highlight being the discovery of an affair with one of the female executive directors – twice this week she'd called me to her office for an urgent 'meeting'.

He had skills that could help me, and I planned to harvest every one of them. The thing I found most useful in his brain, was the knowledge of how to 'Google'. I spent most of my time Googling this city I'd found myself in, looking for any clue that might lead me in her direction. I searched for news articles on prophecies, strange phenomena, unexplained events and so on, but nothing stood out. I even checked back two hundred years for any stories that seemed out of place but discovered zilch. Whoever had hidden her after that attack had done a solid job. The lack of progress jarred me; patience wasn't my strength.

I needed another sign, no matter how small, and as that would only happen when *they* made moves, the best course of action appeared to be a watchful wait. It made sense to have a little fun for now. Plus, the effect that alcohol had on the human brain never ceased to amaze and amuse me.

I assumed there was meant to be a specific time that people left this god forsaken office, but I'd had enough. I headed across the street to the dimly lit bar which I'd seen from the office window and ordered a beer. I wanted a shot of vodka, but it would be gone too quick. The beer would last longer and allow me more time to peruse the establishment.

I felt the admiring glances of women, and quite a few men, everywhere I went. Luck had been on my side when I landed in this body, it was perfect. Women seemed unable to resist Mason with his tall, dark, and handsome vibe, plus I suspected the obvious bulging bank balance helped.

The beer refreshed me after a day glued to a computer screen, but I needed something more. I surveyed the room as I leant back against the bar, a woman, low-cut dress and jet-black hair, watched me. I smiled as I raised the bottle to my mouth and took a long drink, tilting my head back a little further than I needed to. I ordered a bottle of champagne and made sure to flash Mason's black AMEX card as I paid. Then I simply relaxed - three, two, one...

"Hi, I haven't seen you here before. I'm Jasmine," she said as she sat at the bar stool next to me.

"Mason." I looked her up and down. It was rude and obvious, but I didn't care. If she had any self-respect, she'd probably object, but her eyes were on the champagne as I poured a glass and handed it to her. "So, what do you do, Jasmine?"

She drank before she answered, licking the bubbles from her dark red lips. "I'm a surveyor, and you?"

"Something boring to do with money," I said, grinning at her as I settled into the rhythm, confident that she'd be in my bed later that night.

The bar filled up over the next hour or so and as the alcohol seeped into my brain, making this hazy and somehow easier, my eyes continued to peruse the clientele, always on the lookout for the next best option to make my night interesting.

"Have you got more champagne back at your place?" Jasmine asked, interrupting my appraisal of a group who'd just stumbled in, arms linked together.

"I do," I replied, as I ran my finger down her arm. Maybe tonight I didn't have to go through the effort of choosing my favourite, she was already so willing.

"Shall I get us an Uber?" she asked, her eyes sparkling with hope.

I nodded confidently whilst I rummaged through Mason's mind for the knowledge of what an Uber was – I didn't recall this term from my last trip to the human realm. As it turned out, I didn't see much of the Uber anyway as Jasmine threw herself on me the minute we were seated. I mumbled my address to the driver as she straddled my knee and roughly pressed her lips against mine.

Fornication with humans was nice, don't get me wrong,

I'd tried pretty much everything going with both men *and* women, but I always sensed something was lacking and I'd never been able to pinpoint it. It was like a nagging in the back of my head that there should be more. As if I was drinking decaf filter coffee when actually, out there somewhere, was a double shot cortado with my name on it.

Jasmine wasn't on the receiving end of my best work; my mind was too split. Yet she still moaned with appreciation at my every touch. The drama of her annoyed me, the overacting. Did this really boost a human man's ego to have women act this way? Stereotypical displays of fake lust, fearful to claim what they really wanted. I pushed two fingers between her lips to quieten her as my mouth ran down her stomach. I did have to admit to the taste of humans pleasing me, once they were fully aroused, at least.

She pressed against me as my tongue moved inside her, but fate was on my side as I glanced up and out of the floor-to-ceiling glass... that tiny orange light had just flared again and it was close.

I sprang up, shoving Jasmine away from me as I almost tripped in my haste to grab my jeans and hop awkwardly into them whilst simultaneously tugging a T-shirt over my head. Jasmine looked furious; words flew from her mouth, but I didn't listen. My focus was entirely on that flare as I slid my feet, Mason's feet, into brown leather boots and ran to the elevator, anxiously counting seconds as a heat ran from my head down to my toes. I was going to find her; it was almost too much for me to process after the years of shame my father had brought to us. The thought of this, however, did nothing to tame the erection that persisted awkwardly as I fastened the buttons of the jeans.

That tiny flare, so insignificant to everyone else on my plane, had been about six miles north of here. I could run, I could figure out an Uber, but a quicker option presented itself as the elevator doors opened. An unlucky pizza delivery guy swung his leg over the bike, keys still in the ignition, and like a shot I shoved him to the ground.

I was gone in a flash before he even realised. I didn't know these roads at all, but apparently Mason had ridden a motor-bike and I used his memories to process the functions. My own mind focused on the location of that flare.

My heart galloped as I pulled into a tidy street, hidden impulses awakened within me at the thought that she was near. I could sense her; she was enjoying herself...

My teeth scraped at my bottom lips as I rested the heavy bike against a wall with little care. I'd been vaguely turned on by Jasmine but now the ripple that spread out across this area, a wave of sexual longing, was driving me to distraction.

Suddenly, a door slammed, and that longing was crushed under the impact of a fist as it, instead, turned to smothered emotion. A girl, a woman, ran from a house and crossed the road, I could hear her sobs, smell the salt from her tears. I was entirely in the shadows here and didn't dare move in case she saw me. She looked up to the stars then wiped her tears onto her sleeve. Something about the action seemed so innocent, that it gave me a strange sensation, nearer to my heart than was comfortable. She was average height with shoulder length, fine, blonde hair, not dressed extravagantly; it looked like a fairly sensible ensemble. She suddenly glanced back at the building she'd exited in such a hurry and began to walk slowly.

I pursed my lips. It didn't bother me if she walked home alone, but normally human women would be cautious at night-time, the risks to them from their male counterparts being far more numerous than any danger from my plane. I couldn't see any obvious signs emanating from her to hint that she was the one, but she looked emotional and that could have caused the brief flare I saw in the essences that connected the realms. What could have made her change from a state of arousal to anxiety, so quickly?

She wandered as she wiped her eyes and muttered. I followed; she was unlikely to spot me in the dark anyway, but I pulled a minuscule amount of power around me to add to the depth of the shadows. After ten minutes or so, she stopped in front of a tidy house and began to rummage around in her coat pockets, I presumed for keys, as she then headed through a small gate and let herself into the dark building. A scrap of paper fluttered down to the ground from her pocket as she closed the door behind her. I waited until I saw the upstairs lights come on, then vaulted over the garden gate and crept along the path, snatching the paper up and closing my fist around it before I hopped back to the street.

I huddled in a bus stop, just a few metres away and on the opposite side of the road. I could see her house clearly from here, the lights having all gone out again – had she gone straight to bed? There weren't signs of anyone else living there, I'd have been able to hear if she'd called out in greeting as she went inside.

I loosened my fist and held the paper up to read:

Monday – Earlies
Tuesday – Earlies
Wednesday – Day Off
Thursday – Day Off
Friday - Nights

It seemed to have been torn from a larger piece, and I assumed it to be a list of shift patterns, its words written in curled script, leaning towards the right. Along the top of the paper was a printed image of a tree, with an address and telephone number plus website details. *Oak Tree Hospice...*

I smirked to myself as I jumped up and jogged back home, hoping that Jasmine would have let herself out by now. After-all, I had research to do and I didn't want to be distracted...

SEVEN

AMBER

The night seemed endless. I tried to sleep but my mind wouldn't stop. My thoughts swung wildly between the awful day at work, then onto the absolute pleasure I'd felt with Ben, and then the horror as I digested another woman's name. I tried meditation, herbal tea, an audiobook... nothing made me sleep.

Thankfully, I was on a late shift the next day; exhaustion encased me as the sun rose and the day began. I leant against the glass shower screen as hot water cascaded down me in rivulets, the steam billowing and filling the small room, I hoped the heat would massage my brain to life. I tried to focus my mind on the fact that Ben had already let me down, but all I could think of was how it felt to be beneath him, his lips on mine, his hands firm on me, his breath hot and full of need...

My teeth bit into my lip as I closed my eyes and thought of how he felt. I'd never experienced arousal before, this was all new. I hadn't expected it to be so... consuming, and I replayed it over and over in my mind. It was as though my body had been numb before and he had awakened it. This body had never been anything but functional to me, but now I wanted to explore it, know it.

I took a deep breath and swallowed as I ran my hand down my stomach with a slow, dubious touch. I knew this was a thing that people did, enjoying it by all accounts, it just didn't seem very 'me'. But then again, being amorous with work colleagues wasn't very me either. I let two fingers slide between my legs, and my forehead creased up in concentration as I tried to summon that sensation back, but nothing happened. That burn and heat that Ben seemed to bring out in me just wasn't there. In some ways it was a relief, as it had felt too painful at times, almost unnatural.

My eyes flashed open as I shook my head at my own stupidity. I grabbed the shower head and began to wash the vanilla scented oil from my skin, furious at myself for being an idiot, and equally mad at Ben for kissing me like that while thinking of someone else. I'd have to try and stagger shifts at work, see him as little as possible. He'd probably move onto someone else within a week anyway, his next conquest. I mean, he could have his pick of the nurses at work, that was for sure.

I turned the heat up to maximum as I rinsed my legs, my anger rising by the second. I thought of him kissing all the other nurses at work the way he had me. I thought of them underneath him, as I had been, but this time he didn't stop. Before I knew what I was doing the shower head was between my legs as the hot water woke every nerve. In my mind, all I could see was him, as I remembered his tongue teasing at my own, recalled how his weight felt on top of me. I wished he was with me right now.

Steam rose and tumbled around me, as if safeguarding me from prying eyes. I pressed a hand onto the fogged up glass screen as I gasped for breath, the realisation of how my body could feel if I let it, if I allowed him take me there. It took me by absolute surprise. I was humiliated by him using another woman's name, yet at the same time shame surrounded me as I realised I wanted to give him another chance.

I banged my elbow against the screen as loud knocks sounded from the front door, accompanied by the notification of my doorbell as it sounded out from my phone.

I cringed, mortified at my behaviour as I pressed the shower head back into its cradle and twisted the dial to 'off'. Stepping out of the cubicle, I stamped my feet on the mat, trailing wet footprints as I wrapped a large, fluffy, white towel around my chest, and bounced out of the bathroom, running my fingers through wet hair.

"One minute!" I shouted from the top of the stairs as I heard more knocks, fast and insistent. I tucked the towel in on itself under my arm, as I opened the door tentatively and looked around, then my breath caught in my throat. Tall, blond, blue eyed, striking... even his smell was delicious. What on earth did Ben see in me and why was he here now?

He swallowed as he glanced up and down my damp body. "I hoped we could talk... About last night?"

My mouth was open now, my breaths shallow and rapid as I looked at him, truly looked at him. I was unable to tear my eyes away from his as I let the door swing wide open, without a care if anyone on the street saw me resplendently trying to hide my modesty. How did I know him, want him, crave him? Why did these feelings stir within me?

"What are you doing to me?" I whispered into the air hopelessly, for I knew I was powerless around him. He broke down every barrier. He had an authority over me that I didn't understand. I stepped backwards in the hallway as tears of utter frustration built behind my eyes.

He followed, pushing the door closed with a soft click. His eyes hungrily drank me in as he laced his fingers into mine once again and pressed me to the wall. "Will you let me explain it all?" His voice was low, and it positively dripped with desire.

I nodded and pulled him close as I rose onto tiptoes, my mouth seeking the feel of his once more. His breath hit me like a warm jet stream that delivered life and desire, then his mouth crushed mine in an urgent action as our lips clamoured to taste each other. I didn't want him to go slow anymore, as I pushed my tongue between his parted lips, savouring the sigh it drew from him. His hands stroked down the sides of the fluffy towel before rubbing back up on the inside, stroking the skin of my outer thighs and coming to rest on my hips.

I'd never been anywhere near naked with a man. Yet here I was, in just a towel, his hands underneath it, my skin damp from the shower, and I was absolutely enthralled with the moment. I tugged his shirt loose from his jeans, desperate to feel him, my hands insistent as I groped at the warm skin of his back. His hands slid to my waist, holding me firmly and eliciting a moan as I threw my head back. My lips felt lost without his, but he didn't stop kissing, his lips, instead, landed upon my neck as he moved across me and covered every inch of skin with delicate nips of passion.

"Ben..." I sighed, as instinctively one of my knees rose. He shuddered as he drew my face to his and gazed deep into my eyes.

"You used to call me a different name, do you remember?" His eyes were large, pleading.

"I don't know what you mean. What is it with you and names?" That fog had descended on my mind again and I struggled to comprehend.

His eyes flashed as his hands cupped my face before tangling into my hair. "I'm not going to hurt you; I just want you to feel. Do you trust me?"

I nodded and he picked me up, cradling me like an infant as he carried me upstairs. I couldn't tear my gaze away from him and my forehead crumpled in confusion as I tried to look down, but he held my glare in his seductive blue eyes.

"I know you want me to explain," he said as he lay me down on the bed. "It's so complicated, and this is the best way, please trust me."

I continued looking into his eyes as he settled alongside me, and it was as though I saw my past and future within them. I trusted him implicitly. I just didn't know why. I felt unable to vocalise these thoughts and instead simply wrapped my arms around him in affirmation.

He pressed velvet soft lips to my forehead before he pulled his shirt off and snuggled down under the covers with me, tugging at my towel before he tossed it to the floor and pulled my naked body close. "Just let me stay, wake up with me. That's all, Amber."

The sun had been shining but now the room felt dark, things weren't right, but at the same time they felt... serendipitous, as if I was always going to end up here.

His fingers pressed at the centre of my forehead as he rubbed backwards into my hair, over and over. I was like a kitten, pressed into his hand, adoring the touch, and wanting more. He shushed me as the aroma of warm citrus flowed into my senses. His heartbeat pounded into my ear, strong and focused and I lay against the hot skin of his chest, succumbing to something... to him. It was as though I sank into another consciousness, the bed soft beneath me, his arms strong around me. I drifted to a place familiar, yet alien, all at once.

We were in a woodland, but every tree was a cherry blossom and their petals fell upon us like confetti. The air was warm, the sky was picture perfect, and I had not a single worry on my mind. I simply focused on him. It was Ben, but more, so much more. Taller, more rugged, his hair spun with golden strands and the curls longer. His lips were utter perfection, deep and full, a pointed cupid's bow that called out for me to lick it. So, lick it I did. He laughed at the action and pressed me back against the rough bark of a tree, his every kiss sinking pure love into me. I'd never felt as cherished, adored, wanted, needed, as I did in that moment.

"Mireille..." he groaned into the kiss. That name again. I opened my eyes, looking past him as he kissed my neck and held me close. The cherry blossoms gradually gave way to orchards of citrus trees, and, on the horizon, I could see a city that seemed to shimmer in the warm haze of sunshine.

Just then, his mouth dipped lower as he kissed along my collarbone, his hands slid under me and pulled me up towards him. My breath was greedy and fast as he pressed into me. I leaned back against the tree, gasping at the sensation, before grimacing as something behind me caught on the roughness of the bark. A flash went off in my mind, a flare within my consciousness...

Back in my bedroom I sat bolt upright as I blurted out the name, "Barke!"

His eyes were soft with tears as he smiled at me. Tension seemed to drop from him as relief soaked in. "You don't know how long I've waited to hear you say that name again." He stroked the side of my face.

"This still doesn't make sense. I've never taken drugs, but I feel like this must be how it is? My body doesn't feel right, those memories aren't mine. Are they even memories? Or are they hallucinations?"

"They're memories, of us, our home."

"Where is that place? How do I know you? Why are you so familiar to me?" I burst into tears with the exasperation of so many unanswered questions. "Nothing makes sense. I don't understand."

Ben pulled me to his chest and blew out a long, slow breath. "It will make sense, it will. There just isn't an easy way, I want to help."

"Who is Mireille?" I asked between sobs as I tried to control my breath.

He pressed a soft kiss to my forehead before laying back down. "How about I tell you a story, Mireille and Barke's story? Then you stay here with me and sleep. I know it's not bedtime yet but this is difficult, you're exhausted."

As if on cue I yawned and cuddled closer to him, lulled by the scent of oranges once again. "Deal. I love bedtime stories."

"I know you do, my love." He readjusted himself on the bed so that his arms were protective around me under the heavy duvet. "Barke was a man, very similar to me, who lived in a beautiful village. The village was in the middle of a forest and was surrounded by cherry blossom trees. Everywhere felt light and beautiful as the blossoms fell like fragrant snowflakes, and the people who lived there would collect them and make decorations and scented lotions from them. Barke's hallow, his family, consisted of just one person – the girl he'd loved for longer than he could remember, his first love, Mireille."

Ben twisted his fingers around mine, stroking them as he continued, his voice melodic and soothing. I could picture everything so clearly as he described it. "This village, these people, they aren't like the places and people you know, Amber. There aren't jobs and bills, no designer labels or extravagances; people live simply but happily. They eat what they grow, they make what they need. The other big difference is that when two people are bound together in love, it's for eternity, never to be separated. That was Barke and Mireille, they'd been together for hundreds and hundreds of years, they loved their home. One of their favourite things to do was invite their extended hallows, families over, and cook beautiful food to be eaten under the citrus trees in the warm air, the night sky lit up by strings of fairy lights that hung all over their garden. Mireille's favourite food was honey milk bread and she'd bake batches and batches of it for those nights."

I smiled at the thought, licking my lips as the taste of it

seemed to hover upon my tongue. Ben sighed with sadness as the next section of his tale began. "Mireille was the kindest woman, the sweetest, everyone adored her, and she would never upset a soul. She used to care for the sick and the elderly, bring light to their pain. Then one day, some people... ignorant, bad people from another place, decided that Mireille was a threat to them. They couldn't reach her in our village, she was safe, but, in a typical selfless act, she travelled elsewhere. She wanted to pick herbs for a woman who suffered with a disease that damaged her lungs. Mireille only ever wanted to help people. She knew that I..." Ben coughed before he continued, "she knew that Barke wouldn't let her go, so she left when he was busy. The bad people were watching her, and they knew she was alone."

I pressed a kiss to his chest as despair seemed to cascade from him, and he stroked my back in response. "One of them attacked her but she fought back, she was so brave. She injured him and he fled, which gave time for Barke and one of the elders to run to her. She was badly hurt and to bring her back to the village would have put her in more danger. The only way to keep her safe, even though it broke Barke's heart, was to hide her away where they couldn't find her. For her own peace, they hid the memories in her mind, too. Barke had to live with the heartache and the longing every day, but Mireille would be safe and free from the pain and the past."

"That's awful," I whispered, the emotions stuck in my throat.

"It is. But Barke knew that one day he'd be able to find her, one day they could be reunited."

"He sounds amazing, I hope he finds her..." My words trailed away to nothingness as I fell into a restful slumber. Sweet dreams, scents, and tastes overtook everything I thought I knew.

EIGHT

ANWIR

These creatures didn't realise the habits they formed, the patterns they adhered to. It made my life so easy. Just a few days and I knew... I knew where she got her coffee, how long the bathroom light stayed on when she took a shower, the way she gazed at the stars before she drew the curtains each evening.

I still wasn't one hundred per cent sure she was the one, but the odds were in my favour. She was in the right place, at the right time, and that's rarer than most would think. There was also an innocence about her, I couldn't quite describe it, but the air seemed to flow around her differently, people reacted to her, warmed to her, and I found myself wanting to be part of that.

That led me to be outside her favoured coffee shop on a drizzly Friday afternoon. She scrolled through her phone as she waited at the counter, the barista barely noticing her, and I was mystified as to why. Porcelain skin, blonde hair that settled just right, eyes so light, so open to the world. How could every person in here not be entranced by her?

I blew out an angry breath, halting those thoughts, frustrated at myself. I didn't understand why I fixated on her appearance like that, it was just a shell, a body. If she was who I thought she was, she was just possessing like me, albeit unknowingly.

I'm not my father, I won't screw up. The thought careered around my head. I just needed to get a little closer to her, to judge if she was the one. This wasn't distraction, this was research, work. I'd pretty much convinced myself as I timed my next moments just right.

She stepped out of the doorway, clutching her takeaway cup, and I strode forwards, my eyes focused on my phone like every other human in this city. I'd planned the angle of our collision – the coffee set to spill to the side of her, I didn't want to burn any of that pale skin, at least, not yet. But there must be no skin-to-skin contact between us, I couldn't risk that if she was who I suspected; her touch would be toxic.

The cup flew in slow motion, and I played along with the act, reaching out for it but missing. My hands flew up in into Mason's dark hair in faux horror whilst I secretly smiled on the inside. The contents smelled like tea rather than coffee, though, and this surprised me. I hadn't noted it as I'd followed her.

"Fuck!" I exclaimed. "I'm so sorry. I was miles away, it was an important phone call, I..." And then I let my eyes meet hers, allowing the silence to speak its multitude of verses as she gulped. Between the physicality of this body and the presence of my mind, I knew I could overpower her barriers, break through to what I needed.

I expected her to reach hopelessly for the cup, to look around in despair, yet, she didn't. Her eyes met mine, pupils large against the grey blue of her iris as she simply let the drink spill whilst focusing on me. It was as if the world centred in, and then, it was *my* swallow that stuck in my throat.

Before I could react, her hand reached out and gripped my forearm... it was as if everything I had ever known changed.

Every molecule of air was sucked out of my lungs. The crimson blood that flowed through Mason's body froze on its journey. Time paused, waited in wonderment, amazed at what this touch should be, *could* be. I'd been warned, we all had, about what the touch of one such as her would do to us, but this was different.

Her touch burned, but a cold blaze spread, a feeling that penetrated my bones. It ran down to my groin whilst simultaneously massaging my mind and I couldn't cope. I was unable to deal with the explosion of all this ricochet within me.

"Don't worry," she breathed, as her hand rose to her chest and covered her heart. A wave of lust attacked me as I sensed its beat, felt it resonating, calling me. "I didn't look where I was going."

She smiled and a barrier inside of me melted, crashing like an iceberg forever lost to the ocean.

"Let me get you another..." I whispered, my eyes rooted on hers.

"I can't, I—" She glanced down at her watch. "I'll be late for work."

"You mean I've deprived you of caffeine before work? That's unforgiveable!" I exclaimed, regaining some control as I remembered I had Mason's charms at my disposal.

A small laugh escaped her lips, and she looked down with a smile. "Don't worry, it's not a problem."

"It is a problem! You *have* to let me make this up to you, or I will be eternally tortured with the horror of what I put you through." I smiled widely.

"Honestly, don't worry." She waved a hand and started to turn away.

"Will you be here tomorrow? Can I meet you? Buy you breakfast and the biggest coffee they sell?" I asked.

She paused, and I sucked in a breath as I saw her teeth dig into her bottom lip, and a thousand images of how I would kiss her flashed before me.

"Or was it tea?" I asked, desperate for her to stay.

"Hmm?" A flicker of confusion passed over her face before her smile overwhelmed it again. "Oh, the drink? Yes, it was tea. I do like coffee, but I'd always go for tea if there was a choice."

"Well, maybe instead of coffee and croissants, I could buy you tea and... scrambled eggs? For breakfast?"

"Oh, I'm working nights," she said, as a frown creased her forehead, not before I noticed the faintest reddening on her neck.

"This time tomorrow, then? A bite to eat before work?" I tried to remain composed.

"Sure, I tend to pop in most days anyway. Five pm?"

"I'd say it's a date, but I don't think I'm that lucky, am I?" I flashed her my best smile and was rewarded with a laugh before she turned and walked away, looking over her shoulder just once, briefly, before she was lost in the throng of commuters.

That exchange, brief as it was, had turned my mind upside down and there was no way I could face more time at Mason's desk dealing with the meaningless monotony.

I retreated to the penthouse, shooting back a shot of ice-cold vodka before I stepped into the large shower cubicle and turned the water to its hottest setting.

She touched me... She actually touched me, and the toxicity I'd been warned about didn't occur, didn't cause me ill effects. The sleeve of my shirt would have given some protection, but not enough. Was I on the wrong track with this woman? But her touch had done *something* to me. Something I hadn't felt before, and now, all I wanted was for it to be tomorrow, to be in her presence again, to feel a tiny fraction of that.

I slammed my fist against the glass shower screen as I hardened at the memory of how the air between us had felt. Heavy, full of anticipation, longing, and a pure, animalistic urge. A burn of rage grew within my chest as I growled out in frustration. This wasn't me; this was a side effect of this ridiculous human body which seemed to hang onto its pitiful emotions.

As the near scalding water cascaded over me, I let my mind wander back through all the myths and legends, all the stories I'd been told. She shouldn't be able to touch me without damaging me, I couldn't think of a single instance when our kinds had been anything but toxic to each other. The general population didn't even recall the prophecy, but it had always been important to my bloodline, passed down accordingly.

I pulled the words from my memory; they'd been driven there at a young age:

A feather torn asunder
Will call out, through misted skies
Fragmented in his terror
Truth reflected in her eyes

Threads entangled by melody
She will slumber in his domain
Then consent her own demise
Never to see her hallow again

The liar
Will survey his miracle

As the darkness
Kisses the light

All will wane to grey...
All will fade away...

Who would consent to their own demise? I sneered at the very idea as I turned the shower off and stormed through to the bedroom, leaving large, wet footprints behind on the wooden floor. I surveyed them as I sank down onto the bed, my entire body still twitched at the urge she brought out in me.

Grabbing my phone, I returned to the hospice website which I'd devoured in my attempts to learn more about her. This time, I wanted her picture in my mind as I closed my eyes and tried to resolve the yearn that throbbed through my body.

NINE

AMBER

A couple of days had passed since my encounter with Ben. I'd woken up alone, my watch beeping maniacally as it warned me of my low heart rate through the night. We'd slept the day away together and I felt delirious. Like a cat with a full belly rolling around in a patch of sunshine, purring and utterly content. I hadn't been abandoned; he hadn't walked out on me after a one-night stand. He was giving me space, and it was exactly what I needed.

My mind wavered when I was with him and I felt drawn to him. Yet when we were apart, something in my mind didn't settle, as though a piece of a puzzle was missing. Ellie had noticed that I wasn't myself and messaged me before work to suggest that instead of our normal mugs of breaktime soup in the staff room, we order pizza and eat it in her car, so she could interrogate me in private.

Miraculously, we had one of those rare shifts of calmness. Apart from the standard sets of vitals and medication rounds, all the patients were settled for the night.

I was busy with audit paperwork at the nurses' station

when Ellie plonked herself down beside me, spinning the wheeled chair around with a cheeky grin as she placed two mugs of hot, strong tea down on the desk.

"Break time," she trilled. "My car, now!"

True to her word, as we stepped outside into the night air, clutching our mugs, a bemused pizza delivery guy wandered around the car park scratching his head. "I think you're looking for me," Ellie purred, and I couldn't help but laugh as she went into her flirtation zone. It was too cold to stand and watch so I headed to her car, the doors opening with a beep as she followed behind me.

"Sooo..." she began, her eyes narrowed as she switched on the heated seats. "I saw you leave with Ben the other day."

"Yeah, he gave me a lift." I answered, without meeting her eyes as I opened the steamy pizza box.

"Even though your car was in the car park?"

"Erm, yep. Flat tyre."

"But I didn't see you even look at your car, you were too busy holding his hand."

I looked up at her, noticing a cheeky sparkle inhabit her eyes above that infectious smile. "We maybe had a couple of dates, it's nothing, don't get all excited."

"How can you say it's nothing?!" She almost knocked the pizza flying as she hugged me with a squeal. "How long have I been trying to get you laid?"

"Ellie!" I exclaimed. "I haven't slept with him."

"You're going to, though, aren't you? He's hot. Have you seen him in tight jeans?"

"You know that's not my thing," I objected. We'd had this conversation many times.

"It would be, you just need to dive in! I can tell, he has skills." She winked at me, and an unbidden laugh burst from my lips.

"Stop it! That's not an appropriate way to talk about a colleague."

"Amber! Seriously. Forget being appropriate for once, just go get him. When are you seeing him next?"

"Sunday," I replied, as I chewed on my lip. "I'm not sure about it, though."

"What's he like? I've not had much to do with him so far."

"He's amazing at his job," I began.

"You know that's not what I mean. Does he make you laugh? Is he super romantic? Does he ask to tie you up?" She grinned and then bit enthusiastically into a slice of pizza.

"Intense. He's intense. Sometimes it seems like he knows me better than he should."

"What do you mean?" she mumbled, as she swallowed her food down.

"He's vegetarian, like me. He doesn't drink, like me. We danced," I confessed. "And he'd chosen one of my favourite songs."

"That just sounds like you're well suited. Eat up, we don't have long." She motioned towards the box on my knee.

"He lost someone special to him. I'm worried he just wants me to replace her." I rubbed at my temples as a dull ache began to grow.

"You got another headache?" she asked, and I nodded in confirmation. "You need to get those checked out."

"I will, I feel like I have brain fog all the time."

"Me too, but mine are wine induced. How many dates are you talking?"

"Sunday will be the third date, I think, though I'm not sure what's classed as a date and what's just hanging out."

"You know what third date means..." She raised her eyebrows suggestively.

"No! Stop!" I laughed. "Not going there. As if you've ever held out until the third date, anyway!"

"Does he know about..." She motioned towards my nether regions as though virginity was contagious.

"Yeah, he was great about it. He's not exactly a ladies' man by all accounts. Because of this person he lost."

Ellie drummed her fingers on the dashboard. "Sunday, that doesn't give us much time. Meet me before our shift tomorrow night and I'll give you a masterclass in seduction."

I shook my head. "I'm not planning on seducing him, and I can't tomorrow anyway, I'm meeting someone."

Her head twisted around like she was possessed as she grabbed my arm. "Have you been replaced, Mrs Social Recluse? Who?"

I ran my finger over my bottom lip as I thought back. "Erm, you know, he didn't tell me his name."

"What the actual... You *have* been replaced. You're meeting a man you don't know? Is this Tinder?"

"No. A guy knocked my tea over earlier today and said he'd replace it tomorrow." I explained with a sigh; she was reading far too much into this.

"That's absolutely a date. I would've brought wax strips into work if I'd known."

"Ellie, stop! It's not a date, I'm not waxing anything and I'm not having sex with Ben." I said it too harshly, but the words had already escaped me. She dropped her half-eaten slice of pizza back into the box.

"I only wanted to help," she muttered.

I placed a hand on her shoulder and rubbed gently. "I know, I'm sorry. I just... this is new territory for me. I feel a bit out of my depth."

"If you want to talk about stuff I'm here. I'm experienced, promise." She scrunched her nose up mischievously and it set our mood for the rest of the shift as we devoured the pizza and headed back inside.

Ben wasn't the type to be constantly on his phone and neither was I, they'd always been more functional than social for me. I did hope to hear from him, though, which wasn't like me, but our paths hadn't even crossed at work.

He was on my mind as I drew the blackout curtains, pulled my eye mask down and set my phone to play white noise in an attempt to drown out the sounds of the world, as everyone else began their day and I tried to sleep, ready for my second night shift in a row.

I parked up at work and backtracked to the coffee shop. It felt highly unlikely that the man would even show up, it was only a spilt cup of tea after all, and there wasn't any real need for him to replace it. Still, it warmed me to know that good intentions existed, and regardless if he turned up or not, I wanted one of the luscious drinks from this place.

As I pushed on the large glass door, I saw a short queue at the counter. Whilst I pondered what to order, I saw the man in question stand up and wave to me.

I headed over to his small, round table near the back of the shop, feeling self-conscious as I noticed he already had two drinks in front of him. It was all a bit embarrassing over a spill, a simple accident. He remained standing as I smiled and held my hand out, instantly feeling a fool for the over-formalised greeting.

"I'm Amber," I said. "We didn't exchange names yesterday."

His head tilted to one side as he surveyed me with his dark eyes. A lock of almost black hair fell over his forehead, only to be swept away by his hand. I hastily pulled my arm back, my mind filing this as one more example of how socially awkward I was.

I sat down in the armchair, my hands wrapped around the mug as I relished the safety of it, the normalcy of the act which kept my awkward limbs busy. A frown set into his forehead briefly before he, too, sat down and mirrored my act, raising his latte glass to his lips before he spoke.

"Mason, apologies, I thought I'd said. I was mortified about your drink; it must have slipped my mind."

"Don't worry. It honestly didn't matter, there was no need to come and meet me today."

He shrugged; his eyes darted down to the table before he focused on me. "This might sound silly," he began, "but I wondered if it was one of those movie style moments. If I'd been wasting all my time on dating apps because fate was begging me to throw a hot drink at Miss Right."

I spluttered a little on my tea as an amused laugh escaped my lips. "Ha! I can assure you I'm not Miss Right, but I do very much appreciate the drink, thank you."

Mason smiled and the very act softened his features. He had one of those textbook male executive chiselled faces, but underneath I could detect a vulnerability.

"Well, Miss Not-Right, then," he placed his glass back down on the table, "what would you like to eat? Then you can tell me how shocking work was without your caffeine fix."

After again insisting it wasn't necessary and getting nowhere, I ordered carrot and honey soup, a homemade special, that featured every couple of weeks and was pure, homely comfort. Mason ordered the same and we chatted about day-to-day things as we ate. I didn't find small talk with strangers easy when out of my comfort zones, but he put me at ease, and I found myself enjoying the chat, almost as relaxed as I might have been with Ellie.

"Do you live nearby?" I asked.

"In the city centre, it's easier for the office."

"What brought you up this way?"

"Just a client visit." He shrugged. "My job is... I don't know, it makes me feel worthless sometimes. It pays well but there's no sense of achievement if that makes sense?"

I was taken aback by his words and thought that maybe there was more to him under the perfect looks and designer clothes. Was I guilty of judging him by his appearance, his wealth? Those things didn't make him a bad person.

"What do you do?" he continued. "I'm guessing a nurse from the uniform, but I don't want to assume."

"I work at the hospice. I'm a palliative care nurse."

"That must be hard?" His forehead wrinkled as he focused on me, so attentive.

"It's the most fulfilling thing I could ever imagine doing. I lost my mother to cancer when I was eighteen. The nurses were amazing, and I knew then it was what I wanted to do. If I can do anything to ease people's worst times, then I've done a good job."

"Wow..." He shook his head slowly. "That's incredible, but I'm so sorry about your mum. That must have been so hard for you and your dad?"

"I never met my dad; it had always just been the two of us."

"I'm sorry." His hand twitched and raised slightly from the table as if he wanted to reach for me but stopped himself. "I, erm... my father died before I was born, I never met him."

"How about the rest of your family? Are you close?" I asked, conscious of a twitch in his eye.

"No. I rarely see them." His words were blasé, but I sensed him waver. "You were so right about the soup," he said, that confident lady-killer smile retuning. "Amazing!"

I'd had such a lovely time with Mason, but it was obvious we moved in completely different circles and as I was never likely to see him again, I was better off heading to work. I glanced at my watch and reached behind me for my coat, which I'd hung on the back of the chair before I tucked into my soup, not wanting my beautiful new scarf to dip into the thick, orange sustenance.

"I'd best get to work," I said as I stood up and stretched my arms into the sleeves, wrapping the scarf loosely around me. "Thank you so much for this."

"Of course, night shifts must be hard going?" he enquired.

"Not so bad once you're acclimatised to them." I smiled, used to the question from everybody who had a nine-to-five job.

"I'm heading that way, you don't mind if I walk with you, do you?"

"Of course not," I replied, as I turned towards the door, focused on Mason's reflection in one of the many mirrors as he pulled his long, woollen coat on. I could bet it had cost him at least two weeks of my wages, probably more.

"Can I ask a personal question?" Mason looked at me as we wandered around the corner, our pace dwindling as we approached the hospice entrance.

I looked up at him with a nod. "Sure."

"Are you single?" His eyes stayed resolute on mine as a hot flush rushed through me. One more example of the whole world except me being obsessed with chasing love and lust at every opportunity.

"I am, but that's how I want to be. No offence, you seem lovely, it's just not what I'm about."

He looked down; his long eyelashes framed him as he traced his fingers over the beautiful scarf that I'd been gifted only a week ago. He took a business card from his pocket and held it out towards me.

"If you ever change your mind, call me. I'd love to see you again."

I smiled noncommittedly as he strode away, then put the thick, luxurious card in the side pocket of my handbag without a glance. Mason was in a different world than me, and besides, no matter how this situation with Ben played out, I was perfectly content on my own.

TEN
AMBER

Much to my dismay, Ellie had insisted on coming over Sunday afternoon to 'prep' me, in her words. I'd planned to be at the community garden as there was so much work to be done, but Ellie was having none of it, she would have dragged me from there by the hair had I not acquiesced.

It was like a battle of wills except with a lot of laughter, for every single thing she suggested or provided, I countered with something much more sensible, until we met in the middle. I had avoided her home wax kit, yet still cringed with embarrassment as I ran a brand-new razor up and down my legs in the shower.

Ellie smiled as she stood in front of me, satisfied with the results of our compromises. I'd let her curl my hair loosely on the condition we skipped the glittery eyeshadow she'd brought over. I'd agreed to mascara and eyeliner however, and my eyes looked ten times larger as they blinked back at me in the floor length mirror. I'd wanted trousers and she'd brought a mini skirt; this argument had gone on for some time until we'd settled on a dark green skater dress, which I'd forgotten was at the back of my wardrobe. I'd initially added a white cardigan which she'd thrown into the bathroom with a firm '*No*'.

"Can you walk in heels?" she asked, her eyes still running up and down me like a trainer appraising a racehorse.

I shook my head as I replied. "Nope, I don't need heels anyway. You know I don't see the point in them."

An exasperated sigh shot from her lips. "You're impossible, Amber," she said. "Have you still got the ballet pumps I bought for your birthday, or did they end up at the charity shop?"

I smiled and pointed to the wardrobe as she retrieved them with a grin. They were beautiful but I'd never been anywhere nice enough to wear them. Flat, with flexible soles and embroidered with beautiful beads that shimmered under the light.

"These will be perfect."

I slipped my feet into them and leant against her as we looked at each other in the mirror. "This isn't all necessary you know; nothing is going to happen tonight."

"Hmm," she gestured for me to follow as she flopped heavily down on the end of my bed, "I wanted to talk to you about that."

I sat down next to her, my cheeks already burning in mortification at the topic I knew she was about to raise.

"First, don't feel you have to do anything you don't want to." Her eyes lit up, sparkling with mischief. "But, Amber, for goodness sake, please just sleep with the guy!"

"Ellie!" I buried my head in my hands.

"I brought you condoms, he *has* to wear one, no arguments. They're next to the front door, by your keys. You've watched porn, right?" she asked, straight faced.

"Ellie!" I groaned. "No, why on earth would I have wanted to watch porn?"

She laughed. "That's maybe a good thing, because I was going to say, it shouldn't be like porn. You don't need to do all the noises and the acrobatics and dramatics. It should just be... beautiful."

My heart sped up a notch as I heard the dreaminess in her voice.

"Kisses and touches that grow as your bodies just beg to meet. Slowly ramping up until you're just breathless for him, as if his touch could burn you but you'd beg him to do it..." She coughed discreetly as she stood up. "Damn, I think I need to get on Tinder tonight."

As we stood at my front door, she embraced me in a tight hug. "Ring me in the morning?"

"Of course," I replied. "When I'll be here. In my own bed. Alone."

She rolled her eyes and waved nonchalantly as she strode away. "Enjoy! Say hi to Ben for me."

Closing the heavy front door, I leant back, smoothing my dress down over my knees. Ellie was on the wrong track there... completely the wrong track.

♒︎ ♒︎

"Hi." My voice was more of a whisper as Ben opened the door and our eyes met. It was almost as if sparks flashed between them, and I would be pulled to another place. My mind was muddled and foggy yet again, and I seemed unable to think coherently when he was this close to me.

As we headed inside, Ben took my coat, his fingers brushing lightly over my shoulders. I watched him hang it on the stand, as he'd done the last time I was here, but something had shifted – somehow, his touch was still on me, his fingers kneading at my shoulders, even though I could see him in front of me, watching me.

"Are you hungry?" he asked hesitantly. "I was going to cook pasta, so I haven't started it yet."

His eyes took in my face as I stepped forward and as though I'd been possessed, stretched up onto my toes and let my lips glance softly over his. I'd lost control of myself, the air had thickened and although no music played, familiar and beautiful tunes danced through my mind.

His fingers wrapped into my hair as he kissed me back; soft, delicate lips embracing my own. All too soon, the slow action ceased, and he rubbed his nose against mine, his eyes focusing in. I realised I wasn't on my tiptoes anymore, yet my forehead fit exactly against his. I frowned in confusion, while his fingers traced across my forehead, as if to soothe the emotion from me.

"I still don't understand, Ben. All those things you told me about Mireille and Barke, what do they have to do with anything? Why am I feeling these things when I'm with you?"

He laced his fingers through my own, shifting backwards slightly. "It's not something I can explain with words. Will you let me show you?"

I nodded and followed as he led me by the hand into his bedroom. The room was illuminated by bright moonlight. A net curtain blew in the breeze, the leaves and vines which decorated it seemed alive as they moved. I glanced over towards his bed, smiling at the crisp-looking, pure-white bed linen which sat on the deep mattress, under cushions and pillows aplenty.

Ben pressed himself behind me and unfastened the buttons of my dress. My eyelids fluttered as his lips kissed at my neck, glancing touches which barely traced my skin yet set off a burn inside me, which was indescribable. It was as if every fibre of me wanted to join with him.

My dress fell to the ground and his fingers journeyed insistently down my sides, tracing soft and slow from the sensitive skin of my underarms all the way down to my hips. A flurry of kisses trailed down my spine, awakening each vertebra with a silken whisper.

My lungs were full of hot, yearning air as I held my breath. He unfastened my bra and let it drop to the floor in front of me. His fingers pressed in the skin below my shoulder bones, then he dragged them down, towards the centre of my spine. I exhaled as his mouth followed the same line and he placed kiss after kiss on the previously untouched skin there. A burning pain shot through my wrists, and I gasped out loud, my fingers racing to rub at the painful joints.

"Are you OK?" Ben asked, his eyes wide.

"Yeah, I just jarred my wrist," I replied. "I've never wanted anyone sexually. Why do I feel this heat around you?" I was eternally thankful for the darkened room to hide my embarrassed face.

"Remember how I told you Barke and Mireille fell in love for eternity?"

I nodded as I followed him to the bed, grateful as he lifted the cool, white sheets for me. I tugged them up around myself, conscious of my near nakedness, then looked down at my aching joints as he undressed down to tight, black shorts. He took hold of my wrists and pressed his mouth to each before he slipped under the sheets with me, a kind smile upon his mouth.

"Are they sore?" he asked.

"Yes, but stop avoiding the question. What about Barke and Mireille?"

"One minute. Does anything else hurt? I need to know." He ran his hands up my arms, rubbing at my elbows and shoulders as he watched for my reactions.

"I guess all of me feels a little achy, maybe I'm just coming down with a bug. I'm hot, too. I thought it was because of…

this." Heat bloomed furiously across my cheeks. "But maybe it's a temperature. I should go, I don't want to make you sick."

"Don't go anywhere." Ben placed a soft kiss to my forehead. "You aren't sick. Your body is remembering Mireille, she was taller than you. And that's happening because you're here with me."

"Are you Ben? Are you Barke? None of this makes sense…" I wanted to know more, my mind was in a whirl of disbelief, and I couldn't focus through the fog of confusion. I couldn't focus on anything except the need to feel more of him. It was as if a lifetime of having no sexual urges whatsoever had caught up with me, and I was desperate as my body hummed with need.

"I'm yours, forever. That's all that matters…" His words melted away to nothing as his mouth met mine and I sank all my desire into the moment.

I pulled him onto me, my hands stroking up and down his back at speed; I wanted to feel and know him. I gasped for a breath as his fingers twisted into my hair, distracting me momentarily as his mouth moved to my chest. My body had never been awake like this, it was as though everything pleasurable had lain dormant, waiting. This was so good I could hardly bear it and without sentient thought, my legs opened wide and wrapped around his hips.

I cried out as a sharp pain cut through me – as though my hips couldn't handle the stretch as they wrapped around him. That burn rushed down through my joints and I tilted my head to the side and bit on the soft pillow to relieve the pressure and the panic that grew internally.

He ran his hands down to my hips, as if he could sense where the pain targeted me. They felt larger as he rubbed firmly in a circular motion to disperse the heat and discomfort. It shot away through my body, flowing in and around me. A fiery bolt shot straight towards my pelvis, and I was glad for the pillow as a deep moan escaped from my throat.

Ben's hands were back in my hair as he turned me towards him, scattering kisses across my flushed face. "You don't have to hide what you feel," he whispered, his breath sweet against me. "Does it hurt?"

"Yes, but what you did then... that helped, it felt good. I don't understand what's happening."

"Do you want me to stop?" He swallowed deeply as he asked the question.

"No, I've never felt like this before. Does it feel good for you?"

Ben blew out a breath, intertwined with a soft laugh. "Trust me, this feels like heaven."

I lost all track of time as we tangled together in the sumptuous, white space that was Ben's bed. The pain and the heat targeted all my joints, but, each time, he moved to the place and used his hands to force it outwards, dilute it and turn it into pleasure. His teeth nipped at my bellybutton before he sank into the pillow beside me, our breaths mingling together as he stroked my cheek, a contented smile on his reddened lips. We both still had our pants on, and I was all too aware that underneath those thin layers of black cotton, lay the only parts of each other we hadn't now touched.

"I don't want to go too fast. Do you need a break?" he asked quietly.

I looked beyond him, to the moonlight glancing off the delicate curtain as the breeze floated into the room. This time together felt peaceful, and I had no doubts in my mind that I wanted it. The confusion about this whole Mireille and Barke story remained at the forefront of my mind, but it felt distant, I couldn't touch it, so it didn't matter right now. Ben was here; I could touch him.

"No, no break. Just you."

He pulled me up gently, his soft kisses never stopping as he took my hands and placed them on his hips. A low breath shuddered through me with a heady mix of anticipation and nerves as his fingers ran inside the lace of my pants and he gradually pulled them down until they pooled at my bent knees. His eyes focused in on mine with a poised assurance as I copied him, dragging his shorts down his muscular thighs with a gasp as he pulled me close, and I felt him hard against me.

I kicked my pants away with a self-conscious giggle as Ben did the same. He tilted his head to one side and kissed me with a longing as his lips lazily peeled away from my own.

"There's nothing to worry about. I adore you; I'd do anything for you. You're almost there." His mouth was on mine again in passion, and I wondered what 'almost there' meant, but then I was lost in the moment as I felt his fingers circle my bellybutton and begin to wander downwards.

I froze as those fingers traced a line through the hair that they met – should I have taken Ellie's advice and waxed? Was this going to be a major turn off for him? Should I be doing the same to him? This was all so unfamiliar, but I knew that if I started my fingers on their own journey, I wouldn't concentrate on what he was doing to me. And I really, really wanted to concentrate on what he was doing to me.

Apart from that one time in the shower, I'd only ever touched myself in a functional way; I didn't know what to expect as his fingers parted my legs. I hadn't, for one moment, expected the jolt of energy that ran through me as he rested his forefinger on one very specific, raised prominence underneath me. He held his finger there, not moving, just pressing with the lightest touch as I sank my face into his shoulder and sighed deeply. Then, he began to circle and my whole body trembled.

"I want to make you happy, but I don't know what to

do…" I whispered, more to myself than to him, but he moved his mouth to my ear and an almost feral growl escaped his lips.

"You drive me to the edge of impulse. I've craved your skin against mine for two hundred years now. There is nothing you need to do to satisfy my thirst except be here, with me, right now."

His voice purred against me as his forefinger continued to circle and his middle finger slipped lower underneath me, rubbing at wetness I hadn't realised was there, before he cautiously slipped it inside of me.

I thought I would choke on my own breath as the sensation overtook me. A rush ran up my body and circled around my head like a tornado, leaving me dizzy and lost. His one finger circled wantonly inside me as my head fell back in a passionate display. The burn returned, molten and liquid, the pain of it ran down my spine, streamed into my shoulder joints. Only this time his hands couldn't disperse it, as one was melting me internally and the other gripped at my behind, holding me to him. I willed him to run that hand up my back, to stop this torture, but he didn't.

"Just be strong," he gasped, as his finger shifted higher inside me. The rapturous pleasure turned to nausea, his finger now intrusive and wrong, as was the agony of the burn at my back, and for a moment, I was sure this must be death. I screamed as my back rippled. The skin itched as though a thousand parasites dwelled amidst it, just waiting to burst free. I was sure my flesh would tear open, spill onto these beautiful white sheets as trauma blistered through my spine.

My eyes sprang open amidst the chaotic sensations that ensnared me, landing on the mirrored wardrobe to our left; it displayed us perfectly. A sensual, hedonistic, decadent painting of passion, two naked bodies on the bed, writhing together. The reflection was pure desire – except the woman in the mirror wasn't me.

She was much taller, her legs were wrapped around Ben but her long, elegant feet met her own hips. Thick, bouncy curls of honey-blonde hair fell all the way down her back and as her eyes reflected mine, I saw they were an emerald green, nothing like the pale blue of my own. Her back quivered and shook, eliciting deep moans from Ben who now looked more like the man from my visions. He was lost in desire as he scooped up her hair, and an explosion of light pooled out from her back. I was vaguely, dimly aware that a piercing scream flowed from my lips, then, darkness encapsulated me.

ELEVEN

ANWIR

I stood behind a large oak tree, hiding in the shadows, though I knew she wouldn't see me as she casually strolled towards his front door. Following her, darting behind parked cars, and trying to mingle amidst a group of teenagers who chatted and drank from cans, perhaps seemed quite suspicious to any onlookers, but now that I'd found her, I needed to keep her within my sights. She looked like pure temptation as she knocked at his door, one toe twisted into the ground self-consciously, causing the hem of her dress to ripple, as though teasing my eyes with what the lucky guy inside would see.

I still wasn't one hundred per cent sure she was the one, I'd seen no proof, but something in my gut plagued my mind – it insisted I follow her, in search of something specific from her.

A growl rose from deep within me as he opened the front door. He definitely wasn't human; he smelled wrong on some base level. They lingered, all gooey eyed, watching each other for a minute before he invited her inside and closed the door.

A worry bloomed within me, what if he was here to do the same as me? What if he got there first? I couldn't allow my trophy to be taken from me now, not after all this time, planning, sacrifice. Yet, that concern seemed to fade to mist inside of me, as her face replaced it, vibrant, sharp, and beautiful. The thought he could hurt her, scar that skin, was unbearable. I closed my eyes as my mind flicked through images of him kissing her, undressing her, pushing her down onto his bed with a self-satisfied grin.

My nails dug into my palms and left angry crescent indentations in their wake, as I shook my head in frustration. Whatever he had planned for her, I wanted to see. The woman had burrowed into my mind; she must be the one, she must be.

The blinds were drawn, and I could see muted light behind them, but I needed more. I had to help her if he was hunting her, because she was *my* prey, mine alone.

I focused some dark threads of power which enabled me to scale the gate that blocked the dim side alley that ran between the house and its neighbour. Landing silently, I glanced around the corner of the building, scoping out the rear of the house.

It was just a garden, I could smell the pollen from the flowers, the decomposition of the leaves and mulch on the floor, but the only thing that interested me was the whispering coming from inside.

I made my way warily to a large fire burner which took pride of place in the centre of a patio. Squatting behind it I raised my head, resting my chin on the brickwork as I surveyed the house from this angle. The luck of my ancestors was with me tonight as my eyes focused in on the large, open window. A sheer lace curtain was all that lay between me and the two of them.

I closed my eyes to hide the telltale gleam of power as I focused on enhancing my vision. I had to be cautious - unwanted attention from home or anywhere else was the last thing I needed. A satisfied sigh flowed into the night air as they opened, and I took in the miraculous sight that was Amber Carmichael. It was even enough to distract me from the stench of him as he let her dress fall to the floor.

A hot burn flashed high inside my chest, entirely uncomfortable. I knew what this was, but I didn't want to give it a name; it wasn't an emotion that someone like me should feel. Besides... no matter how much I would like to be in his place, I wouldn't be able to touch her. So maybe this was as close as I could get, therefore, it made perfect sense to enjoy my front row seat. I'd simply make sure to memorise every second for my own personal playback. Maybe I'd find a woman to take home afterwards, they were easy enough to seduce around here.

I blurred him out, pictured myself there, instead. Her teeth sank slow and languid into her bottom lip, the plumpness of it pulling into her mouth before it sprang back out as she turned. There was no way I could save this up for later, my hands dropped and unfastened my trousers; I was harder at this moment than I'd ever been in my entire life.

A grimace of pain tainted her face and all I could think of was how it would feel to hurt her, to ease the pain and then bring it back, harder each time until she begged for more. This seemed to be what he was doing, only in a gentle way, I had to harden it up for my own mind as I focused on the perfection that was her body.

The bastard covered her with a sheet as they climbed into bed. Glimpses of tangled flesh were all I got now, but it didn't stop my mind placing me in the scene, I longed to run my tongue and teeth over every inch of her, to draw moans with my every touch.

They kneeled on the bed together and my hand gripped harder at the sight of her tangled-up limbs. His hand snaked underneath her and I would have bitten his fingers off just to taste her upon them. She looked towards the flimsy material that swung in the open doorway and it was as though her eyes met mine; I forced my tongue to the roof of my mouth as I pressed my lips together, stifling the noise as I came longer and harder than I'd thought possible, simply at the sight of this naked goddess of a woman.

A piercing scream split the night air in two and I shuddered with panic as my eyes sprang open: Had she seen me? No, she was staring, aghast, in a mirror, but what had caused that blood curdling cry? For a moment I feared he'd killed her, taken my role, but he had a look of horror on his face as she collapsed down onto the bed, like an angel falling from the clouds.

I reached out for the blanket that covered a day bed next to the fire pit and wiped my hands clean on it, my heart hammering against my ribs with apprehension, worry, desire, confusion. It all felt like too much.

Tears ran from his eyes as he called her, over and over in an attempt to rouse her. She'd fallen so fast it could have been narcolepsy, if not for that scream. What had caused it?

I zipped myself back up and continued to watch as he shook her shoulders. He buried his face into her neck and rocked her like a baby before pulling her onto his knee, cradling her lovingly. "Please," he begged, "Mireille, wake up. Just wake up."

I threw my head back and looked up at the stars, my mouth gurning into a ridiculous grin at the significance of the knowledge he'd just unknowingly given me.

Mireille.

Mireille, you absolute fucking angel. It had been one of the last words my father murmured according to my elder relatives in the terror, yet nobody knew why. Now, I knew. She was the one. I could finish it now, end this prophecy. In all honesty I didn't even believe in the damned thing, but I'd lived my whole life with the shame of his failure and now I could wipe it all out.

If this... man... knew what she was and he wasn't here to kill her, I could only assume he was also from the angelic plane. Maybe I could get a two for one that would not only wipe out the shame but elevate me to a God-like status at home. I'd have anything or anyone I wanted after this.

Except for her...

I punched the brickwork in front of me as the ridiculous thought flashed through my mind, then cursed myself for the noise as my eyes flashed back to the open door. Nothing to worry about, though, he was entirely focused on her as her eyes fluttered open like delicate butterfly wings and a gasp of breath escaped her lips.

She crawled backwards, crab-like on the bed, away from him, as she shook her head and sobbed. He reached for her, his head bowed as if begging for forgiveness.

"Please, let me explain," he sobbed, as she jumped up with her back to him, tugging her pants up her legs, leaving the waistband tangled as she fumbled with her bra clasp, hands shaking too much to fasten it. I longed to reach out and do it for her, to help her with this simple act.

He reached for her again and this time she slapped his hand away, grabbing her dress in a clenched fist and holding her shoes aloft as she fled towards the front of the building.

"Fuck," I exclaimed, as I launched myself over the gate. They were too preoccupied to worry about a noise out here and I would need every ounce of power I could get for whatever else the evening may bring my way.

"Amber, please, stop!" he exclaimed, as I heard the front door burst open.

"Stay away from me. I don't want you anywhere near me!"

I edged around to the front of the house where she stumbled on the front step, pulling her dress together and stepping into her shoes. I knew where she would go, and I needed to get there before her. As he continued to beg and she prepared to flee, I used a burst of speed to run towards her house, sticking to dark shadows. It was only a few minutes away, I slowed to a standstill and fixed my hair before wiping my hands on the back of my jeans, grimacing at the grubbiness of them as I pulled my phone from my pocket.

I began to stroll casually in the direction I'd just come from, concentrating, so I could time this just right. The smile on my face widened uncharacteristically as I approached the corner and counted in my mind. Three, two, one...

"Ouch!" I exclaimed, as her foot landed heavy on mine. She recoiled; her hands flew up into her hair in confusion. "Watch where you're going."

"I'm so sorry," she sobbed as she tried to edge past me, her eyes firmly on the ground as she wiped at them.

"Amber?" Her eyes flicked up and met mine, darting between them in confusion before she took a breath, her panic subsiding.

"Mason? What are you doing here?"

I took hold of the sleeve of her dress, careful to not touch her skin as I leant back and looked her up and down. "I'm just heading home from a friend's place. You're crying, what's wrong? Have you been attacked? What's happened?" I let the words fade out as I looked beyond her, down the dark street for some assailant I knew didn't exist.

She shook her head as a fresh flood of tears sprang from her eyes. I snatched my hand back as she raised her own to wipe them away, within millimetres of me.

"I don't know how to explain, even to myself." She shuddered and took a deep breath as she looked at me, her eyes huge with fear. Even in this state she tried to smile, and it was as though a slither of ice broke off from my heart and ricocheted throughout my body.

I coughed and tried to ignore the worrisome sensation. "Let's get you somewhere safe. Shall I call a cab? Where do you live?"

"I don't want to go home," she mumbled, before a defiance crossed her face. "He might follow me."

"We can worry about who 'he' is later. Want me to take you to a friend?"

She shook her head; she looked utterly lost, and a deep part of me ached for her. "I don't know where to go."

"I know you don't know me very well, but you can trust me," I lied, and it lay heavy in my chest. "Come to mine and we'll figure it out from there."

Those big, Bambi-like, blue eyes looked up at me and for some reason I couldn't catch my next breath. I could sense her thoughts jumble up with indecision.

She nodded gratefully, I removed my jacket and placed it around her shoulders before swiping for an Uber with the app on the phone, which I was growing more and more accustomed to.

The drive was fifteen minutes at the most, but she curled her legs up under her on the back seat and seemed to instantly fall asleep. I was fascinated as I watched her eyes zap around behind her pale eyelids, her nose twitching as her hair tickled across it. At one point she bit her lip and murmured, and I swear if that Uber driver hadn't been with us, I would have had serious issues restraining myself. Whatever damage she would do to me would be worth it to feel her, just once.

She didn't awaken as the car pulled up outside my apartment block. I threw a twenty towards the driver by way of a tip on top of the automated payment and asked him to wait as I dashed into the opulent lobby and snatched up one of the thick blankets from the wicker baskets that sat at the side doors, to be used in the garden terrace on chilly evenings.

Running back to the car with its idling engine, I wrapped

her in it, again careful to avoid skin-to-skin contact. Her phone lay on the back seat. I pushed it away, happy as it slid under the passenger seat; she wouldn't need it.

I swaddled her in my arms like a new-born, before carrying her up to the penthouse, as if she were my bride, my prize, my... angel?

TWELVE

AMBER

Normally, I'd awaken with crystal clear thoughts, ready to go, and psyched up for whatever events the day might bring. No wandering around the house bleary eyed in search of caffeine with grunts in lieu of actual words for me – I just woke up, I'd always been the same.

Today was different. I stretched; my eyes remained closed as a smile crept onto my lips at the touch of luxurious sheets that seemed to hug my body. It was as if the bed cushioned me, wrapped around me protectively. With a deep, fulfilling inhale, I slid under the covers as the scents of cedarwood, lime and something that resembled bourbon washed over me, delicious, inviting, and warm.

Resurfacing, I blew out the long, slow breath, it must have been an amazing dream last night to wake up this sheltered and serene. My eyes fluttered as they opened, then I paused, my forehead creased in confusion as I surveyed my surroundings— this was not my room.

I had pride of place in an enormous bed. The sumptuous sheets I'd been relishing were midnight black with a silver-grey pattern criss-crossed around them. A full-length window dominated the wall to the right of me, a magnificent view of the city on display. Wherever I was, it was a high floor. The room was immaculate with modern furniture and fitted wardrobes positioned to compliment the space.

I sank my head between my hands as I tried to recall. I'd walked to Ben's, but this definitely wasn't his ground floor flat. Had he taken us to a hotel? My fingers delved through my hair as I attempted to fit the images of last night into something that made sense, but that brain fog was on me again. My anxiety peaked as I wondered once more if there was something seriously wrong with me. Physically and mentally I'd felt messed up lately and I couldn't put my finger on what the problem was.

I gulped down my tension as I lifted the sheet, praying to myself that I wouldn't be naked. What if this strangeness I suffered from had led to some awful mistake where I'd spent the night with a stranger? I wore a large, white T-shirt, but my pants and bra were in place underneath. From the corner of my eye, I spotted my dress and shoes on a plush, beige armchair at the side of the bed, alongside a white waffle robe and a handwritten note.

I stood, feeling the warm wooden floorboards beneath my toes. How expensive must underfloor heating be in a place like this? Slipping my arms into the lavish robe, I fastened it tight as I glanced around, perturbed, as if some stranger was going to jump out and frighten me. I reached for the note, rubbing the thick paper between my fingers as I began to read:

Amber,

I hope you slept well. You were exhausted last night, I was worried the dress would inhibit your sleep, I promise I kept my eyes closed while I swapped it for the T-shirt.

*I'll be in my office, two doors to the left of this room. Let me know
when you're up and I'll make breakfast. I'm worried about you.*

Mason

A memory came back to me— crashing into Mason on the
street, my eyes full of tears. He'd looked after me, let me come
back here because I didn't want to go home. Ben and I must
have fought, but I couldn't quite recall the details.

I tiptoed into the en-suite bathroom, reticent to disrupt
the silence which seemed to dominate this place. A new toothbrush had been left for me I noted, as I splashed cool water
over my face. My fingers combed through my hair, pulling last
night's curls to the ends. Sucking a breath in, I decided it was
time to look for Mason.

Cautiously, I inched the bedroom door open and glanced
left and right. The hallway was conservatively decorated, with
elegant wall lights situated between each door. The beautiful
wooden floor continued out here and as I stepped onto it, the
soles of my feet were warmed once again. As instructed on the
note, I knocked on the second door to the left. The scrape of a
chair was followed by footsteps, and the door opened wide.

The fog in my mind flowed away as I gazed into his honey-
brown eyes, set underneath the longest, darkest eyelashes I'd
seen on a man. He looked different here than he had in the
coffee shop, more vulnerable. The dark stubble he sported
suited him and his near-black hair made him more approachable as it fell softly against his forehead. He was taller than I
remembered, too, and I felt tiny here in front of him, in his
robe that was too large for me.

"Amber," he said, relief in his voice, "glad to see you up.
How are you feeling?"

I shuffled my feet awkwardly as I answered. "Good, a bit confused but, wow, your bed is comfortable."

A soft laugh escaped him. "Yeah, I thought I'd give you the best bed. Let me just send this email and I'm all yours. Make yourself comfortable."

He gestured down the hallway before turning back to his desk with a kind smile. I sucked my top lip into my mouth as I headed through the open doorway at the end of the hall.

If I thought the bedroom was luxurious, the living area was on another level. More floor-to-ceiling windows let in an extraordinary amount of light, and they continued around the corner of the room, giving the impression you could see the whole of the city. A deep, chocolate-brown suede sofa curved into the embrace of the corner of the room, encircling a walnut coffee table, and a large television which hung on the wall. This blended into the kitchen, full of glossy, cappuccino-coloured cupboards and immaculate steel appliances.

I ran my finger over a coffee machine as complicated looking as any I'd seen a barista tackle. Mason and I truly did live in different worlds. I'd bet this place had cost ten times what my cosy home had, and that would be without all the luxurious items he'd filled it with. I jumped, disturbed from my pondering as Mason headed in, his feet bare under dark denim jeans. The T-shirt he wore looked similar to mine and I couldn't help but smile as I imagined a wardrobe full of identical attire.

"Nice to see you smiling," he said, as he walked behind me and flicked some switches on. "I'd offer coffee, but you like tea, right?"

I nodded, not sure how to behave whilst alone with the man who'd looked after me, even though I couldn't remember what had upset me in the first place.

He pushed a beautifully carved wooden box towards me, his eyes seeming to drink me in. My finger stroked over the intricate detail of roses and vines before I lifted the brass latch. The box housed a multitude of tea bags, all labelled and strung, enticing as a selection of penny sweets would be to a small child. I flicked through the options before I pulled out a Keemun variety and passed it over to Mason, my fingers trembling. He dropped it into a ceramic mug, beaker style, without a handle. I sucked in a breath as he stretched past me, almost brushing my arm with his as he pulled an identical teabag from the box.

"Take these to the sofa," he said, as he placed a jug of hot milk onto a tray alongside the mugs. "I'll be right with you."

I curled my legs up under me on the soft material, infinitely glad Ellie had made me shave; surely this sofa would reject anyone with hairy legs or cellulite, everything in here was beautiful, Mason included. I clutched the tea between my hands, savouring the heat as I gazed out the window, watching life carry on below us. Cars, people, relationships, jobs. It was strange to witness the everyday from this vantage point.

My stomach growled as the scent of warm bread travelled towards me. "Sorry," I mumbled with a warmth rising up my cheeks as Mason sat next to me, placing a larger tray on the table with piles of toasted, crusty bread next to plates, knives, a butter dish and tiny but luxurious pots of different jams.

He beamed from ear to ear, and the crinkles around his eyes brought a whole new dimension to his face. "You sound ravenous, dig in. It's nice when someone has an appetite."

I took one of the thicker pieces with raggedy edges and began to smother it in butter, a weakness of mine, before glancing through the jams and adding strawberry and vanilla; it was from a store way out of my price range. "Am I allowed to eat on the sofa?" I asked.

He laughed as he reached for a piece himself, smothering it in a bitter, shredded marmalade. "Of course. You can do whatever you like here, it's a rule-free zone."

I'm sure he hadn't meant it in a sexual way, but a blazing heat spread from my chest to my forehead. I concentrated on my breakfast, hopeful he wouldn't notice, suddenly all too aware of how loudly I chewed.

"So," he said, in between mouthfuls, "who upset you last night and do I need to go spill their drink, too?"

I laughed to detract from my embarrassment. "This sounds stupid, but I can't quite remember."

He paused, placing his plate down on the table. "That's not good. Had you had a lot to drink?"

I shook my head, brushing the crumbs that had fallen onto the T-shirt down onto my plate. "I don't drink. I remember I went to a friend's place, and after that it's all a bit foggy."

"Did you go out somewhere? Could you have been drugged? There's a lot of weirdos around. Do we need to get you checked out?"

"No, I think I just had a disagreement with my friend. I'm not good with conflict. I'll check my phone, see if he's been in touch."

"I don't think you had a phone when you bumped into me. Just your house keys in your hand, I've left them on the hallway table."

"Strange," I mumbled, as I reached for another piece of toast and added the same accompaniments.

"Is strawberry your favourite?" Mason asked, nodding his head towards the jam jar I'd just sealed back up.

"I love strawberries." More heat flooded my face, his gaze so intense, his whole aura seemed so strong.

"I could get used to mornings like this." He grinned; those eyes entirely focused on me once more. "A gorgeous woman in my T-shirt, sipping Keemun and getting strawberry jam all over her beautiful lips." He reached forwards and slowly wiped a thick, cloth napkin over my mouth, showing me the smear of jam that graced it after his touch.

I held my breath the entire time as my mind tried to keep up with the flashes and urges that snaked around my body. It was as though all my internal organs had just plummeted into the bottom of my stomach, converging with a deep ache that somehow felt so very good.

Part of me was shifting, I couldn't explain it, but Mason put me at ease. He even seemed to help with the brain fog I kept experiencing. I walked over to the tall windows, breathing deeply as I looked down on the world.

I sensed him approach me. His fingers traced up the sides of my arms so lightly it felt like magic. As I glanced down, I saw he wasn't actually making contact, yet his fingers hovered so close to me he was surely touching the fine hairs that stood on end as electricity seemed to surge between us. It was as though he could take over my body as every nerve came to life and I begged to feel him.

"Why do I feel like I know you?" he asked, his voice husky and dripping with need.

"I don't know," I whispered in reply, fearful my breath would fog up the glass as my body went into overdrive. "You don't know me, I'm sure. I'd remember if I knew somebody like you."

"What do you mean? Somebody like me?" I noticed a quiver in his voice.

"You have this... presence," I gulped. "An effect, I'd remember it."

"Is it an effect you like?" he murmured, his breath teasing my ear.

"Yes..." The sound barely left my lips as I trembled at his proximity.

"You smell like breakfast and my bed, all tumbled together. I wish you were here for breakfast every day,

Amber." His mouth moved to my other ear and a shiver ran through me. "You tear my resolve in two."

He stalked around me, breathed me in, inhaled me, like a predator scoping out his prey. And I wanted him to catch me, I wanted to submit to him. His lips hovered over my neck, directly over my pulse, which throbbed with my quickened heart rate. My knees felt as if they would buckle, and I pressed my palm flat against the glass of the window to steady myself.

"If I was allowed to touch you," he whispered, "you'd be writhing in pleasure over my fingers within two minutes."

"You can touch me…" I gasped, desperate to feel him on me.

"I wish I could." A long sigh streamed from his mouth as he stepped back from me. "I need to finish some work. Why don't you relax? Help yourself to food, TV, shower, whatever you need. I'll be an hour or so, and then I can take you home or figure out what you want to do. Does that sound OK?"

I nodded, my eyes intent on the window as I knew my face would give away my arousal. I felt as if the entire city must be aware of how I felt, as if it surged out of me. How had he turned me on like that with simple words and proximity? "Thank you for being so nice to me. You barely know me, you're so kind."

"I think that perhaps, I know you better than either of us realises." He grabbed his mug and headed back towards his office.

I closed my eyes as I inhaled a deep breath of his scent, immediately thinking of his bed, as it trailed after him. Nothing made sense, but I felt secure here. Mason made me feel safe, whatever that might mean— safe and utterly full of lust.

THIRTEEN

ANWIR

Adevilish grin cemented itself onto my lips as I reclined in the ridiculous office chair that inhabited this room. I was used to instigating blushes, but the way Amber had trembled, her hand pressed to the glass, the flush of her skin... I wanted to do more. I wanted to know how to be like her, to roll around in her bed, wear her clothes, get inside of Amber Carmichael's body and mind.

A shiver trickled down my spine as I recalled her face when I'd opened the office door that morning, those large, blue eyes staring up at me, the creamy skin of her legs on display from underneath that white robe. I would have given up every woman I'd ever touched to be able to be with this one, just once.

With a frustrated sigh I forced the image away, I'd been so careful to avoid any skin-to-skin contact, I couldn't take the risk. But why did she always have to look so fucking inviting? Even the way she held the mug of tea between her delicate hands; would she hold me so delicately? I wondered. It had taken me an age to get her undressed and into bed last night, touching her only through cloth. What I'd give to just have her naked and mine.

There was no work for me to complete, I'd seen some angry emails fly in as I taught myself to navigate this computer, and I assumed I was fired but it didn't matter. Mason Donoghue was deceased, it was just that nobody else knew yet. What I needed to do now was gain Amber's trust, let her settle, grow confident, confide in me.

It was all part of my task, purely the task... No ulterior motive whatsoever.

Ninety minutes later, ninety long minutes where I'd waited patiently as she tiptoed around, I headed back into the living room. I was impressed I'd managed to stay put, and when I felt the thrum of the hot water pipes underneath me as she showered, it had taken all my willpower not to barge into the bathroom. The thought of her naked, hot water streaming down her, was almost too much to handle.

Amber was curled up on the sofa in a patch of sunshine, watching some programme about herb gardening on a bizarre channel I'd never noticed. To be honest, though, there was only one section of channels I tended to frequent on the rare occasions I did watch the contraption – it seemed Mason had similar tastes to me, and quite the subscription package.

"I thought these might be handy," I said, placing some jeans and an off-the-shoulder blue jumper down on the seat next to her. I'd found them a few nights back in the spare bedroom, with some old photographs and other female clothing, never knowing I might have such a beautiful need for them.

"Your girlfriends?" she asked, with a tone she tried to hide.

"No, no girlfriend, remember?" I frowned playfully. "My sister stays over when she's in town, always leaves spare clothes here. I thought we could get some fresh air together, and you might not want to wear last nights dress or my robe."

"Fresh air sounds good. If I'm in your way, though, please just say, I can go."

"You would never be in my way," I reassured her. It should have been a lie, but for some reason, I felt the truth in it. "I know a lovely place about half an hour away. We'll see if the walk clears your mind, then I can take you home and make sure you're safe. If that's what you want…" I let the open ending of it linger, an invitation that didn't need to be spoken.

"How did I not know this was here?" Amber gazed around, open mouthed at the castle ruins as the sunshine scattered shadows onto the moss underfoot.

"Sometimes there are amazing places just out of our sight. We need to look a little further than normal, it's too easy to wander with our eyes seemingly open, but taking nothing in."

She glanced up at me, a bemused expression on her face. "If there was ever a living example of 'don't judge a book by its cover', it'd be you, Mason."

I laughed lightly. "What do you mean?"

"You're just… so much deeper than I would have expected. When you bumped into me," she blushed as she spoke, "I thought you were just another city executive in a rush, not a care for anyone except yourself and your image. But you're not, you're so kind and so deep."

"Careful, Amber." I winked as I guided us down an overgrown path. "You sound like you're warming to me."

The pink flush on her cheeks deepened and we wandered

further down the path, stopping to sit on a low wall atop a hill, which graced us with views of the countryside below. I'd seen the way she gazed out of the apartment windows; this was a woman who liked a view.

"So," I began, "let's start from the beginning, figure out last night. Otherwise, I can't let you go in case you're in some kind of danger. You were so upset." I rubbed the middle of her back, careful to only touch the soft jumper.

"My friend, Ellie, came over to help me get ready because I was going to Ben's."

"Who is Ben? Your boyfriend?" I felt an edge creep into my voice.

She shook her head. "No, just a friend from work. We've been out a few times but... he's not my boyfriend. I went to his place; he was meant to cook dinner for us. Then, I don't remember what else happened."

I slid my hand from her back and focused my eyes upon hers, angling myself so the sun's glare wouldn't blind her. "Do you think he hurt you?"

She swallowed heavily. "I think we had an argument, but I don't sense that he hurt me."

"That's not normal, to not remember, though. How well do you know this guy?"

"He's worked with me for five or six weeks now. He would have been police checked before he got the job. They're very strict on that. He's a bereavement counsellor, he's a nice guy."

"Yeah," I shrugged. "The bad guys are the best at acting nice." My stomach flipped painfully as I realised what I was saying, doing – takes a bad guy to know a bad guy. I let out a long sigh before I continued. "What's his surname?"

"Hagan."

I pulled my phone from my pocket, opened up Google and entered – *Ben Hagan Bereavement Counsellor*, then held

OLIVIA LOCKHART

the phone out tentatively, urging her to take it but keeping my hand at a safe distance.

For the next ten minutes she searched different terms, adding more and then less information, but nothing appeared for this specific Ben Hagan. I held my smile back as I saw her face crinkle with confusion.

With impulsive decision she deleted the search and typed in a new word – *Barke.* Various Wikipedia entries and brewery websites appeared but she scrolled passed them, a look of frustration on her face. Her thumb returned to the search box and this time she searched for *Barke meaning.* She rubbed at her forehead as she read an entry defining it as *'blessings'.* Then she handed the phone back to me with a sigh.

"What's Barke?" I asked.

"I'm not sure," she replied. "Just a word that keeps floating around my head, I don't know why."

"Maybe it was from a dream. Listen..." I paused for a moment, "I don't want to worry you but your Ben Hagan, he doesn't seem to be legit." At that moment the shrill ringtone of my mobile sounded out. "One moment, sorry."

I stepped away, cancelling the call before I pretended to answer; I wanted to give her a couple of minutes to think on this new information. In all honesty, I also needed the time to compose myself. I was so sure it was her; I should just finish this now. Even if it wasn't her, one human woman gone would be no loss, there were plenty more, she was nothing special... Except she was.

I raised my face up to the sky, the sun warmed it as the breeze rustled my hair. I'd been here too long, and I wondered if it was turning me soft. Now was the perfect time, this place was deserted. I should just get it done.

"Sorry about that," I said as she stood up. "Fancy a climb? The view's even better up there." I pointed up the steep steps of the rubble that rose behind us.

"Sure," she replied. "Then I'd better get home."

I nodded. "Ladies first."

A heaviness settled on me as I followed her up the aged stone steps. It was an unwelcome emotion - almost regret, but for an act I hadn't carried out yet. I had no appetite to drag this out, to enjoy it, when we got to the top, I'd just push her to the jagged ruins below. There was no need for explicit violence.

As she reached the top step, she turned to me, smiling down. "Mason, thank you, thank you so much for being so nice to me—" She squealed as she tripped on the uneven steps and plummeted straight into my arms.

The urge to step back was instant, to let her fall, but an instinct in me sprang to life as my arms reached out to grab her, and time slowed as a hot panic rose within me.

She fell against me, her face pressed to my neck. I could feel the dampness of her lips as they sank against my skin. Then, I was transported, lost, found, replaced... completed.

We were under a blackened night sky, sparkling pin pricks of light illuminated pockets of the darkness. A wild, rough wind blew her hair out behind her as I gazed upon the beauty in front of my eyes. It was Amber - but changed. Her long hair blonder as it curled, the green flecks in her eyes expanded to fill the entire iris, dusky pink rosebud lips that begged for me to kiss them.

I moved forwards, desperate to touch her, but she stepped back with a sinful smile, toward the edge of the skyscraper I now realised we stood atop. My heart stopped as I reached for her, wrapping my hands around her delicate wrists as I held her, saved her from the deadly fall. Her white dress billowed around her as I tugged her back to me, holding her steadfast as my every fear vibrated internally.

"Amber, I can't let you fall."

She ran a finger down my cheek, her eyes burned into me. "What if I want to fall, Anwir? What if I would fall over and over, for you?"

My heart exploded within me as I heard my true name tumble from her lips. A name as unworthy as mine on lips as miraculous as hers. How could that be? How could any of this be?

"I love you," she whispered, her eyes closed as she shifted towards me. Tears ached in my throat as I longed to return the words. "I know the words don't come naturally to you, so show me."

She reached behind her and unfastened a clasp, her dress fluttered away on a sharp gust of wind and left her entirely naked in front of me. I groaned deeply as my lips met hers, soft and tentative at first as I absorbed the taste of her, honey and vanilla, pure life and love; softness.

My hands tangled into her long hair as she kissed me with a passion I'd never felt, her tongue danced with my own, her teeth scraped my lips and she poured every ounce of love, the only love I'd ever felt, into me. I sucked on her mouth, wanting to absorb her as I ran my hands down her back, hardening as my fingers traced over the silken feathers that protruded.

We ran, we leapt into the darkness together. The wind tore at our skin as it whipped our bodies, but our eyes never left each other, we were joined and nothing in any world could separate us.

I blew out a gust of hot breath, blinking as the vision ended, yet the goosebumps that covered my body remained. No time had passed, her lips were still against me where she'd landed from her stumble. Instantaneously, I wrapped my arms around her, holding her to me as I pressed my face to the top of her head, breathing in the scent of her hair, letting her flow into me.

How was this happening? If she was the one, I would be burned by her touch. Yet, if she wasn't the one... Nothing made sense. Everything pointed to her being the angel, so why could I touch her? A demon should not be able to hold an angel like this, I should have blistered skin and a toxic taste in my mouth, but instead, I had the strangest, warmest glow in my chest. It troubled me, yet at the same time, I craved more of it.

"I'm so sorry," she gasped. "I'm so clumsy. Are you going to keep saving me like this?"

She bit her lip as she asked the question, her eyes wide open, full of honesty and trust, and I knew, I knew in that moment that I would never be able to hurt her.

She remained in my arms, and I ran one hand up her back, stroking my fingers up the nape of her neck and into the downy hair that grew there. Soft, featherlike, she was divine. I marvelled at the fact I could touch her, and now I didn't want to stop.

My fingers moved to the side and traced her hairline, running over her ear before flowing down her jaw and coming to a halt in the middle of her chin as I smiled at her. She ducked her head down so my finger met her lips, those rosy full lips which plagued my thoughts. I stroked along the length of them, savouring the dampness as she opened them slightly, her breath heavy as my finger traced the silky inner skin.

For every erotic encounter I'd had in my life, every fornication and moment of lust, nothing had ever come close to how I felt as I stroked her lips. My eyes closed of their own accord as I pressed my forehead against hers.

"You have no idea how badly I want to kiss you," I whispered.

"I'm so confused about what's happening to me," she

replied, rubbing her nose against mine with an intimacy I hungered for.

"I know, and that's why I won't kiss you. Yet." I sighed despondently as I stepped back from her. "Let me take you home, make sure you're safe."

Within the hour I'd checked her house, made her tea, and said goodbye. Promising to call her later, on her landline, to make sure she was safe. I longed for her to come home with me, but this was going too far, this lust was heavy and unbidden. I needed to get some perspective and there was only one way I could do that.

FOURTEEN

AMBER

After Mason dropped me home with a comforting hug that we both seemed loathe to end, I tugged all the curtains closed. This gut instinct that something was very wrong wouldn't budge and anxiety bubbled up in me. What if it was I who had the problem? Or was the only issue the fact that Mason left a weight that I felt only he could lift?

Physically, I was so different these past few weeks, the aches and pains, the sensation that my body was going through some kind of second puberty, none of which felt normal. Add to that the fact I was slave to utterly lustful thoughts about not just one man, but two, after a lifetime of feeling nothing in that respect, was a huge worry. If I'd had my phone, I would have been on Google looking up brain tumours or hormonal disorders, so maybe it was a blessing I had no idea what I'd done with it.

There was also a good chance it was a mental health issue. Maybe I was losing my sanity, falling under a variant of schizophrenia or bizarre psychotic delusions. I had blanks in my recent memories; I was still unable to recall the events at Ben's house.

I stood under the hot shower for far longer than normal the next morning. I wasn't in the right frame of mind for work, unable to snap out of this melancholy. One thing continued to bring a smile to my lips, though: Mason. As he'd caught me after my stumble – which could have ended so badly – his eyes had drawn me in, the way his hands felt on my back, on my lips, tangled in my hair.

I sighed angrily as I turned the shower off and stepped out, rubbing myself briskly with a towel. Frustrated and confused as I just went round and round the same concerns. I needed to see my doctor, that much was clear, I'd ask for some time off later in the week.

To add to my low mood, I had no time to stop at the coffee shop, and my mind was wondering if Mason might go there today. I smiled at Lucy, who was working on reception, as I headed into the bright lobby of Oak Tree Hospice. She cradled the phone between her cheek and shoulder as she mouthed to me, "June wants to see you."

Dropping my bag and coat into my own office, I picked up my iPad to check the occupancy and handover notes, then headed straight to see June.

"You wanted to see me?" I asked, as I stepped into her office.

"Sit down, I won't keep you long." She glanced at the clock above the office door. "You know I don't beat around the bush. The past couple of days... there's been something off with you, is there anything you need to talk about?"

A sickness settled in my stomach; was I now in trouble at work on top of everything else? I'd never, ever been in trouble at work, at school, anywhere, it would devastate me to let anyone down.

"I've felt a bit off, to be honest. I was going to ask if I

could take some time off later in the week, when I can get a doctor's appointment." I looked down at her desk.

"You know you can always reach out to me. You're the best member of staff I have here, you mean a lot to everyone. If there's anything we can do to help with whatever is wrong?"

I shook my head as I glanced up, battling tears, although I didn't know why. "It's just a virus most likely. I'll be OK. I'm sorry if it's affected my work, I didn't mean for it to."

"Your work is brilliant as ever. I have an obligation to look out for my staff, though, Amber, and it seems to me that since that lovely young girl died, you've struggled."

My eyes met June's as she mentioned the patient. "Her name was Rebecca." My tone was aggressive as I spoke the words and I immediately regretted it.

June tapped her pen on the desk as she considered me. "I think we need to get you an appointment with Occupational Health. Rebecca was the same age as you, wasn't she? I can see why that would affect you in this way. I'll do the paperwork, but until the appointment comes through, I think you should take some time off. Try and relax, practise some self-care."

"Am I being suspended?" I gasped as the nausea in me threatened to overspill.

"No, nothing like that. I have a duty of care; I need to make sure you're OK. This job we do, it takes its toll on our own health."

"I understand, I don't think I need it, but I do understand your position. I'm here now, though, and it looks busy," I glanced at the patient admissions chart on my iPad. "Can I work this shift?"

June nodded. "Of course, I'll get all the paperwork done now. Please don't think this is a reflection on you. Your health is too precious to put at risk."

I was in a daze as I wandered back to my office to amend the rotas for the rest of the week. I made a call to the doctor's surgery while I was there and arranged an appointment for three days' time, before I busied myself with the shift and patient care.

By the time I had chance for a break, my feet ached, and I took the opportunity to recline on the comfortable, familiar sofa in the staff room, cradling my boiling hot mug of tea, and wondering who had eaten all the nice biscuits. I glanced across to the door as I heard the tell-tale squeak of the hinges, and my breath stalled as Ben entered the room.

"Amber," he said with an urgency, as he walked directly over to me. "I've been trying to call you; I came to your place, but you weren't there. What happened? Why did you run off? You've not replied to any of my messages, I didn't know if you were OK or…"

He finally ran out of words after his outburst. I looked at him quizzically. "Sorry if I worried you, I lost my phone. I hoped it might be at yours. I've not seen it since then."

"It's not at mine, I would have heard it the amount of times I've called and messaged."

"Did you drug me?" I asked, my eyes travelling down to the tattered coffee table covered in biscuit crumbs and tea stains.

He lifted my chin, so my eyes met his. "Amber, I wouldn't ever hurt you. How could you think that?"

"The whole night is a blur; I came round for something to eat and then the next thing I knew I was waking up in a friend's apartment. I can't even remember what we fell out about or why I was so upset. I need you to explain."

"Things got a bit heated," he glanced around self-consciously, "in the bedroom. I think you just panicked. I wanted you to stay so we could talk, but you insisted on leaving. Then I haven't been able to get hold of you since; I've been out of my mind with worry."

His eyes seemed so sincere, the blue of them almost

sparkled in the brightness of the room, but my mind was clammy and slow.

"What friend?"

"Pardon?" I asked in confusion.

"You said you woke up in a friend's apartment. What friend? Ellie? Does she know?"

"No, not Ellie. Not anyone you know."

His forehead creased and he scratched at his neck as he pulled back from me. "Can we try again? Definitely just dinner, won't go near the bedroom, I promise."

"I don't know," I replied, dropping my head into my hands as I took a deep breath. "I'm so confused. June is making me take some time off and meet with Occupational Health. I feel like everything is messed up and I don't understand."

"Just meet me as a friend then, that's all I'm asking. Let's go for lunch tomorrow. Or a picnic in the park like we mentioned last time? And you can talk to me about everything that's worrying you." He placed his hand on top of my own and I smiled as the warmness of him soaked into me.

"That sounds nice," I said, as I brushed a loose, blond curl from his forehead.

Just then the door squeaked as a group of nurses walked in, chattering and laughing as they rushed towards the kettle and fridge. Ben ruffled my hair lightly as he headed out, back to work with a smile. I found myself in a daydream once more as the others sat down. A daydream of the two of us at the park, laughing, as the sunshine bathed us in warm rays.

For the rest of the shift, I didn't mention to anyone that I'd be taking a break, I felt awkward about it, as if it were some form of punishment, despite June's reassurances. I locked all my files and iPad away in my office and headed out of the doors, pulling my jacket on as I glanced at the ominous-looking rain clouds that seemed to be blowing in.

Ellie was just finishing a phone call; the signal inside was notoriously bad, and staff often lurked out here on break times to catch up on calls and messages. "Amber," she called over. "I'm still owed an update; don't think you've got away with it by not replying to my messages."

I smiled as I headed over, my clumsy fingers hastily pressing the buttons on my jacket together. "Nothing much to say, we're just friends. I lost my phone, sorry, didn't mean to ignore you."

"Hmm." She eyed me with suspicion for a moment before her gaze was drawn behind me, and her mouth dropped open dramatically. "Holy fuck... I think my ovaries just exploded."

I twisted my neck around, eager to learn what on earth had drawn that reaction from her. I couldn't help but bite my lip to quell a smile as I spotted Mason head across the car park, his hand raised in a wave.

I looked back to Ellie who waved in return, a trance-like expression painted across her face. "He's waving at me." I laughed, elbowing her in the side. "That's Mason, the guy I told you about, who spilled my drink."

"You didn't mention he was mind blowingly hot. Is he single?" she panted. An emotion I hadn't felt before passed through me, a queasiness, an unwillingness to share that information. I didn't like it; it felt territorial and very not me.

"Erm, I'm not sure. I'd better go see what he wants. I'll call you tomorrow." I winced, as I realised I had no phone, no numbers, but I didn't have the energy to deal with that right now.

She continued to stare at Mason as I backed away, stifling a giggle, and turned to meet him on his path towards me.

"This is a nice surprise," I beamed as I spoke, genuinely happy to see him again. "Hopefully, neither of us is going to fall or spill any hot liquids today?"

Mason smiled at me, that dangerous smile as his white,

straight teeth showed, and a tiny dimple appeared in his chin. "Maybe I already fell," he said quietly.

My face must have flashed bright red, I was so unsure of how to react. Was he flirting? Was he teasing? I had no idea. I coughed, shivering slightly. "What brings you here?" My stomach dropped in case he was here for the obvious reason, the situation everyone dreaded. "You're not visiting someone are you? I'm sorry, I didn't think."

"Shh," he said with a kind smile, as he rubbed his hand up and down my arm. "No, the only person I'm visiting is you. I got you a gift." He held out a paper bag from a well-known department store. I was excited but simultaneously confused.

"Why?"

He shrugged and for a moment I saw a flash of a cheeky little boy, the type who would get away with all his mischief thanks to the charming smile on his face. "To be honest, I think it's a selfish gesture. I wanted to get your number, and I can only get it if you have a phone..."

I lifted the sleek, rectangular box out of the bag, my eyebrows wrinkled up. "That's way too generous, you shouldn't have done that."

He ignored my protestations as he continued. "I had them set it up, just switch it on and it's all ready to go." I ran my hand over the box with a smile, it was so much fancier than my old one. "Amber, why is she staring at me like that?"

I laughed as I turned and saw Ellie, still rooted in place. "Apparently, the sheer sight of you made her ovaries explode. You want her number instead?" I made a joke of it, but I really didn't want him to say yes.

"I've already got the only number I want. Shall we give her something to stare at?"

I tilted my head to the side, confused at what Mason meant, before he wrapped his arms around me and hugged me tightly. He took a deep breath as my head settled underneath his chin. Thoughts of Ellie and new mobile phones left my mind as in return, I sank against him, his scent immediately causing the sensation of being in his bed again. I shocked myself as a singular thought crossed my mind – if only he'd been in the bed with me.

"You got time to grab a drink?" he asked, as he released me from the embrace.

I was caught off guard. I'd never been popular, the one with plans, yet now I had Ben, Ellie, and Mason after my time.

"Erm, sure, no plans to rush home for."

"In that case, want some dinner with that drink?" His dark eyes were wide and hopeful as he looked at me.

I paused before I answered. I had no reason to refuse but I was unsure if I had the confidence to say yes. I settled for a nod and glanced back to see Ellie giving me the thumbs up as Mason linked his arm through mine, and we walked towards the high street, leaving my faithful old car behind as we discussed what type of food would be nice.

I peered back over my shoulder once more, sure I could feel eyes on me from the staff room, but it was just my imagination; the window was bare.

FIFTEEN
ANWIR

I rested one hand against Amber's across the middle of the table as we faced each other, nestled at the back of the Italian restaurant on the high street which she'd nervously assured me had been fantastic on her work's Christmas party a couple of years ago. Reassured that I could touch her, I found myself unable to stop, my fingers constantly wanting to trail over her skin, and I had to restrain myself or risk scaring her away.

When I'd asked where she wanted to go, she seemed so unsure of herself. It didn't appear as if she had much of a social life and I couldn't discern why - she was absolutely beautiful, kind, sweet, and funny. I pulled my hand back to my drink, hoping to quell the taunts, thoughts, and voices that plagued me. The space she inhabited in my mind grew exponentially, day after day.

The knowledge that I could touch her had firmly embedded itself into my mind and the thought consumed me. I'd hardly slept last night; thinking about her endlessly was exhausting and I knew I had to see her today. This had never happened before and I didn't welcome it, yet I pandered to it. At a time that I should be heading home after having destroyed her, I was instead buying her lemon and basil tagliatelle and wondering if she'd let me kiss her later. It was laughable, and very not me.

After I'd seen Amber home last night and made sure she was safe, I'd fallen into a foul mood. My feelings about her were utterly alien and they brought back too many dark thoughts of my father – had he failed to kill her for the same reason? Did he long for her as I did? The thought I might have anything in common with him disgusted me and I needed to do something to rid myself of that sensation.

Two hours later I'd been undressing two extremely attractive, eager, and agile blondes in my bedroom. I'd chosen women who looked as close to Amber as possible, but the reality was neither of them held a torch to her, with their thick make up and low-cut tops. They tried too hard, whereas Amber exuded beauty without even knowing it, and they were invisible in comparison.

I tried to get into the zone, to forget who they were or weren't and just lose myself in the sex, but as I took a deep breath against one of the pillows, Amber's scent flowed into me. It was the beautiful aroma of vanilla and honey that always seemed to accompany her. I was repulsed that I'd brought other women here, allowed them to taint that memory of her.

I'd flown into an absolute rage, snarling at them to get out. They fled, terrified, as I threw their belongings out the door after them, slamming it so hard a faint crack appeared in the thick, dark wood adjacent to a hinge.

Once I'd calmed, I'd called Amber on her landline, as promised, to check that she was settled. I spent far longer than was necessary wishing her the sweetest of dreams, my soul warm every time I made her laugh or sensed her smile down the phone. The rest of the night had been spent finishing off a bottle of whisky as I ran over and over my own idiocy and wondered what to do.

I needed to get back on track, as Amber seemed to trust me now. When I'd kicked her phone under the seat of the Uber, I was just thinking of keeping her away from *him*, but with a new phone I could contact her, I could track her, I would have an excuse to see her again. What I hadn't planned on was asking her out to dinner and sitting here, staring at her beautiful face like a lovesick puppy.

"I spoke to Ben today." She volunteered the information.

"Ben? The friend from the other night?"

She nodded. "I still don't know why I can't remember, but he said we were..." Her face flushed scarlet before she continued quietly. "He said we were... getting intimate, in his bedroom, and I freaked out and left."

I was repulsed as I remembered the sight of the two of them. I'd thought at the time it was as close as I'd get to intimacy with her, but I knew now that I could touch her, too. If I'd been aware of it that night, I'd have forcefully dragged him off her. "Do you think it's the truth?" I asked.

She bit on her lip, lowering her cutlery to the almost empty pasta bowl. "It sounds as though it could be true, I do get... sort of freaked out by situations like that."

"By intimacy?" I asked, as I stirred at the turn this conversation was taking.

"I'm not like normal people, I've never had sexual urges. I've never..." She lowered her voice even further, her eyes scanning around us. "I've never slept with anyone."

I blew out a low breath to calm the absolute fire that had awakened underneath the table. Not only was she absolutely fucking perfect, but she was also a virgin. "Does he know this? Was he trying to force you?"

"I don't think so. I do feel things when I'm with him, I'm

just not used to it. Ugh, I don't know what I'm saying, ignore me. You don't want to know this."

"I do want to know because I want to help you and make sure you're safe. And I don't think that guy is good for you. He had no internet presence, remember? Nada, that's not normal, and then you've got these memory gaps when you're with him."

She nodded and took a drink of her sparkling water. "I know it doesn't look good. I honestly don't think he's a bad person, though."

"There's one other problem," I said, as I gulped the deep, red wine from my long-stemmed glass.

Her blue eyes met mine, pupils wide with anxiety. She worried so much, I wanted her to never have to feel that way again; I longed to keep her safe. Such an idiot, how could I keep her safe with my history, my heritage?

I glanced down towards the table as I gathered my thoughts, before looking up at her. "I'm maybe biased against him, because I…" I sighed sadly. "I wish I was the guy who gave you those feelings. I meant what I said the other day, about wanting to kiss you. I can't stop thinking about it. It's like you drag me closer to the edge, every single day."

This time she held my gaze, and I could see the blush still threatened under her pale, porcelain-like skin, but she held it under control as her eyes drank me in. I couldn't tear my gaze away from her, even as I felt her hand settle on top of mine, the warmth and goodness within her seeping into me.

"I wanted to kiss you, too, when I so gracefully fell into your arms, "she chuckled. "But I'm just so confused at the moment. I don't deserve how nice you are to me."

"You deserve so much more than me, but that doesn't stop me from wanting you. Would I ever even stand a chance?"

"You're in a completely different world to me, Mason. Guys like you, don't have girlfriends like me."

"Guys like me... you don't know what I'm like." The reality of this situation weighed heavy as I placed a pile of notes on the table to cover the bill, plus a hefty tip. "Come on, I'll walk you back to your car."

I wrapped my arm around her shoulder as we wandered down the high street. When I glimpsed our reflection in a shop window, the image struck me of how right we looked together. Nobody from my plane knew I'd come to kill her, other than the lesser ones, and they wouldn't even remember by now, be earning their pennies doing nefarious deeds for others already. Maybe this *could* be something?

It wasn't me she liked, though, it was Mason, and that's what I needed to remember when I went home. I needed to go home and leave her alone, for I knew without a doubt I couldn't hurt her. This was the only way, before my terror discovered that failure ran in the family.

Amber surprised me as she wrapped her arms around my middle after unlocking her car. "Thank you for dinner," she mumbled into my chest. "I had a lovely time."

"Me too," I said, as I rested my chin on her head, holding her close. As I breathed her in, I closed my eyes, eager to memorise this moment and the feel of her. I knew I had to leave and that the crushing pain would take over my chest.

She pulled back slightly, much to my dismay. "Hey, Mason..." I heard her say. I began to open my eyes to look at her, but before I did, she kissed me.

Her soft lips brushed delicately against me, locking us together as mine slowly moved against hers. I'd never kissed like this before, and it burned me up from the inside. We barely moved as the thin, delicate skin of our mouths pressed together. I felt her bite on her bottom lip and I smiled as I nudged her and instead, nibbled gently on it myself. She moved her arms up around my neck and began to press a multitude of tiny, sweet kisses across my mouth.

Every single thing about this woman was utterly, fucking adorable.

A deep sigh escaped her lips as my hands slid down her back, and I pressed her carefully against the car, entranced. She pulled me closer, and I took the signs of enjoyment to heart as I deepened the kiss, letting my mouth wrap around hers as we tangled together, a true, soulful kiss. I knew I'd never experience the likes of this with any other.

With her face in my hands, I scattered slow, full whispers from my lips down her cheeks and across her neck, stopping to feel her pulse against my mouth as her accelerated heartbeat sounded out in tandem with my own. She shivered as I nipped at her collarbone before returning to her mouth and letting my tongue slide alongside her own. She met me and matched me in urgency and wanting.

How could I have ever guessed it could feel like this? I didn't have words; this was so much more than a kiss, and I couldn't comprehend where these feelings that flooded into me came from, as if borne from nothing. Surely, they must have existed before today, gathered at the edges of the universe before they flew to us, summoned by our mingled breath?

A car drove in and passed us, its headlights disrupted the moment as we pulled away, our lips clinging to each other's for the briefest moment before Amber stumbled. My arms steadied her as she giggled self-consciously and buried her head in my chest.

"I'm so sorry," she muttered.

I took her hands in mine, interlacing my fingers with hers. "Amber, my attraction to you, it isn't just one way, is it? That was…" I didn't have a word to finish that sentence, nor did I need to as she placed one solitary kiss upon my mouth again.

"Sexy as hell?"

I grinned. "Yeah." I shifted my legs, not wanting her to be put off by how hard I was right now, turned on by her, the kiss, the moment, the sheer magic of this whole situation. "I swear I've tasted you on my lips before…"

"Can we go back to yours?" she asked with a gulp, wide eyed and utterly alluring.

"Yes," I replied, as I raised her hands to my mouth, kissing them both before I climbed into the passenger seat. An absolute wreck of nerves, anticipation, and lust, plus, a heat that spread out from a central point within me, a warmness I had no word to describe – I'd never felt it before.

SIXTEEN

AMBER

My fingers whitened on the steering wheel as I gripped it tight. Why on earth had I asked to go back to his? How was I going to explain away how uncomfortable I was when we got there? What if that weird ache appeared again like it had with Ben?

There was no comparison between the two of them. When I'd kissed Ben, it had been nice, I'd liked it. But when I'd kissed Mason... I couldn't even describe the sensation, I'd been lost in it, and that's why I'd asked to go back to his.

I knew I'd end up full of regret but somehow it was worth it, to be close to him, to spend time with him. He was intoxicating, yet it only made me more certain that I had some sort of hormonal imbalance, going from having no attraction to anyone in the world, then being attracted to two guys in the same month. I made a mental note to mention it to the doctor when I had my appointment.

The rain poured down. I loved the sound on the glass, that persistent tip tap interrupted by the swish of the wipers breaking the silence that somehow echoed within the car. The continuous drum of heavy raindrops against the windows only added to the excitement of being in such close proximity to Mason. I licked my lips as I remembered the feel of his own upon them, and from the corner of my eye I spotted him sneak a glance at me, a small, but unmistakable smile flickering across his mouth.

"Where should I park?" I asked, breaking the hush that still soaked the inside of the car.

"There's an underground car park," he replied, pointing to an entrance at the left of his building.

"I feel bad that we just went out for dinner, and I was dressed in my work clothes. I'm sure you're used to glamorous ladies?"

Mason raised an eyebrow at me, his mouth pulled to one side as he sucked on his gum. "All you need to know is that I wouldn't change anything about you."

I followed him to the lift, clutching the paper bag with my new phone inside, without a clue as to what I would do once we were inside. He pushed the button for the twentieth floor and as the doors closed and the whoosh of the rapidly rising lift began, our eyes met.

We seemed to communicate so much as we stood gazing at each other for that minute that stretched into an eternity. Like a spell had fallen upon us both and we didn't want to escape.

"You and I..." Mason whispered, "we're a collision. Probably not meant to happen, but we fell through every gap until we landed here, together."

I felt myself glide towards him, like he pulled me with delicate strings, then everything blurred. His mouth was on mine, his fingers were in my hair, he walked me backwards towards his front door as he fumbled in his pocket for his keys. My breath was caught up in my lungs as he slammed the door closed behind us and pressed me against the wall. I heard the clatter as a table was knocked down, its contents spilling all over the floor, but I didn't care, I just needed more of him.

I wrapped my arms around his middle, tugging his shirt loose so I could touch his skin whilst my mouth moved down to his neck, dark stubble prickling at my lips in a delicious way which I could never have anticipated. He slid his knee between my legs and as he brushed against me, I gasped for breath. This was pure pleasure like I'd never, ever known, not with Ben, not with myself, nothing had ever felt like this.

He pinned my hands to the wall and pressed his knee harder against me as his mouth covered mine. Only when he gave me a second to breathe did I manage to utter some lost words. "Mason, I'm not going crazy, am I? This *is* happening?"

His kisses slowed down as his hands let me go. He swiped my hair away from my forehead, his thick eyelashes fluttered as he regained his breath. I couldn't help but let out a disappointed sigh as he moved his knee from the place it was so welcome.

"Why are you stopping? Please don't stop."

He smiled at me as he led me over to the sofa. "Trust me, I don't want to stop. But, knowing what I know... I can't be your first. I don't deserve you, I've done awful things in my past, but I won't do them to you. I refuse."

"What do you mean? You're one of the nicest people I've ever met."

He sighed, and his hand shook a little as he ran it through his now dishevelled hair. I couldn't take my eyes off him, I felt greedy. It was as if he were a drug, and I was desperate for another hit.

"There are things I want to tell you, but I'm not sure where to begin. I don't want to scare you or upset you."

I took hold of his hands. "I wouldn't think less of you, what is it? I already feel like I know you, yet I want to know more. I want to know the real you, I want you to know the real me." I sighed. "Sorry, I sound like some desperate teenager, don't I? This isn't what you need."

I stood, as if to leave, but he pulled me back down, his eyes wide with emotion. "Please don't go. Stay, Amber."

As I lowered myself back down on the sofa, he visibly relaxed. I pressed a kiss to the wrinkles of worry that had indented themselves on his forehead and he looked across at me, stroking my hand as he began to speak.

"How open minded are you? Can we be totally honest?"

"I may not have had a wild life, but I'm not a judgemental person. People's lives are complex, it isn't black and white."

"You do so much good, you're like a shining light. And I... I've hurt people, physically and emotionally. I don't bring light or goodness to people, I hurt them, and I move on. I'm worthless, and I can't entangle your life into that."

"I'm sure that's not true—"

"It's absolutely fucking true," he snapped, interrupting my protestations. "You have no idea. My father was a failure of a man and all I do is follow in his footsteps no matter how hard I try to sidestep them. I mean, look at me now. Here to complete a task, and instead I find myself falling in love with a woman I can't ever have."

His hands cradled his head as he pulled at his hair. My mind whirled in confusion. He was falling in love with me? Surely, he didn't know me well enough, but then, my experience of it all was severely lacking.

"I know everything about pleasure, lust, sex, fucking," he continued. "But absolutely nothing about love. Nobody has ever loved me, and I've never felt love for another. Until now. Until you."

"I've never experienced romantic love, but I felt encapsulated by the love of my mother from the day I was born. And I'm surrounded by the most heart-breaking love every day at work as people say their final goodbyes." I gulped, sucking on my lip. "But I've known nothing of sex, of bodies, of what people can do to each other. And I've never wanted to. Until now. Until you." I smiled at him as I copied his words and was rewarded with a dazzling grin.

"I want nothing more than for us to teach each other what we know. But I'm not the one to show you. I'm not the one you're destined for."

"Who decides who we are supposed to be with? Do I not get to make that decision?" I asked.

"Not if you're already bound."

I let out a long sigh. "Why does everyone speak to me in riddles?"

"What do you mean?"

"Ben..." I replied, "from work, it's the kind of thing he talks about. He tells me stories about different places, and it confuses me."

"What's the deal with you and him?" Mason asked, attempting to look nonchalant, but the tiny tremor in his voice gave him away.

"I don't know. He seems to want to court me, but something feels off. Especially after that night I don't remember."

Mason burst into laughter. "Sorry, did we go back to Victorian times? He's 'courting' you? Do you have space on your dance card for me, madam?"

I joined in his laughter and slapped him on the arm playfully. "Too many historical romance books. You know what I mean."

He grabbed me and pulled me to his chest in a delicate embrace. "I still can't get over the fact I can touch you."

I twisted around and placed a single kiss to his lips. "Of course you can touch me. When I asked to come back here, I hoped you knew what I meant. I want you to touch me, Mason."

He threw his head back against the sofa, and a growl of frustration escaped his lips.

"I know you don't usually drink, but will you please have one glass with me? There are things I need to tell you and it's not going to be easy."

A flash of lightning lit up the sky, an incredible sight through the tall glass windows of the penthouse. Moments later a tumble of thunder rippled through the air, I almost felt it was responsible for the goosebumps upon my arms, but Mason caused more of them than all the thunder in the world ever could.

"I love thunder..." he mumbled.

"Me too," I said, as I stroked my fingers across his neck.

"Shall we talk on the roof? Get closer to the storm?"

I nodded and he placed a kiss on my hairline, shivering slightly, before he grabbed two long-stemmed glasses and an expensive looking bottle. He led me to the fire doors, next to the elevator we'd been in not long before, and together we ascended to the roof.

Seventeen

Anwir

Was I doing the right thing, attempting to explain it all to her? I should have just taken her to bed and then sent her on her way, before leaving this place and heading home. I'd used more women, and men, than I could count, so why couldn't I do it this time?

It was difficult to admit, but I awoke each morning with an ache because she wasn't next to me. I couldn't bear the thought of existing this way, so needy, so lost without her.

I grabbed a large, snug blanket from a basket, identical to those in the lobby, and headed over to the comfortable rattan furniture which was housed under a covered pergola. The rain pounded down but it couldn't touch us in here, we were perfectly placed to experience the storm, the only light that illuminated us being the soft glow of the LED lanterns that were strung diagonally around the roof of the structure.

We sat sideways; eyes trained on each other. Amber tucked the blanket around us as I poured two glasses of deep, sultry red wine. This wine had been tucked away in Mason's office, Château Margaux 2004 – it looked expensive, it tasted delectable. If this beautiful creature was going to have her first drink of wine, it should be a good one. Not like the vinegary, bitter drinks of home. I imagined that where she came from, everything was delicious, but I'd never know, I could never go there.

She broke me from my trance with a soft murmur. "So?"

"Try the drink first," I encouraged, as I stroked her hair behind her ear.

She tentatively raised it to her lips, and I longed to lick the remnants away. Her eyes closed as she tilted her head from side to side and let the small sip of deep, dark liquid travel around her mouth.

"I can taste oranges..." She smiled serenely and raised the glass for another sip. "And black cherry, it feels warm. I like it."

She took a third sip, opening her eyes to look at me. Her smile through the glass of ruby liquid was enough to bring me to my knees. It was as though every second I fell deeper, accelerated towards a terminal velocity that would crush me. Was this what insanity felt like - a sharp tumble into some unknown abyss where love and lust nestled together amongst dark, unknown depths?

"Do you ever think there's more than just this world? Other places, times, beings?" I asked.

She nodded. "I do. I don't know what exactly, but I've felt strangeness at work, when a person passes. Or when they're close, more so when they're close."

My mind whirred with options, how to get to the point without scaring her, without alienating her or making her think I was unstable.

"This," I gestured around us, to the sky, with golden timing as a flash of lightning lit up the skyscape, "this planet. It has... layers. We're here, on this layer, or plane. There are two other planes."

She watched me intently as the tiniest vertical line

appeared on the inside of her right eyebrow, and I knew she suppressed a frown.

"These layers all exist at the same time. Time moves at the same speed, but the places are separated. There's a barrier between them, a barrier that humans cannot see or cross. If the planes were stacked on top of each other, the humans would be in the middle."

"So, who would be the bread in this human sandwich of planes?" she asked with a bemused smile. Perhaps she thought this was just some conspiracy theory, which maybe wasn't the worst outcome; I could let it settle in her mind. "Who lives on the other two planes?"

"Angels and demons." I replied, matter of factly. "Angels live in the sunshine and demons live in the dirt."

"I don't believe in heaven and hell. Nothing is that black and white." She jumped, spilling a drop of wine, as another peel of thunder rumbled louder and closer. The rain hammered onto the roof and Amber cuddled in closer to me, pulling the blanket higher up to keep us warm.

"Heaven and hell are purely human fiction, nobody of any race will be there to greet you when you die. The stories and legends of angels and demons have come about from ancient history, from times when the races crossed into the human plane; humans are rather prone to drama. Angels and demons can travel to the human plane, the middle plane, but not to each other's, luckily, because they've been at war for a very long time."

"I suppose that would sort of make sense." She wrapped her fingers around mine and I rubbed softly at her cold skin in an attempt to bring warmth to it. "How do you know all this? Is there any proof?"

I sucked a deep breath in and squeezed her hand. "You and I are the proof."

There was silence. I let it sit, allowed the words to mould

into her mind, form an idea of what I was trying to get across. I inhaled through my nose and the ozone of the storm flowed into me. There were so many things I couldn't stand about this plane, but I had grown very attached to the fresh air.

"I'm completely bewildered," she began. "But... the way you speak to me, it just sounds right, I can't get enough. I want to know all of this, all of you, Mason."

"What if I told you I wasn't human?" I turned her face to mine, her beauty not dimmed at all in the shadows of the night, and slowly kissed her, savouring each second in case it was my last.

"I think it would make sense," she said, her lips against mine. "Because you're spectacular. Of course you're an angel."

I ripped my gaze away from hers as a pressure crushed down on my heart. This was where I'd lose her, where her natural instinct to detest me and my type would awaken.

"You mentioned black and white before, it isn't that simple. You can't write a whole species off as good or bad. Look at humans! Angels and demons have been at war for so long, but at least we don't go to war on our own type. Nothing has killed more humans than other humans, with their pointless wars and their false religions."

"Mason, it wouldn't matter to me what you were. The way I feel about you, I've never experienced it. It's like I was meant to find you."

"Amber," I held her tightly to me and spoke into her ear, "you've never been attracted to any of them because they're human. You're not. You shouldn't be attracted to me because you're an angel... I'm not."

Her body shuddered but she didn't move away from me. I was ready to lose her, yet somehow, she was still here with me. After a moment she reached for her glass, taking a long sip before she passed it to me. The gesture meant everything, that she still wanted to share even with the knowledge of what I was. That warmness spread within me again and released some of the crush upon my chest.

"Normally, I'd think this was foolish nonsense. But things lately... have happened to me that make no sense. Can I tell you? If you know why, will you answer?"

"I'll never be anything but honest with you. Which is hilarious, given my name."

"What's your name?" she asked, her teeth sinking into that plump bottom lip again as she faced me. "Your real name?"

"Anwir," I replied. "It means liar." My stomach sank in shame. What was I even doing here, hoping to be with someone like her?

"What's my real name?" she asked with a loud gulp, placing the glass back on the table.

"Mireille."

At that moment a blinding bolt of lightning hit further up the road, so strong it shook the entire building, and the accompanying thunder growled its anger out across the city, booming and seemingly eternal.

Time between us stopped, as Mireille observed me, and our truth, for the first time.

EIGHTEEN

AMBER

A s surreal as this was, I sensed his honesty; there was a naked truth to his words. I gazed into his eyes and saw fear, enough to petrify a person.

"Don't be scared, please. I'm not leaving," I reassured him.

He pulled me into a tight hug and his vulnerability tore a hole in me. He'd said nobody had ever loved him, how could that be? He drew me in, melted me, intrigued me, burned me.

"I need you to tell me more. Somebody else called me Mireille, recently. Why do I not know this name? Is this some weird witness protection? Amnesia?"

"Not quite. You were put here to keep you safe though."

"So, I'm an angel? That's what you're telling me?"

"Yes, but not in the way you know them, from a human mind. You're just a being from the angelic plane, but you've been here for a long time."

"And you're from..." I let the words peter out, not sure of how to phrase this and not wanting to offend him or make him feel worse than he obviously did.

"The demon plane. If you do want to leave, I understand."

"I don't claim to understand what's happening here, in

any way, shape or form. But the one thing I do understand is that I don't want to leave you. I need you; I want you. Wherever you're from, your ancestry, that's not your fault and it isn't something you should be responsible for."

"You said someone else called you Mireille?" he asked, as the lightning flashed again. "Was it Ben?"

I nodded. "Is he a demon, too? A bad one? Is that why I get these memory blanks? Is that why he's been so... persuasive? To try and corrupt me?"

"I don't know this for sure, but I'm pretty confident he's an angel. I think he's been sent to take you back home. You must have some history with him, for him to be given the task."

"What were you sent here for?" I asked.

"I wasn't sent, I chose to travel here. To right a wrong, an event that my father messed up."

"What if I don't want to leave here? Don't want to go with Barke?" My voice sounded stubborn and defiant.

"Is that his real name?" asked Mason, as a cloud of sadness descended upon him. "You're remembering, aren't you?"

"I think so, but that's all it is. A memory. That doesn't mean I want to go back there. Maybe I want to go with you."

"You can't travel to my plane. And I can't travel to your plane. There isn't anywhere we could be together. I have to let you go and I'm trying to do it in the best way. I'm trying."

"We can just stay here together, then. We have choices, if you want to try this, we can."

The heavy rain now seeped through the sodden roof; I wiped wet splodges from his forehead as he spoke to me, that cloud of despair not lifting at all.

"If we stay here both sides will come for us. They'll destroy us. You see, I shouldn't be able to touch you. Angels are toxic to demons, my skin should blister and burn when I touch you, but it doesn't. Your kiss should smoulder my lungs to ash, but it doesn't. That's dangerous and neither side will stand for it. They'd kill us both, they'd hunt us."

"So, why can I touch you?" I whispered, desperation tinged at the edge of my voice.

"I haven't figured that one out," he replied, resting his forehead against my own as his warm breath washed over me.

It was as though that breath deposited tendrils of smoky lust into my mind, and now, they threatened to consume me. I couldn't think about anything but him, I tortured myself with the imagination of his touch all over me, his effect on me, how to get more, always more. He was like a drug, and I wanted to consume him entirely.

"You don't know love and I don't know lust," I whispered into his ear, biting gently. "Maybe we only have this one night, who knows? How can anybody know? I want you to teach me pleasure, and I'll show you how it feels to be loved."

My breath was greedy and fast as I waited for his response. His eyes flicked between mine, his mind in obvious turmoil. Yet he didn't speak, he seemed unable.

"Anwir," I loved the feel of his name upon my tongue, it dripped from my mouth like dew from heaven. "You deserve love, you should always have been loved. How about tonight, I'll teach you how to make love, and you teach me how to fuck?"

I shocked myself at the use of the word, but I had to have him. I couldn't leave this place without him. A further bolt of lightning struck, but the thunder lagged behind as the storm drifted away. Almost as if it didn't want to watch this act, so private, so sacred, that it could only be between us. Even if it could only happen once, even if it killed us, I knew it had to be. We, Anwir and Amber, had to be.

Shaking himself out of his trance, Anwir grabbed my hand, and we ran, laughing in the rain, back down to his apartment. As if we were just giddy, innocent teenagers, for one night, at least.

≈≈≈

"Can I ask something of you?" Anwir said, as he led me through the dark apartment towards his bedroom, the same room I'd slept in just nights before when I'd felt like a different person.

"Of course," I replied, as lightning lit the room aglow.

"I don't know how this will go, it's never happened before, an angel and a demon, to my knowledge at least. If I should change in anyway, please don't look at me. I couldn't bear it if you rejected me, not after everything you've made me feel." His eyes were downcast. "I've shielded us, we're safe... from them."

"Anwir," I saw another brief shiver run through him as I used his true name, "I would never reject you. I see nothing but beauty in you. Can you do something for me?"

He nodded, wrapping my hands in his.

"Keep calling me Amber. I don't want to be Mireille. I don't want to be the woman who can't be with you."

"Deal," he said, low and husky as he reached for me, his lips landing upon mine as soft as snowflakes drifting down to earth.

I was completely out of my comfort zone; this was new territory. My mind was jumbled with his words and the confusion of the past few weeks. Yet I knew, none of it mattered. If all we had was one night, I wanted to live every second of it.

My eyes fluttered closed at the sensation of his lips as they touched mine... and I found myself exploring every bit of his mouth softly and slowly. I unbuttoned his shirt, let my fingers trail over his skin as it was exposed. Once every button was open, he shrugged the shirt off and I wrapped my arms around him and inhaled the heady scent of his chest as I lowered my ear and listened to his heartbeat, strong and steady.

"I know you say we're different," I said, raising my mouth back up to his ear, "but your heart beats just like mine, your lips kiss just like mine. And I love you, as if you were mine."

He froze for a moment, then lowered his head to my ear in return. "Amber, I'm yours. Completely yours. I've never said the words... I..."

He gulped and I stroked his cheek, pulling him to face me as I placed a kiss onto his lips. "You don't have to say it because I know it. All you have to do is accept my love, accept that you deserve it. Then show me how that makes you feel."

It was as if a timer went off and we hurriedly undressed each other, giggling at our clumsy fingers and thumbs as clothes and underwear were discarded to the corners of the room. Anwir walked to one side of the bed, naked, and I forced myself to keep my eyes on his face as I tiptoed to the opposite side, a giddy smile ever-present upon my mouth.

I sighed at the sensation as I slid between the freshly laundered sheets, so smooth and cool against me. Yet the pleasure of the sheets paled away as Anwir kissed his way up my arm, holding himself above me with the biggest, dopiest grin on his face.

"Hi," he beamed.

"Hi," I replied, my heart bursting into overdrive at the sensation of being underneath him, the sheer amount of skin that touched skin now setting off impulses and triggers around my whole body.

"I like you being in my bed..." he purred as his mouth moved down and kissed the top of my shoulder, before licking at my collarbone. "After you stayed the other night, I could smell you here, it was extremely distracting."

"Mmhmm," I mumbled, unable to put any intelligent

sounds together as his mouth moved down lower, teasing on its travels before his tongue met my nipple and I bunched the sheets up under my fingers.

"You like?" he asked, teasingly, as he moved to the other side and repeated the action, growing in firmness as his teeth indented my now hardened nipple ever so slightly.

I tried to speak but no sound escaped my mouth as I arched my body. He pressed me back down, returning to my mouth for a kiss and allowing his tongue to entangle with mine.

"I know you're struggling for words right now, but if you want me to stop, I need to know that you'll tell me. You have to want this one hundred per cent because we can't take it back."

I bit my tingling lip as his eyes sank into mine.

"I would tell you; I promise. But I don't think I'll want you to stop. Do we..." I felt mortified at what I was about to say, which was ridiculous given that he'd just had my nipples in his mouth. "Do we need protection? I'm not on any contraception; certified virgin, remember?"

"As if I could forget, feeling the pressure there. And no, demons make babies the same way humans do, but angels don't. You don't have to worry about catching anything, I've always been careful." He pressed a kiss to my forehead. "It's your choice, give me a minute, I'll grab something."

"No." I tilted my head to the side. "Just you, I only want you." A playful smile worked its way onto my mouth. "If I tell you I love you again, will you keep kissing me?"

"I will, but tell me first, are strawberries still your favourite food?"

I laughed as my fingers stroked the outline of his ribs. I marvelled at the feel of them having never touched a person like this. "They are," I said, kissing his neck.

He bit at my ear lobe before he replied, words that travelled directly into my mind like a flame that ran white hot along a wick. "If you want me to stop, say strawberry. I'll stop immediately, but if I don't hear that word I'm just going to keep going. And Amber, every time I eat a strawberry from now on, instead of tasting it, I'll taste you."

He shot down to my neck, kissing the gulp that stuck in my throat as I answered him.

"I'll keep it in mind, but I won't say it." I let my hand travel further down his back, scraping my fingers against him as I did so, wanting him entirely and eternally, so sure that I could gorge on this man forever.

"Stubborn woman." He tickled at my side, eliciting sharp giggles which quickly ceased as his mouth licked down my breastbone and all the way to my naval, where he proceeded to place soft kisses that grew firmer as he moved. His teeth scraped against my hip bone, as if he wished to taste every inch of skin, skin that grew hotter by the second.

Anwir flipped me onto my stomach and straddled me. "You are so beautiful," he murmured as he bent forwards, pushing my hair up and placing the lightest of kisses along the nape of my neck. He then layered them down my spine, and I felt his fingers rub underneath my shoulder blades and I tensed - remembering the image I'd seen in Ben's mirror.

"Amber," he said, as he moved beside me and wrapped me in a hug. "I promise you're safe."

"I only ever feel safe when I'm with you." My voice trembled as a solitary tear slid from my eye.

"Then stay with me, always," he murmured, as he moved back on top of me. "I love you."

I smiled at the words he'd managed to say as he wiped the tear away with his finger. Then the air in the room stilled, as if a magical curtain had lowered itself over us, protecting us. If all this talk of planes were true, I didn't care on which one I was right now, he loved me and I felt it in every atom that made up this form, whether it was mine or not.

The glide of his hands all over my body felt like silk caressing my skin. He touched me and explored me in ways that I knew existed but had never expected to feel. His fingers were so delicate as they slipped inside of me, opening my mind and body to new waves of pleasure.

I tried to reach down to touch him in return, but he grasped my hands and placed them at my sides. "Later," he sighed, his words vibrating against me as he continued his actions, and I melted deliciously underneath him, desperate for more.

He kissed his way back to my mouth, his fingers entangled with mine as he looked down upon me. "Completely sure?" he asked, his eyes beseeching me.

"In a million lifetimes, I could never be surer of anything than I am of this, Anwir." Every time I spoke his name it was as if I could see my love flow into his heart, then pump around his body, slowly but surely eroding away all the negativity he had within him.

He buried his face into my neck, squashing himself against the throb of my pulse as he reached down with one hand and positioned himself, just inside me... the barest hint of air separating us.

Then his hands were in my hair as he peppered kisses across my lips and cheeks, his eyes watched me with a mixture of concern and adoration as he pushed inside me, slow and gentle.

I tensed, not through mistrust of him, but with nervousness of the unknown. "I can stop anytime you want me to. Breathe, Amber." He moaned discreetly and my heart melted with love for him.

"Don't stop," I pleaded as I took in a deep breath, begging the oxygen to flow through my body, relax my muscles, soften myself against his hardness as I willed him deeper inside me. The sensation as he stretched me and moulded me to him was breath-taking, the twinges of pain only adding to my rapture.

His breath shuddered, a noise caught in his throat, and the sound of it at my ear nearly finished me off there and then. I wanted to burn the feel of this into my mind and relive it over and over. My arms and legs instinctively wrapped around him, holding him to me, as if fearful that he would flee and leave me without this experience again.

His voice murmured as we fell into a rhythm, a flow that was unique to us, only us. "I love you so much, I feel like it's going to overwhelm me."

"Me too, but I'd welcome it." I gasped as his speed increased at my words. The realisation that we were making love burrowed into my mind, birthing a glow that spread throughout me as I ran my fingers down his chest. It was as though our souls had been contained our whole lives, bound with delicate strings, and as we joined together, they disentangled and wove a new pattern, binding our hearts together eternally.

As I fell beneath him, I didn't care about his form, his lineage or past – he was pure love to me, love, and this new feeling. He created an insatiable urge to have him within me, it gnawed at my bones, and I was desperate for him to touch me everywhere, to take that urge and replace it with his touch, his soul. I wanted to tell him all about it as he lit my body up and brought me to life.

NINETEEN

ANWIR

What had that been? My mind raced, threatening to bubble over as it tried to comprehend what had just happened. I'd never felt anything like that, I was far from a stranger to physical pleasure, but that... That was something else. A deeper, stronger connection than surely could ever have existed before last night. How could anyone feel this and not want to shout it from the rooftops, to run gleefully and tell every person they saw how amazing life was when you were in love?

Her every kiss healed wounds I didn't know I had. Each stroke of her fingers soaked goodness into me, where before I'd only seen bad. Looking into her eyes as we'd been joined together... she overtook me, overwhelmed me and I knew I'd do anything for her. I'd sacrifice the whole world to keep her safe. She saw me, she truly saw the real me and she loved me.

My heart and my soul had blossomed, tripled in size as we lay in the bed staring into each other's eyes. Smiling, I stroked my thumb down her face. She was awe inspiring; so natural and beautiful with her reddened cheeks, swollen lips and that blonde hair messed up as it fell around her face. Waking up next to someone I loved was beyond my wildest dreams, dreams I hadn't known I even longed for.

"I was worried I'd hurt you," I said quietly, placing a kiss on her shoulder.

She shook her head as she answered. "You didn't hurt me at all. All you did was make me realise that for my whole life I've been nothing more than a shadow. I've not been truly alive, until now."

"I wish we could be like this, always. I'd banish every clock in existence to stop time for you, for us." I pulled her to my chest, closing my eyes as I embraced the feel of her against me. I'd never known anything could feel like this; I struggled to swallow my emotions as the realisation hit me that my entire life I'd been using people, discarding them, when instead I could have sought out... this. Although, wherever would I have found her? It would have been impossible.

"How can this be wrong?" she asked. "Why would they hunt us for this?"

"It isn't wrong. They're just bigoted idiots full of hate. Nothing about us being together is wrong."

"I think your name is beautiful by the way, Anwir," she said as she relaxed against me.

Every time she spoke my name, used the word love, pressed her fingertips or lips to my skin, I grew inside. As if I'd spent my whole life hunched over, eager to avoid notice, but she straightened my spine, she made me proud. She made me want to embrace every minute of life and never waste a second again.

Yet, there was something I couldn't swallow down, a breath that wouldn't reach the places it should. A heavy ball of lead had lodged itself in my throat as the thought that I dreaded drove itself into the forefront of my mind. I had to leave. For as pure and magical as this night had been, it had put her in danger. What right did I have to make love to her, when it could only lead to pain? I was such a fool to think we could have one perfect night, because I craved more, an agonised want that I knew would drive me insane. The angels would come for her and the demons would come for me, and we'd be torn apart.

Amber's breath had slowed, her heartbeat was sedate and settled as she pressed against me, falling into a delicate sleep in my arms. I couldn't help but smile at the snuffles and noises she made as she slipped into a dream, but at the same time they broke my heart.

I'd never expected to fall in love, and I'd never imagined for one moment that it could be so painful, so consuming, and yet so addictive all at once. For I had fallen so deeply, so quickly, so hard for this woman – but that was the problem. She wasn't simply a woman; she was an angel. There was no place for us to be together, she'd end up hurt and I couldn't let my selfishness, the flaw that had plagued me my entire life, cause her harm.

This one perfect night was all I could have if I wanted to keep her safe, and she needed to be safe. My entire life I'd been selfish, only cared about myself and the stupid reputation of my terror, but love had turned that around. Love had made me selfless, for I *would* put myself through the agony of never touching her again, I'd send her back to that angel, to him, if it meant that she would be safe.

One thing hadn't changed, though, that being the hatred and repulsion I felt for my father. He'd tried to murder her, over some foolhardy ancient prophecy that made no sense. If he'd been sober, better at his job, less distracted, he might have succeeded, and I'd have never known peace like this within me. Thankfully, he was an absolute fuckup, and this glorious creature who slept against my chest had defeated him.

What would she ever think of me if she knew?

I craved sleep. I longed to slumber beside her, share her

dreams, awaken to her smile. But I had to stay awake, I had to remember every second of this, the sounds she made, the way she smelled, the touch of her upon my skin. I would never experience it again.

For hours I lay there with her, my eyes raw with fatigue, my throat choked with emotion. An almost invisible crack had appeared on my heart, the heart once shrivelled and barely alive, that now swelled with love, lust, life, and blood. I knew the crack would grow, and it would kill me, but I had to do this. For Amber.

As the sun began its languid journey into a new day, I slid away from her. She reached out in her sleep, and I pressed my pillow into the warm spot my body had just vacated. The crack on my heart deepened as she wrapped herself around the warm, feathery pillow, took a deep breath and smiled as her breaths decelerated to that of deep sleep once again.

I summoned a small amount of power, which jolted into me with a shudder. I was not fully in control as this tsunami of emotion battered against me. With the power, shaky as it was, I moved silently, not causing the slightest of tremors as I collected my clothes and dressed.

At the bathroom sink, I reached for a toothbrush from the ostentatious, heavy, glass tumbler that Mason kept them in. Then I froze, gawking at myself in the mirror. It seemed the most mundane act, but if I brushed my teeth, I would remove the touch of her from my mouth and I simply couldn't bear to do that.

I remained silenced, so didn't hear the shatter of the glass under my hand as my fist slammed into it. The pain shot up my arm as shards of the thick glass drove into my skin, allowing viscous, dark blood to flow into the gloss-white sink below. My gaze didn't flicker from my eyes as I let the pain grow, hoping in vain, that it would distract me from the splinter carved deep within my chest as the fissure in my heart widened.

To draw this out longer than necessary would only make it worse and risk her waking. Let her have her beautiful sleep, and although she may hate me in the morning, she'd be home and safe soon.

I stepped backwards out of the bedroom door, unable to wrench my gaze from her sleeping form. I was utterly torn between wanting to imprint this image of her onto my retinas, burn it into them as the sun would, and also darkly wishing I could never think of her again, for my heart couldn't take the anguish, the grief.

In the end I had to lower my eyes as I turned and closed the bedroom door, before I solemnly left the apartment, leaving my keys and phone, knowing I wouldn't come back here ever again.

The only things I took with me were a large wad of cash and a tortured heart that dripped excruciatingly with regret and agony.

Twenty

Amber

I knew where I was the second my brain flashed with consciousness, before my eyes opened, before a single muscle in my body moved a millimetre. Anwir. That one word was a sunrise in my mind as I awoke, remade during the dark, stormy night we'd spent together.

My nose wriggled from side to side, a large smile formed underneath it as the scent of him travelled to my brain in a delicious swirl of love. He smelled amazing, a spicy concoction of black pepper and vanilla, just enough to tingle, yet warm me at the same time.

I stretched out my toes, revelling in the sensation of my muscles coming to life, as if I were aware of each individual one whilst a delicious stretch travelled up my body. The stretch continued up my legs, pulled at my sides before I arched my arms up over my head and yawned, slowly blinking my eyes open. My thighs ached as I squeezed them together, forcing my teeth to sink into my lip at the memory of how he'd made me feel. I longed to do it all again. It was as though I was a champagne bottle; all my lust had been held back, denied for so long, and he was the one who'd popped the cork.

Now, I simply couldn't stop the bubbles of desire that exploded from me.

The room was bathed in dim light, as if it was neither night nor day. I squinted towards the tall windows and took in the dense fog that covered the surrounding buildings. Due to the height of this tower, we were inside the thick mist.

The weather was of no consequence; I had nowhere to be. I would happily stay here with this amazing man as I continued to learn about his body and soul. There were no doubts how deeply entwined together we were.

I rolled over, a silly, excited grin on my face, wanting to share with Anwir how incredible I felt. Yet, I found the other side of the bed empty, his pillow lying lengthways down the bed alongside my body.

Pulling myself up, I rolled my neck from side to side and surveyed the room, wondering where he'd gone. The conversation about strawberries drifted lustfully through my mind as my stomach rumbled, and I hoped he'd gone to make breakfast. He seemed to like to feed me, take care of me.

My own clothes lay scattered across the floor, but Anwir's were notably absent; if he'd got dressed, that was a situation I would have to remedy. I grabbed a white T-shirt from the wardrobe and inhaled deeply as I pulled it over my head and stretched my arms into the soft cotton.

That blissful underfloor heating welcomed my bare feet as they touched down, toes jiggling playfully as I made my way to the bathroom, feeling every inch the sexual goddess as memories of last night seemed embossed upon my skin. As if any innocent passer-by would look at me and see the absolute delirium that he'd bestowed upon me, over and over again.

It took a moment for my brain to register the image that greeted me. A toothbrush, discarded in the sink, surrounded by the thickest, sharpest fragments of glass. Whatever had broken seemed to have shattered into a million jagged pieces. I was frozen to the spot as alarm bells replaced the warm sensation I'd bathed in. Laced within that glass was a deep, crimson liquid that could only be blood.

The way it had dripped amongst the glass shards emphasised it, making it seem like more. I knew from my nursing experience it wasn't a deadly amount, by far, but it was enough to have come from a bad wound that likely needed stitches. Why hadn't Anwir woken me if he'd hurt himself? As my brain began to piece together every possibility, I noticed that scattered droplets of blood trailed out of the bedroom.

"Anwir?" I called as I strode out of the door, worry prickling at my skin, leaving me with goosebumps for very different reasons than the previous few hours. The hallway was silent save for the hammer of my heart in my chest. I sprinted towards the kitchen, following the trail of blood as I called his name, but he wasn't there.

"Anwir!" My voice rose in pitch as I dashed from room to room in search of him, only to find every room hollow and empty. The fog outside the windows continued to circle, stifling the air in this place as I turned on the spot, around and around in confusion.

My eyes landed on the paper bag from the department store, and I leaped for it, grabbing the phone, and finding Anwir's number, the only number in there so far, even if it was marked as Mason. I waited anxiously as the call connected, only to hear the heavy buzz of his phone vibrate on the coffee table, my name illuminated on its display. His keys were next to it. Where would he have gone without keys and a phone, why was he bleeding, had he been attacked? Maybe the wound was so bad he'd gone to hospital. But... why without me? Why without his things?

I fell backwards in a slump, luckily close enough to the sofa for it to cushion my landing. My soul seemed to know his, yet of his actual day-to-day to life I knew little. I had no idea where he might be, who he might have gone to. Last night had been perfection; he loved me, I felt it, he wouldn't have just left me unless it was something urgent, of that, I was sure.

Shivering, I decided tea would help, and stroked my finger over the intricate wooden box once more as I selected an English breakfast teabag and drowned it in boiling water. Transfixed as the amber brown, misty swirls escaped from it into the clear water, my mind focused in on the mundane to stop the troublesome thoughts that plagued me.

I checked each room again, for a note or a clue, but there was nothing amiss, nothing new. I grabbed the duvet from the bed and dragged it to the sofa, curling up under it in an attempt to stop the trembles that had set upon me, this time purely through fear rather than lust. Cradling the tea that I knew I wouldn't drink between my shaky hands, I waited, eyes on the door, desperate to understand what was wrong.

By midday the fog had cleared, but I hadn't moved. His mobile buzzed multiple times with messages, but without knowledge of his passcode I couldn't access it. Anwir's phone? Mason's phone? I had no idea whose it even was.

All the things he'd told me – maybe he was unstable or had a personality disorder or delusions. Or perhaps he knew exactly what he was doing, and this was some weird seduction game. I groaned at my own stupidity as I threw the covers aside and trudged back to the main bathroom, refusing to acknowledge the ensuite with its blood-stained mystery. Every footstep felt too heavy, as if I weighed double, and the effort exhausted me.

Slumped on the toilet with my head in my hands, sobs overtook me, and a tear splashed onto the marble tiles. I was pathetic. No wonder he'd gone, I was just a silly girl he'd seen as a challenge, and I'd played right into his hands. He told me his name meant liar... But why had he left me in the apartment? That made no sense, surely, he would have seduced me at my place and then snuck out, left me with no way to track him. It was all so damned confusing, and my brain ached with the mental strain.

No matter how many of these thoughts and theories flew through my mind, I couldn't wholeheartedly believe any were true. What we had was real, I knew it.

Washing my hands, I shook my head at the sight that greeted me in the mirror. My drawn, pale reflection looked ten years older; any glow the passion had given me had soon dispersed. I wasn't attractive enough for someone like him, how could plain, boring Amber ever be? Maybe that's why he'd jumped on this Mireille scenario, he needed someone like her: magnificent, but also absolutely imaginary.

I almost choked on my breath as I heard the front door click open, and quick as a flash I shot out of the bathroom and sprinted back towards the door, cursing myself for my abandonment of my post under the duvet.

"Anwir?" I cried out as I rounded the corner, sliding to a halt dramatically before I could throw myself into his arms. It wasn't him.

A middle-aged lady in a beige uniform stood in front of me, holding a mop and a basket of cleaning products. "Sorry, love," she said, brusquely. "Twice a week I come here to clean, name's Rachel. Didn't mean to surprise you, the place is normally empty." I saw her eyes glance to the bedcovers strewn across the sofa as she spoke to me. "Is Mr Donoghue here? I've never met him, guess he works long hours to afford a place like this?"

"I... erm..." I tugged his T-shirt down, hoping it covered me sufficiently as I tried to compose an appropriate answer.

"You his girlfriend?" she asked with a slight scowl as she looked me up and down.

"It's not a good time to be honest," I replied, ignoring her question. "Could you leave it for today? You'll still get paid, I'm sure."

"I don't know, I don't want to get in trouble with the boss..."

"Wait there." I ran to the bedroom and grabbed a twenty-pound note from the pocket of my trousers which still lay on the floor.

"Here," I panted, as I thrust it at her. "Go and treat yourself to a nice coffee and a sit down. Mr Donoghue and I are..." I bit my lip and willed my cheeks to colour up; it wasn't a difficult task. "We're busy, in the erm... bedroom. He's a little tied up right now, if you know what I mean."

"Oh!" She guffawed as she pocketed the money. "Why didn't you just say so? Enjoy, and don't worry, I'm the soul of discretion." She let herself out with a wink and I could hear her chuckle as the ding of the lift rang out in the hallway.

I threw myself face down on to the sofa and let every tear flow, soaking into the duvet, diluting that beautiful smell of him and making me wonder if love was worth this.

The fog persevered as day blended to evening, blocking out the light of the stars as time ticked on and today became tomorrow. I didn't move and Anwir didn't return. My eyes throbbed painfully with exhaustion as morning arrived. No delicious wake up this time, though, no hope; just despair and disappointment. Ellie had once told me men were just disappointments, I recalled, sadly.

I couldn't stay here forever; it was all too obvious he had

left me and didn't want the awkwardness of explanations. He'd got what he wanted and was done. But what if he was hurt somewhere? What if the demons or angels had come for him? Like he'd warned.

I dressed, splashing cold water on my face before I grabbed the phone he'd bought for me. Just in case he called or messaged, if I were so lucky. I scolded myself for being so needy, but I slipped his T-shirt into the bag, too, folded neatly, in case I needed comfort from it.

A heaviness settled on me as I closed the front door and headed to the underground car park. I'd been right when I awoke yesterday morning; I had changed, just not in the way I'd first expected.

Back in my car, I wanted to drive to Ellie's. I wanted her comforting arms around me while she told me men were all the same and made me hot chocolate with whipped cream to cheer me up. I wanted to talk about how good it had been and how bad it felt now. But I was too ashamed, and it was too complicated to begin to explain. Angels and demons... it shouldn't be true, but life was upside down and it seemed as feasible a reason as any other.

Instead, I turned the car towards home, my mind groggy and overwhelmed as I swore to never tell anyone about this. What an idiot, the woman who lost her virginity and her heart in one night, to a liar.

TWENTY-ONE

AMBER

A series of loud, persistent bangs jolted me awake, but my brain was reluctant to rise with the same urgency as my body. I didn't remember climbing into bed, didn't remember arriving home, but I was under my covers and back in Anwir's white T-shirt. A glimpse towards the window told me it was still light outside, at least I hadn't slept the entire day away as I was overtaken by exhaustion and my predicament.

The commotion seemed to sound from my front door and showed no signs of stopping. I shook myself from my sleepy daze, grabbed a robe and headed down the stairs.

"Who is it?" I asked tentatively, as I reached the last step and peered cautiously through the glass hole which allowed a view of the front steps.

"Amber, I've been worried sick. It's Ben, let me in."

I could see his face was drawn with concern as I unlocked the door and opened it, pulling my robe tighter around me. Ben looked me up and down, his face still and focused.

"Hi, sorry, it's not the best time." I began to say.

"You're asked to take some time off work and then you

disappear for two nights, after you're seen with some guy in the car park. I was about to go to the police. For fuck's sake..." I'd never heard him sound so tense, certainly never heard him swear. He swept his hands through his hair, pulling it back as his blue eyes bore into me.

"I'm sorry, I didn't think. Come in." I held the door open and let him walk past me into the house. "I'll make some tea."

As I busied myself with the kettle and mugs, he took a seat at the dining table, drumming his fingers with the occasional mutter. I sat down opposite and pushed a navy-blue mug in his direction, before raising my own to my lips and blowing on the steam.

"I take it you still haven't found your phone?" he asked. "I've been ringing and messaging. I came here a few times to try and find you. I've been to the park, the community centre, Ellie's house, where have you been?"

His tone niggled; I shouldn't have to answer to him. A couple of dates and some heavy petting did not give him any claim on me. "Work told me to take some time to look after myself, I needed to get away. I didn't realise I had to ask permission."

His eyes didn't falter from mine as he sipped, seemingly numb to the hot temperature of the tea. "I didn't mean that you had to ask permission, it would have just been nice to know. We were meant to go for a picnic, remember?"

"Oh." The conversation on my last day at work reappeared in my mind. "I'm so sorry, with everything that was going on, it slipped my mind."

"As long as you're OK, that's all that matters." He reached his hand out and placed it over mine protectively, but somehow it didn't seem right now. I pulled back, standing up to reach for the biscuit tin as an excuse, as I placed it between us and nibbled on the first one my hand grasped at.

"That was very rude of me, though, I'm sorry. Another time?" I asked, eager to keep it casual.

"Tomorrow?"

"Um..." I tried to stall, unsure how to answer, but knowing my heart would absolutely not be in on this.

"Just as friends, I know that what happened at mine was too much for you."

"Sure. OK." I sipped the tea.

"Where did you go?" he asked, persistently.

"To stay with a friend," I replied, as my stomach sank at the memory.

"Anyone I know?"

"I doubt it. Have I missed much at work?" Having swung the conversation back to work, I breathed a sigh of relief as he filled me in on the standard events that made up days at the hospice, which led to generic small talk, the only type I could deal with right now.

We finished our drinks and I yawned dramatically, rubbing at my eyes. "I'm sorry, Ben. I'm worn out."

"Don't worry. Shall I pick you up tomorrow? Eleven?"

I agreed as we headed towards the front door.

"I'm sorry if I worried you," I said. "Thank you for checking on me."

Ben pulled me into a tight hug, and as my arms wrapped around him, tears pricked at my eyes. I wanted nothing more than to hug Anwir right now.

"You know you mean a lot to me; I'm sorry things have been confusing." He kissed the top of my head and I bit into my gum, using the pain to stop the tears that still threatened to overspill from my eyes.

"You smell different..." he said, as he inhaled, his lips hovering just above my hair.

"Must be my friend's shampoo, different brand," I said, as

I pulled back from the hug. He looked me up and down, his eyes intense.

"Yeah, must be." He frowned, then blasted a charming smile out again, as if nothing was wrong. "See you tomorrow. Looking forward to it." He blew a soft kiss towards me as he meandered down the path and onto the pavement.

As I closed the front door, I leant back against it and let the tears flow once again. I missed Anwir so much, I could still feel him all over my body, but I knew it would fade. And the thought of him fading away with it, tore me up inside. I knew where I needed to go to let this emotion out.

There was one person I would have been able to talk this over with, but she wasn't here anymore. "Mum," I whispered as I rubbed my finger over the cold stone of her memorial. "I don't know what's going on anymore, I wish you were here."

Jennifer Carmichael – I traced my finger over each letter of her name, letting her voice and face flow into my memories. "Seven years... Do I even remember your voice correctly or is it just something my mind made up now? Has my whole life been false? Are you even my mum? I can't think, my mind is overflowing with all of this."

I pressed my forehead to the cool, impersonal stone as I knelt on the damp ground, all too aware of the hushed whispers of passing mourners as they respected my grief. What an imposter I felt... Yes, I missed my mum every single day, my heart longed for her to be with me. I'd still been a child at eighteen when I lost her and found myself alone in the world, but every one of these tears today was either for Anwir, or formed purely out of self-pity over this ridiculous situation I found myself in.

"How do I find out the truth, Mum? It would be easier if he'd made it all up, slept with me and left me. I'd be an idiot but that would be the end. I don't think he made it up, though. Did you know? What I am? What I was?"

I looked up to the sky as I rubbed at the tense muscles of my neck, every bit of me still thirsting for Anwir's touch. "I do love him. I wish this was normal, and I could bring him home for dinner to meet you. I think you'd love him, too; he has..." I closed my eyes as I reminisced. "He has this aura, it absorbs into me, leaves me warm and content. He's so unassuming, he has no idea how kind and wonderful he is."

On a whim I unravelled the scarf from my neck and wrapped it around the base of the headstone, tying it elegantly. "To keep you warm, green was always your favourite. Even if all of this is true, and I'm not even human, I'll never believe that you weren't my mum. You filled me with love and security. I miss you every single day. I love you always."

"Amber?" A voice called out. I twisted around, wiping at my eyes with my sleeve.

"Ellie..." My eyes focused on my friend and every tear in me welled out at speed as I blubbered and sobbed, unable to draw a full breath through the onslaught of emotion as a barrage of salted tears slid out of me. She held me until I calmed, never one to judge or try to rush what a person felt. "What are you doing here?" I stuttered as I managed to compose myself.

"You're not the only one who tries to attend the funerals you know?" She smiled as she wrapped my hands in hers. "You're cold, I've got coffee in the car, come on."

She helped me up and gave me a moment as I blew a kiss to my mum, promising to come back soon, then we headed towards the car park, arm in arm, a smattering of persistent sobs making themselves known every few seconds.

"I heard about work," Ellie said as we huddled in her car,

and she poured coffee from a flask. "Has it brought everything back about your mum?"

"That never really leaves me. I just feel lost, Ellie. Like I'm in the wrong place, but at the same time, I don't know where I'm meant to be."

"Has hot bad boy got anything to do with this?"

A loud guffaw escaped my mouth as she brought a genuine smile to me for the first time since I'd awoken without Anwir. "Excuse me?"

Her eyes had that sparkle dancing in them again as she spoke. "The guy who met you from work, you know who I'm talking about. Tall, devastatingly handsome, definite bad boy vibes. Where did you two wander off to together?"

"He's hot, that I admit, but he's not a bad boy." I sipped the warm coffee as I tried to compose myself. "He's an absolute sweetheart really, just doesn't show it to the world I guess."

"Oh, I see, but he shows it to you?" She wriggled closer to me. "Amber Carmichael... did you just admit to fancying someone?"

"It's not that simple, sadly."

"Why? Because you had a couple of dates, that you're not even sure were dates, with Ben? Doesn't mean you have to marry him! And I've noted you avoided the question about where you went."

"He's travelled out of town now anyway, not worth stressing about it. I'm going to meet Ben tomorrow but just as friends, I don't want it to be anything more than that. My mind is too messed up."

"I'm worried, you sound so unsettled, it's not like you."

I sighed deeply before draining the coffee. "I don't feel much like me at the moment, to be honest. Do you mind driving me home? I just want to go soak in the bath, try and relax."

"Of course I don't mind. Want me to stay over with you?"

"No," I shook my head, "I'll be fine, and I know you have work tomorrow, you need all your energy for that. Heard some selfish woman went off sick and left you short staffed."

"Hey," her face scrunched up, "you are not selfish for taking care of yourself. I don't want to hear that again." She pulled me to her, hugging me tightly, her dark ponytail tickling my face. "I'll always be here for you, even if you don't reply to my texts."

"Oh?" I rummaged around in my bag. "New phone, put your number in."

She entered her details into my contacts and a sense of irony washed over me as I saw she'd named herself 'Guardian Angel Ellie'.

"We all feel a bit lost sometimes, Amber. Let's do something together at weekend, take your mind off things."

"I love you," I said, as I flung my arms around her neck. "What would I do without you?"

"Love you too, daft girl. Come on, let's get you home."

Despite having slept until late, I'd fallen straight back into a slumber as soon as my head hit my pillow post bath. By the time I needed to be ready for the picnic, I felt a little more in control of myself, but the ache in my chest never wavered. The sun burned high in the sky, shining bright, which felt wrong. How could the world be so beautiful and warm, when my heart felt so cold and abandoned? I pushed the thoughts aside as I chose a long, sunshine-yellow maxi dress and kept my hair down, thinking I could at least give the image of happiness externally.

"Morning." Ben smiled brightly as I opened the front

door, grabbing my sunglasses and handbag from the hall table. "You look much better than last night, positively glowing."

"Was nothing a good sleep couldn't fix. Do we need to stop and get anything for the picnic?"

"All under control," he said, as he held his arm out. I linked mine through it, noticing the wicker basket in his other hand, and we began to wander slowly in the direction of the park.

"I know it's not been long since we were here," Ben said, "but look how everything has grown in that time."

I smiled as I saw all the blossoming buds and shoots, this truly was an amazing time of year for nature. It was reassuring, yet painful, to know that life carried on as normal, even though mine seemed to have ground to a painful halt after just beginning to start.

Ben led us to a quiet corner of the park. Situated well away from the crowded children's play area, and the larger fields full of impromptu football games that seemed to spring up between groups of teens and young adults. He placed a striped picnic blanket on the ground and motioned for me to sit.

"Madam," he smiled, as he held his hand out like a maitre'd and passed me a small bottle of sparkling, raspberry lemonade, somehow still cold.

"Thank you." I smiled as I unscrewed the metal top and sipped, watching him spread out delicious treats – cupcakes with baby pink icing, perfectly cut finger sandwiches, crudités with hummus, and a tub of sliced strawberries.

"Ellie told me these would be your favourites." I sensed him look up at me as my eyes were trained on the strawberries, Anwir's words hurtling around my mind and bruising my heart further.

"Definitely," I replied. "This looks incredible." I reached for a cheese and tomato sandwich finger and observed Ben as he leaned back against a large oak tree. Any passing female would be drooling, as he looked every inch the perfect boy next door, an atypical angel, as the sun drew out even more shine from his blond hair, the ends still curled perfectly. His azure eyes seemed enhanced due to the light blue of his short-sleeved shirt, with his tanned, muscular arms crossed casually on his legs. I knew now, though, that I felt nothing but friend-ship for him. Maybe I could put a word in for Ellie, it was about time she had a good guy in her life; surely an angelic guy wouldn't do her wrong.

"Can we have an honest conversation?" I asked.

Ben frowned quizzically. "Of course, what's wrong?"

"You know that story you told me? About Mireille?"

He nodded as he dipped a carrot stick into hummus and motioned for me to continue.

"Was it true?" I asked. "It wasn't just a story, was it?"

He chewed on his lip for a moment before he answered. "It's not easy to explain, and it happened a long time ago, but yes, it's true."

"Am I Mireille?" I asked, defiantly, looking directly into his eyes.

"Right now, no. But a part of you was, is, could be again. If that even makes sense."

"And what was Mireille to you? Someone special?"

"She was bound to me. I guess that's the equivalent of a marriage here, but more meaningful, stronger. A binding doesn't get broken, you don't just divorce your way out of it."

He looked uncomfortable, but I was aware he was oblivious to the information Anwir had told me. Despite seemingly having abandoned me, I was convinced that Anwir had spoken the truth, as implausible as it sounded, and I was eager to know if Ben would be as forthcoming.

"But you're so young, and you said Mireille was a long time ago?" I took another sandwich as I watched him closely.

"It's not easy to explain, Amber. I wish you'd just let me show you what I meant, the other night."

"How can you show me the past? I don't know what's going on, I don't know what you want from me. I want to be your friend, I want to trust you, but weird things keep happening with us."

"Maybe you just need to have faith and trust me. It will become clear, I promise it will."

"Are you saying that in some other time or place, you and I were bound together? Married?"

He nodded, shuffling away from the tree he'd leaned against as he moved closer to me. "You started to feel it the other night, I know you did, but you got scared. I understand that."

Lying had never sat easy with me, but I wanted the truth, and I felt like allowing him closer was the only way I'd get the information I craved. Maybe it would even help me locate Anwir, but I was going to have to summon acting skills I'd never used to pull this off.

I plucked a cupcake from the enticing selection, purpose-fully running my finger through the soft pink icing, before I licked it off. "So, you want to be more than my friend?"

"I don't think I could live with just being your friend. Do you remember Barke?"

"Yes," I said, as I nibbled at the cupcake, purposefully spreading icing on my top lip.

A small laugh escaped with his next breath as he contin-ued. "In the same way you have a piece of Mireille in you, I have a piece of Barke in me, a bigger piece, admittedly. And the love he felt for her, I feel for you."

I gulped, moving closer to him, dreading what I was about to do, but needing to do it anyway, needing to get any kind of clue about this bizarre situation and how it could lead me back to the man my body and mind craved.

"You love me?" I asked.

"I love you," he replied, as he reached out his finger and wiped the icing from my lip before slipping it into his own mouth. He'd said it so easily compared to the stuttering struggle Anwir had with the words. Yet there was no feeling behind it, it was empty and vague.

"I... I don't know you well enough to return that sentiment. I'm sorry."

"You don't have to say sorry, it will all make more sense to you, with time."

"Are we reincarnated then? Is that what you're trying to tell me?"

"Not quite. I know I said we could come here as friends today, but please, can I kiss you?"

"I don't know..." My throat felt constricted as I tried to hold back tears; there was only one person whose touch I ached for.

"It'll aid your memories. I just want to help you."

I nodded, mentally wrapping a bandage around my heart as I knew this kiss wasn't right, it felt unforgivable to let someone else's lips touch where Anwir's had been. But if Ben was right, and this helped my memories, things might make more sense. Any essence of Anwir left upon me was surely gone by now anyway...

I leaned forward to meet him, his eyes still trained upon mine as his features blurred in proximity and I felt his warm, sweet breath hover above my lips. I pushed mine out to meet his, remembering how tantalising his kisses had felt before, how enjoyable... but now, after Anwir, they felt empty.

As he intensified the kiss, his fingers drifted into my hair and he muttered about how beautiful I was, how he'd missed me, all the things I'd heard before which were slowly starting to join up to create a clearer picture in my mind. I opened my eyes, observing him. He was completely lost in this, and abruptly, the air stilled around us.

The warm breeze that had skimmed over my bare shoulders stopped, the rustle of the leaves was no more, the happy laughter that travelled this way from the children's play area, simply ceased.

His mouth travelled to my neck with a deep, satisfied sigh and I took the opportunity to glance around, even the perfect white, fluffy clouds had paused their journey across the calm sky. An unnatural event was in progress, and I knew that it was Ben's doing. I should have felt scared, been wary, but all my mind kept telling me was that this could lead me to Anwir, or at least draw his attention.

So, I kissed Ben's neck in return, trying to fool my mind that he was Anwir, with varying degrees of success as I arched up towards him, encouraging his mouth to my collarbone as his hands slid up the sides of my thighs, bunching the thin cotton of my dress around my hips.

"This is a bit public..." I whispered, forcing a gasp from my lips.

"Nobody can see us, trust me. I keep telling you, you just have to trust me, Mireille."

I let the name slide as he pulled us down onto the blanket together, facing each other, then he wrapped an arm underneath me and returned his kisses to my mouth, deeper than before, unyielding, as his tongue explored me.

I struggled against him, pulling back to press my lips to his ear in a whisper. "What will happen if I trust you, Barke?"

It was as though a bright light within him signalled a message as I said his name. He wrapped one of his legs firmly around mine as he replied, "You're so close, so perfectly close. It has to be today; I can't wait any longer."

"What has to be today?" I asked, and a slither of panic formed in my throat as I recognised that 'Ben', whoever he was, did not seem to be in control right now. Barke's name seemed to have polarised the atmosphere in this spot.

"Hush," he commanded. Not softly and sweetly, but as if my words were an annoyance, a distraction. Before I could utter another sound, his tongue slid into my mouth, and I heard the rip of material as he tore the back of my beautiful, sunshine coloured dress. I tried to move but his leg was tight around me, the muscles of his thigh keeping me in place as his hands rubbed below my shoulder blades.

At first, the sensation was akin to a massage, but his actions began to burn as his fingers pushed deeper into the muscles and flesh, kneading it as though I was dough, not a living person who he could hurt. The familiar burn and ache spread throughout my body and my mind flashed back to his house, when he'd eased this for me, a memory I'd suppressed. Not today, though, he had no intention of easing my discomfort. His hands didn't stray once from the two areas of my back, as he pressed harder and deeper, as if trying to burrow inside me, gouge something out of me.

His mouth let mine go as a deep, sexual rumble grew in his throat. Every time I tried to move, he pinned me tighter. My breath gasped as I was forced against his chest, and that compression hid the scream of pain that flew from my lips. He dragged his nails from the top to the bottom of my shoulder blade, but they felt sharp, like a knife slicing me open, tearing me apart. He repeated the action on the other side, still holding me to him, his chest soaked with my tears and wetness from my mouth as I tried to scream, tried to speak, but could ultimately do little except struggle for each breath, as the singe of agony threatened to split my back in two.

"I knew this would work if you trusted me," he sneered, a dark edge to his voice that I hadn't heard before. "I know, Mireille. I know that you've been with him. That you've defiled yourself with him."

My eyes opened in shock as he pulled back momentarily, his arms continuing to hold me in place.

"What? I..."

"I didn't say you could speak." He flipped me onto my back as he spat the words out. A pain shot through me as I felt something angular and sharp dig into me from the ground below. Barke held a hand over my mouth as his arm pushed upon my throat, causing an acrid bile to rise within me. My vision blurred as tears streamed from my eyes, and my chest heaved with the effort of trying to gulp in the air that my body screamed out for. Then everything darkened, as if night fell on the ugly scene, and all I could think of was Anwir. The supposed liar, the one self-titled as a demon, the only one who could save me, the one to whom my heart and soul belonged.

TWENTY-TWO

MIREILLE

I'd been so excited when my parents told me a bonding ceremony had been arranged. Angelic children were so rare; I was about to turn eighteen and there'd been no other children delivered to our town since me. Because of this rarity, bindings were arranged between families across the realm, to ensure that the tradition continued, and in the hope more children would be blessed upon the couples.

My future life-mate was called Barke – it meant blessings, and this made my heart warm as my father had always referred to me as his 'little blessing'. Barke was much older than me, but again, this wasn't out of the ordinary. With children so few and far between, an age gap of a couple of a hundred years was fairly standard, and that's what we would have.

Barke lived on the other side of the realm from my childhood home, in a picturesque village nestled amongst citrus groves, high in the hills above the capital city. The villa he'd built was beautiful, with its terracotta floor, whitewashed exterior and lush, green garden which always seemed to be bathed in sunlight. I moved there immediately after the binding ceremony. My heart ached as I said goodbye to my parents, but I knew this was my new life, I'd been prepared for it since I was young. It was how things worked in our society; you weren't bound by love, you loved the one you were bound to.

I only met Barke three times before I moved in with him, and one of those was the ceremony itself. Yet, I had no nerves, a naïve young girl who'd never known badness, and Barke put me at ease. He was so gentle, approachable, and utterly charming. Plus, as an eighteen-year-old girl, the fact that he was the truest definition of classical, male beauty, was a major bonus. Six and a half feet tall, tanned, muscular and perfectly proportioned – his eyes matched the bright blue skies that always seemed to grace the citrus groves, and his thick, blonde hair fell in curls, curls that I wanted to wrap around my finger as soon as I laid eyes on them.

We'd stood side by side at the ceremony and I was enthralled by our reflection in the floor-to-ceiling mirrors behind the ceremonial table. The two of us together were picture perfection; every guest there commented on it. My blonde hair matched his in colour, as ringlet curls sprang down to the waist of my delicate, blush-yellow gown. My eyes were a deep emerald-green, and next to his sky-blue, I imagined them as the ocean meeting the sky on the horizon. The things the mind of a besotted teenager will imagine. Even the height difference between us felt right, as when he hugged me for the first time, I noticed how the top of my head sat under his nose, and he breathed in the scent of me, deeply.

When he brought me home to the villa and gave me space to put my belongings away in the bedroom, I stood perfectly still, staring at the large bed which dominated the room. A breeze blew in through the open window and twisted the voile curtain, wrapping it around the intricately carved wooden posts which formed the four-poster, reminding me of the silks that circus dancers would perform with. Barke entered behind me, treading softly as he rested his hands on my shoulders and turned me to face him.

"You don't have to worry," he reassured me. "First of all, we become friends, we work all this new life together out, and we move on when you're ready. Until then, my room is next door."

And that was how the most magical few months of my life began. He treated me with utter reverence and respect, and I willingly slipped under his spell. Tiny seedlings of adoration had been planted in my heart and with his every loving action, they sprouted to life, buds and blooms that grew with wild abandon. He brought me my favourite tea in bed in the mornings, left notes around the house to make me smile. When he sensed I was homesick he'd take me outside after dark to look at the stars, holding me close as he wiped my tears whilst I regaled him with fond memories of my childhood. He didn't want me to be lonely, so he introduced me to the other families in the village, encouraged me to make friends, but I was always drawn to our alone times. My favourite moment of every day being the picnic lunches I packed, when I went to meet him as he worked in the orchards. We would sit in the shade of the citrus trees, the warm sun on our skin as the scents of the oranges and lemons drifted over us. It was here I learned to trust him physically, as well as emotionally. As we ate our favourite foods, his fingers would caress my skin, he'd bite on his lip, and I could sense his desperation to kiss me. Day by day we'd journey further and further into each other, until within four weeks I allowed him to caress my wings, asked him if he could finish his work early that day and join me in my own bedroom, make it *our* bedroom.

For a year we lived in absolute paradise, completely lost as we fell in love, deep, solid love which I'd craved and needed. He was my everything, and I knew how he idolised me. We seemed compatible in every way as we drove each other to the depths of desire each night and awoke with absolute love and adoration every new morning. We'd hold lavish feasts, when the families from nearby would join us to eat under the stars, fairy lights strung from citrus tree to citrus tree as we dined al fresco, warm breezes upon our bodies as the countryside rang out with sounds of laughter, love, and friendship.

If there had been a contest for angelic inspirational couples, we would have been the stars in first place. Things changed so slowly, shifted so subtly, that I didn't stand a chance.

It began with jealousy, he would claim that the other men in the village were attracted to me. It was easier to avoid social gatherings than deal with his wings flicking angrily against me, as he slept facing the wall, rage seething from within, leaving me unable to sleep in the dark atmosphere of the room.

I strived to help the older angels, who couldn't work for their food as we did, couldn't repair their houses, but he said I pandered to them, made them lazy. One day I defied him; he forbade me to help a particular lady, yet I went anyway once he was out in the orchard, unable to leave a soul struggling when I had the means to help her. She had the most awful cough and I used lemons and honey from our orchards and beehives to make her a tonic. He accused me of theft. I questioned how that could be if everything we had was shared, and he laughed. He convulsed with laughter, long and harsh, telling me that nothing was ours, everything was his, including me. The binding was basically a contract, and I belonged to him for eternity. I'd stolen from him, and I needed to pay.

Hours later, I barricaded my bedroom door as best I could as he left my room and went to sleep in his old bed. My nose bled underneath an eye that was swollen shut and bruised, but it was nothing compared to the agony he'd left between my legs as he forced the point home, over and over, that I belonged completely to him, only to him.

As the years passed, my boundaries grew blurred, and I accepted his mood swings. The shock of that first night became something I closed my eyes and mind to as it happened, for he rarely made love to me anymore; the nights of rage and violence seemed all he was capable of. The only time he acted like the loving, adoring man I'd fallen for, was when we were in company.

I'd cry to myself under those same starry skies he used to take me to see, pray to anyone who may listen that my beautiful parents would never see the life they had unknowingly bound me into. To the outside world we were still perfect, nobody knew what went on inside of our villa, and Barke was confident in the fact that I would never admit my weaknesses, for he had fully convinced me that usually, it was my fault.

An angelic lifetime spans hundreds of years, but I was eager for change and travel as we approached our hundredth anniversary. He, however, held no similar desires. He was the main man in this village, the respected one, and he revelled in it. Once a month he would travel to the city for regional meetings with the other leaders, discussing taxes and policies, working hard to make life better. I envied him that small freedom. He was also convinced that if we stayed here and I learned how to behave, we'd be blessed with a child of our own, despite the odds being against us. I begged the universe not to allow that to happen, to not inflict him upon a tiny child.

The lady whom I'd first got into trouble for still deteriorated, slowly, but surely. I knew of a herb, grown in the human plane, that could help her. Barke had, of course, refused to let me travel there. I knew I had a chance, though, and the next time he went to one of the city meetings, I planned to go and gather as much as possible and stockpile it for her.

As soon as I landed in the human realm, I drew the cold air into my lungs with a satisfied sigh. Yes, it had taint, it was full of pollution, but it was real, and it was different, it made me feel alive. I'd landed in some ancient human ruins, which laughably, by angel standards, were still new, but the research I'd managed to surreptitiously conduct in a library in the nearest town, told me this was where I would find the herb.

I could never have known an attack was imminent that day, but, if I had known, I would have travelled anyway. For my existence with Barke was not a life, and I'd have felt no sadness at my journey ending. I plucked the herbs from the ground, placing as many as possible into my home-woven basket, until I felt a rush of air behind me. It broke my heart, but the thought that ricocheted through my mind was that this was Barke, come to punish me for my disobedience.

Angry words snarled and twisted through the air.

"Liar. Liar. Liar. Liar."

I twisted around in surprise with a petrified scream, raising my wing in front of me in defence as I saw a demonic face rush toward me. A crushing, torturous pain embedded itself into me, and I could only look on in horror as deep, red blood flowed amongst my pure, white feathers.

I stumbled backwards, the hooded figure advancing upon me once more. Despite not fearing for my pathetic existence, a survival instinct grew within me. I reached for a feather that hung limp from my injured appendage and tugged on it with all my might, wincing at the jolt of pain that shot along my wing bone and up into my shoulder.

My vision was blurred and blackened, as if I had descended down a long tunnel. I knew I had one chance. I struck down with the feather, leaving the pointed end exposed, and felt it connect with something, someone. An ugly scream permeated the air and then I lapsed into unconsciousness, vaguely aware of someone lifting me, but too weak to care if it was friend or foe, and unsure of who I classed as which anymore – after all, it would be far from the first time that Barke had had to deal with me being knocked unconscious through violence.

AMBER

My throat was clogged and raw as I opened my eyes. Tears burned me like acid as they dripped inwards, too stubborn to fall externally and give him the satisfaction of knowing what he did.

"That must feel better?" Barke asked, surveying me casually.

"What must feel better?" My voice was croaky and weak as I replied.

"Having your wings back, you finally manifested them."

I flexed them, blanching at the pain as they extended from my shoulder blades.

"You aren't thanking me, then?" he asked, a menacing edge to his voice. "Because you disobeyed me, over a few fucking herbs for some meaningless old crone, I've had to cope for two hundred years without you. Two hundred years, Mireille. I love you, what do you think that's done to me?"

I gulped and it was as though my tears were glass that cut into my throat. Every memory was now fresh and vivid, and I knew I needed to appease him to get through this in the most painless fashion.

"I'm so sorry, I didn't think."

"You never think." He grabbed my cheeks between his thumb and forefinger and squeezed tight as his eyes focused close in on mine, imprisoning me in his grasp. I knew I couldn't hide my fear at this close range.

"As if it wasn't bad enough that the elders had to put you in a human body while you healed, while the threat was dealt with. As if that stain upon you wasn't enough. I now find out you've defiled our bond by fucking someone else." He spat the words at me, angrily. I looked down at the ground below me, recognising that we were still in the park, fearful of how far he would go this time.

"I didn't have my memories, I didn't know. But you've shown me now, Barke. I remember our bond, how I love you."

He pulled me to him, pressing a soft kiss to my lips. "I love you, Mireille."

"I think I need to just go home and recover from this. It's all confusing."

"Back to the citrus grove?" He smiled and stroked my face, as if butter wouldn't melt, a far cry from the man who'd bruised every inch of my body, over hundreds of years. The way his personality seemed to switch so easily between two halves terrified me, and it made him all the more dangerous as I struggled to keep up with which half I was dealing with.

I nodded, playing along. "I need to go back to Amber's house first, though, there are things I need."

"Put your wings away," he commanded. I glanced left and right at them, focusing hard as I managed to wriggle them, but nothing else happened. "For fuck's sake, Mireille," he huffed impatiently.

He reached for my back and shoved on each side, hard. I whimpered as the wings retracted within me and saw his do the same.

"We'll go there now; I want to talk on the way."

His eyes closed for a moment as he drew in a long breath, and the breeze began to flow again. The world around us came back to life from its temporary slumber, as he wrapped his fingers around mine and led me out of the park and back in the direction of Amber's home.

"It's been horrible without you," he said. "I know that I lose my temper too quick, and I'm not patient enough with you, I promise I'll be better. Being without you has taught me so much. I harassed everyone until I was allowed to come and get you, but they kept telling me to wait."

"I'm glad they changed their minds," I lied, attempting to keep my voice steady as I spoke. "How did you manage to get the job at the hospice?"

"Humans are idiots, I've told you this before. A little bit of wining, dining and oral sex, and that woman from HR signed all the paperwork I needed her to."

"But..." I wanted to ask why it was acceptable for him to have done that, yet not me, but fear froze my words as I changed tact. "You're here now," I replied, hatred for myself rising as I continued to appease him, keep him calm. The promise of him being better made nausea well up. It was a promise I'd heard before and knew he was incapable of keeping, or even attempting.

He stopped in the middle of the street, holding my face in the same position he had before, but this time with a gentleness as he placed soft kisses across my lips. "I know you weren't in your own mind when you slept with him. I'm going to forgive you, in time."

Tension radiated into my limbs; my throat choked up again as I was too scared to respond.

"To show you how much I mean that," he continued, "I'm going to let you say goodbye to him."

"What?" My eyes shot upwards and met his own, passing by the amused grin that rose up on the left side of his mouth.

"You can say goodbye, and then you come home with me. You know you can't live on this plane. It was just a means to an end."

"I have no idea where he is, though."

"I do, I can take you there now if that's what you want."

My heart pounded so hard I thought I would surely die. I wanted to say yes, but what if this was a trick, and he'd punish me if I gave the wrong answer? My eyes flashed from left to right as I looked at him, seeking any clue as to what I should do.

"Don't panic," he said, as he stroked my cheek. "There's only one condition."

I sighed, knowing that as with everything else, there'd be a condition or a bargain.

"I don't trust you," I murmured. "There's bound to be more than one."

"Are you calling me a liar?" he asked, running a finger down my spine before it leeched across to my shoulder blade.

In spite of my fear, I let the words rush out of me, in disgust. "I would never grace you with that name."

I heard the crack before I felt the pain, as his palm slapped across my face, almost knocking me into the road. My hand shot to my cheek which felt as if a thousand sharp needles had just penetrated it. I kept my eyes fixed firm on the ground.

"Why do you have to make this so difficult?" he said through a clenched jaw, glancing around to make sure nobody had seen. "I thought that rebellious, spiteful streak had been knocked out of you long ago. I blame your parents, mollycoddling you the way they did."

A heart-wrenching ache stabbed through me as I begged and prayed, again, to anyone who might listen, that my beautiful parents would never know of what had become of me. That they fell asleep each night thinking their little blessing, their darling angel, was happy, warm, safe, and loved.

"I'll let you go, but the condition stands. You have to ask him for the full story of why he travelled to this plane. Don't

try and wheedle out of it or trick me. I will know. You understand, don't you? I always know, Mireille."

I nodded; my heart sank as I slipped back into my old
ways. "Thank you, Barke."

He smiled and kissed the top of my head. "You're
gorgeous when you behave."

Then he led me in a different direction, towards the
grimier part of the city centre, a place I didn't normally
frequent. We walked in silence, still holding hands, just a
normal couple to all intents and purposes, yet I felt as if the
weight of all three worlds was on my shoulders.

"He's in there," said Barke as we stopped outside an Irish
bar that I'd heard of, but never been in – O'Shaughnessy's.
"I'll find you later. Enjoy your... goodbye." He smirked at me
as he turned and walked away, I fought against the buckle that
threatened to swipe my legs out from under me. My entire
body trembled as I sprinted inside, panicking as I looked
around for the bathroom sign, then running towards it, tears
spilling down my cheeks as I burst into a cubicle and heaved. I
threw up until my stomach muscles burned with a pain akin
to what I'd felt when my wings emerged, and the very memory
of *that* moment caused me to retch once again.

As I splashed cold water on my face from the grimy sink, I
examined my reflection. It was Amber who looked back at me,
but my mind was Mireille, and I was sure the green flecks in
Amber's eyes had expanded. A war raged within me, between
my fear of Barke and my love for Anwir. I was in the middle,
being ripped apart, and there was seemingly nothing I
could do.

Twenty-Three

Anwir

Each solitary hour felt as though it had stretched to days since I'd closed that apartment door behind me. I'd tortured myself for every second, in dimly lit corners of questionable bars. Each time my mind set itself on returning to her, I downed another drink, drowning the thought out. I knew I had to do this for her, no matter how it hurt. The concept that I'd found someone more important than myself was still disturbing as it settled within me, yet I liked how it felt, how it gave me hope.

I should have left this plane already, gone home, and tried to move on, but I didn't think I'd ever be able to. What life was there back there, after everything I'd experienced? Everything she'd made me feel. I downed a shot of tequila as she crossed my mind, like some perverse drinking game for the broken hearted.

Without a care for what anyone around me thought, I allowed my forehead to crash into the tacky table in front of me, wondering how many bangs it would take for me to find peace from this suffering.

"Mind if I join you?"

I looked up to see the young barmaid who'd served me for the past couple of hours shimmy into the booth next to me.

"Don't expect good company," I replied with a shrug.

"This place is a total dive, you don't look like you belong here," she said as she placed two beer bottles down on the table. I reached for one and clinked it to hers by way of a thank you.

"I don't belong anywhere, that's the problem."

"I see a lot of this, you'd be surprised. Love-life or money trouble?" she asked, very matter of fact.

I glanced up bleary-eyed, already irritated. "Love-life. That shit needs a warning label. I'm not interested in you, by the way," I snarled, wanting to warn her away, to keep anyone vaguely decent away from me.

"Hey, don't flatter yourself. I'm not interested in you!" A sharp laugh escaped her mouth. "It's just that sitting here with a couple of beers is infinitely better than the cess pit they call a staff room. I like listening to people's stories, it might help?"

"S'not much of a story," I slurred as I rubbed at my face. "I fell in love with someone who deserves better than me, then I left her, now I'm fucking miserable."

"Why is it up to you to dictate who or what she does or doesn't deserve?" she asked, a defiant edge to her voice.

"Sounds like something she'd say," I mumbled into my beer bottle as I took another swig.

"What's her name?"

"Amber," I sighed, wanting to just press my head to the table again.

"What did she say when you broke things off with her?"

"You're so fucking nosy."

"Yep," she replied, "but I have free beer, remember?"

"Fuck's sake..." I picked at the beer mat in front of me as I tried to explain. "She didn't say anything, I left before she woke up."

"Seriously? Maybe she does deserve better! That's the lowest." Her mouth turned down at the edges in distaste as she pulled her phone out of her pocket and swiped through an app.

"Well, what would you have done? If you're oh-so-knowledgeable?" I snarked.

"Have an honest conversation? Why do guys find that so difficult?!"

"Because I'm petrified of losing her, but I'm even more scared of what I'll do to her if I stay."

She rubbed my arm for a moment, but I found no comfort in it. The only touch that could comfort me was gone. "When did you first realise you loved her? I'm a sucker for a love story."

"Think I loved her before I knew her." I snickered at my own idiotic words. "But I guess, when it struck home, was when I told her my name. From the second she knew my true name, she never called me Mason again. Not once, she just saw the real me. Nobody else ever did." At this point my head hit the table again as a crushing blow reverberated into me, pounding out from my heart. How could missing someone, aching for someone, turn into a physical pain? It made no sense.

The barmaid continued to talk but I ignored her, until a minute or two later I felt the booth rock as she departed. My mind wanted to replay the moments with Amber that I longed for: her kiss, her fingers around mine, that beautiful vanilla scent that seemed to flow with her. I took a deep breath and just for a moment, it was as if she was in the room; my mind knew her scent too well and right now, it was torture.

"Time to go, you've been drunk for hours. Don't need anyone slumped at a table, putting the punters off." I squinted up at the words as I felt two pairs of arms take hold of me, one each side, and drag me towards the exit. I didn't put up any resistance, I was limp, and this wasn't likely to be the last bar I was ejected from, it certainly wasn't the first.

A cold breeze blasted over my face as I closed my eyes against the brightness. I'd lost track of days and times at the bottom of the first bottle.

"Anwir?" A voice behind me called out, timidly. My heart stuttered as I turned. The barmen dropped me to the floor, and I saw her. My Amber, watching me, mouth agape, as the door slammed closed.

Within seconds she was outside and throwing her arms around me. She sobbed into my shoulder as I held her to me and buried my nose into her hair. I could feel myself sober up as I battled between euphoria and desperation.

"What are you doing here?" I said, my mouth at her ear as I couldn't let this embrace end.

"We're in danger," she whispered, so lightly I could barely make out the sounds. "Can you hide us?"

Unable to stop my lips from seeking her out, I pressed them to hers, and every hole in my heart closed over as I did so. I drew on a thread of power, pulled it slowly, tried to delicately weave it as I encapsulated us both, shielded us from all the worlds, not just this one. The power felt different, thin as gossamer but ten times as powerful as before, there was no time to question that now, though. "Don't let go of me," I whispered back, as I transported us to the place where we'd been happy.

<hr/>

As the dizzy sensation eased, I opened my eyes and glanced around. We'd landed in Mason's bedroom, the last place I'd left her. The blinds were pulled down, leaving the room dim and warm. It was tidy, the bed was made neatly, and I wondered if that had been Amber. My heart sank as I cursed myself for the way I'd left her, but then, my mind emptied again as Amber realised where we were and crushed her lips against mine.

There was no need for words, apologies, explanations at this moment as I marvelled at how it felt to be reunited with her. I knew my heart had broken when I left her, but I hadn't realised a physical piece of my soul had been torn away too, and here she was, breathing it back in to me with every kiss.

My hand tangled into her hair, holding her to me as our mouths danced together. I never wanted to stop tasting her, feeling her warmth against me. I was absorbed in her and how she allowed her love to flow into me, soothe me.

She tugged at my shirt, and I smiled against her kiss as she began to unfasten the buttons, her fingers teasing at my chest. She bit on my bottom lip as I grinned, and the smallest of giggles escaped her mouth and filled my mind with joy. Pressing my hands to her hips I gathered the silken material of her dress between my fingers, pulling it up until it bunched inside my fists, at which point I momentarily tore my lips from hers as I lifted the dress over her head and tossed it aside.

Amber pulled me straight back into the heady, decadent moment as we tangled together, her hands insistent as she tugged at my jeans, pausing on my hips as she slowed for a moment, tucking her thumbs inside the elastic of my pants. She sighed, contented as she pushed them to the floor and I mirrored her action, rubbing the delicate material briefly between my fingers, aware that nothing would ever feel as good as her skin.

Her mouth moved to my neck as she pushed my hands back to her hips, her own reached behind her as she unclasped her bra and dropped it to the floor. My kiss met her neck in return, and I revelled in the sensation of her strong pulse under my lips. There was no barrier between us now, every skin cell in my body called out to have hers pressed against it, to feel her form against mine.

I stepped us towards the bed, stopping as her legs touched the cushioned divan base. Gently, I guided her to lay down, her hips just on the edge of the bed as her legs dangled. I used my mouth to kiss a pathway down her chest, lingering for an extra moment on every spot that made her gasp or press herself towards me; this would be a slow journey and I wanted to taste every second of it for eternity. My fingers massaged at her hips in slow circles as my tongue grazed the skin of her stomach, so light it left goosebumps of anticipation. I felt drawn into her, she called me, and I had to answer.

She stroked my hair between her fingers as I sank to my knees, placing a kiss on the inside of each knee, alternating between her legs as I moved higher up her inner thighs, sometimes light, and barely there, sometimes sucking or nibbling on her skin. I wanted to make this last forever, yet at the same time I longed to reach the destination.

I blew out a long breath as I paused and felt her shiver when it reached into her. I'd done this hundreds of times, but it had never mattered before. Now, though, everything had changed. To be in this situation with a woman I loved who, for reasons I couldn't fathom, loved me just as fiercely, was bewildering. Add onto that the fact that she was an angel, and if it weren't for the strength of feeling within me, I'd assume that this was all some awful joke, at my expense.

I placed a solitary, long kiss onto the very centre of her and she relaxed against my mouth as I breathed her wholly into me. She perfused every vital organ within me with her scent, her feel, her being; she was me and I was her as I sank into the motion and rhythm of her desire.

To an outsider she may have seemed silent, but her body communicated with me on a baser level. As a flick of my tongue caused a tremble down her thigh and the slightest scrape of my teeth drew a shiver up her spine, I used every subtle sign to learn and adapt and make this everything she deserved. At the point I allowed my tongue to glide gently inside her, her fingers tightened in my hair, pulling me in and without words, asking for more. The moments grew in intensity, yet no matter how fast I moved, how firm my touch, it was never without love – I hadn't realised two people could show such ferocity and passion in a moment, yet still be encapsulated in absolute adoration. When she'd spoken about making love and fucking, she hadn't realised, and neither had I, that the two of us could combine those very different acts into the absolute perfection that unfolded in front of us right now.

Her breath was swift, accelerated with low and captivating moans as I reached my hands up for hers, interlacing her fingers with mine and resting them on her warm stomach as her thighs tightened in anticipation. I covered her with my mouth and let my tongue tip her into a rapture that gave me every bit as much enjoyment, as her taste flooded my senses, a sensation I knew I needed more of. My new addiction wasn't any chemical substance, it was her, this euphoria, as she pulsated with desire against my tongue.

Remaining between her legs, loathe to leave this patch of heaven, I placed gentle kisses all over her as the trembling climax slowed and her body relaxed below me. Her breaths were now slow and deep, and as I rose from my knees, I fell another chasm deeper in love with her. Amber's face was perfectly relaxed, a sultry, happy smile dancing casually on her lips. Visible, even in the dimness of the room was the slightest indentation in her bottom lip, which she'd been biting through her pleasure.

She slid backwards on the bed, until her head landed on one of the deep pillows and I followed above her, chasing every kiss from her mouth, pinning her there with my tongue against her own as we settled into the new spot. Placing her palm on my chest she pushed me up, rising with me so we kneeled, face to face, lips brushing against each other.

"When we're apart," I began, "it's like a slow suffocation, then you come back, and all the air rushes into me."

"Are you drunk?" she asked with a coy smile.

"You sobered me up. Don't worry."

"What if it's different this time?" she whispered.

"It will be different every time. That's not bad." I smiled and rubbed her shoulder. "I want to feel this a thousand times with you."

"The word still counts, right?" she asked, a subtle tremor to her voice.

"Of course, I won't hurt you, I could never hurt you."

My words faded away as she kissed me, twisting around so that my back pressed against the padded, extravagant headboard of the bed, my legs stretched out straight as she wrapped hers around me and nibbled on my ear lobe.

"I want to see your eyes." Her voice sent goosebumps down my entire body as she held her face close to mine; her pupils were enormous in the darkened room as she held my gaze, communicating everything between us as she silently ordered me to keep them trained on her own.

Her fingers brushed my stomach as they teased their way down before taking hold of me. A shy smile decorated her mouth at my intake of breath as I felt her soft hand run tantalisingly up and down my length, then, she guided me to her. Those angelic eyes possessed me as she lowered herself down, and every millimetre felt as though I lost myself all over again until I filled her completely. She wrapped her arms around my neck, then neither of us moved, lost in the magic of this, as our eyes drank each other in and I felt myself throb within her, desperate for her.

She kissed me and the fervour consumed us. My hands ran

up and down her back as she rocked upon me, a ridiculous pride surging in me as she took control and moved as she needed and wanted. The very fact that she had that faith and trust in me warmed my soul.

I could feel she was tantalisingly in reach of what she needed, of what we both needed, as she ripped her mouth from mine, gasping for air before she pressed it to my neck. She whimpered against me and in panic I tried to slow her down, pressing my hands to her hips, petrified to hurt her.

She wrenched them away, then clung to me again for stability. "I didn't say the word."

I buried my face into her shoulder, squeezing her, willing myself not to succumb just yet, desperate as I was to feel any release inside of her.

"I love you, Anwir," she murmured against my hot skin as beads of sweat dripped down between us.

"Never as much as I love you," I gasped into her ear, surprising myself at how easy the words I'd never been able to say flowed. I pressed down on her shoulders, pushed myself as deep inside her as I'd ever been and heard her cry out as she tightened around me.

My brain swam in delirious bliss as my eyes closed against the room which seemed to pirouette in a spin. I couldn't feel anything except the sensation of being joined with her. How could my worthless body be one with this deity? My muse, my one, my passion, my everything.

Our breaths slowly calmed as we held each other, and I smiled sleepily as she kissed a bead of sweat from my forehead.

"I don't generally do this with men who are thrown out of bars, just so you know," she joked, before her eyes widened. "Why did you leave me?"

"I wanted to protect you, from me, from them. I just wanted to keep you safe."

"You don't walk out on someone you love. You don't know how I felt when I realised you were gone."

"Me loving you puts you in danger. I thought removing myself was the best thing to do. You deserve better than me." I looked down, full of shame, but she cupped my chin and forced our eyes to meet.

"What I deserve is my choice, and I choose you, I choose to love you." She poked me in the arm as she spoke.

"Forgive me, I honestly only thought of you." I ran my hands up her back and froze. "Amber..." I whispered as my eyes wandered from hers and took in the majestic sight.

Her face was perfection, flushed and red, but relaxed and devoid of tension in the soft aftermath of our love making. Her shoulders shuddered with a tremor of desire that continued to pulse through her. And, to each side of those beautiful shoulders, protruded a wing. Wings so magnificent it was as if they'd been sculpted, the very definition of flawless.

She swallowed, then her eyes closed as a look of humiliation crossed her face. "I'm so sorry, I'm not good at controlling them yet, I didn't mean for you to see—"

I pressed a finger to her lips, my eyes rushing back to meet hers. "You never, ever say sorry for being you. I'd love you with three heads, no eyes, purple skin, weird caterpillar feet..." She laughed and I kissed her nose before continuing. "You don't ever have to hide from me."

"I love how easily you say that now." She pulled my hand to her mouth, letting her lips glide softly over my fingers.

"Can I touch them?" I asked.

She nodded, letting my hand drop from her mouth as she pressed her lips together. I sighed, momentarily lost as she lifted herself off me and sat down on the edge of the bed, her back to me. They were even more beautiful from this vantage point, and it was one more aspect of her that I longed to explore and fully understand.

I shuffled close behind her and placed my hands on her shoulders, rubbing reassuringly as I let my fingers journey outwards. I shuddered as they touched the first feather, white as snow and as soft as if spun from cashmere, just for her. She quivered and I slowed, waiting for her to ask me to stop, but no words were uttered.

I stroked their length and breadth, mesmerised. They were fluffier next to the bone, like baby feathers, growing longer and silkier out towards the edge. Somehow, they felt weightless, yet also full of power. After a minute or two, I gingerly wrapped my arms around her from behind, concerned in case they were sore. Her wings graced me like a gift as they pressed against my chest, absorbing my heartbeat into them.

"You're incredible, don't ever forget," I said as I kissed the side of her face. "It makes me sad, I was taught from such a young age to hate angels, that their wings were ugly and corrupt. They're not, they're part of you, and nothing about you could ever be ugly or corrupt. I could bury myself in these wings for eternity."

Tears began to flow down her cheeks and I jumped off the bed, kneeling on the floor again to face her as I took her hands in mine. "Amber, please don't cry. I love them, I love you."

"I need to tell you how I got them, but I don't want to ruin such a beautiful moment."

The automatic timer on the blinds buzzed, an infuriating reminder that Mason had strict sleep cycles. I shielded my eyes as they slowly raised, allowing the daylight into our haven. I blinked as I looked up at Amber, the sunlight glistening against her eyes.

"Who did this to you?" I growled, as I saw fresh, raw bruises on her neck, a graze across her left cheekbone.

"I told you, we're in danger..."

Twenty-Four
Amber

How weak was I? The moment I'd set eyes upon Anwir I'd thrown myself at him like a needy ex-girlfriend. At the point I should have demanded an answer as to why he'd abandoned me like that, with no word, I instead jumped directly into his arms, followed by his bed.

A delicious shiver teased me at the thought of what we'd just done. It felt surreal, as if something that good surely couldn't have been caused by another person's hands, mouth, and other... appendages. Whilst caught in that spell, I hadn't had to think of the painful reality of this situation, but now those truths pushed against my mind, insistent and sharp.

"Are we safe here?" I asked.

Anwir nodded. "We're shielded. I know you're new to all this. Other angels and demons would be able to see sparks or flares we create on the human realm, but I've shielded us, nobody will spot us. What happened to you? Is it my fault?"

I shook my head, reaching out and stroking the stubble on his chin, the scratch of it against my fingertips bringing an instant smile to my face. "Not your fault, but we really do have to talk. As much fun as that was..." I motioned my head to the bed behind me with a smile.

He stood, pressing a kiss to my forehead as he did so. "I'll make some tea. You get some clothes on and meet me on the sofa. You know where the T-shirts are."

I laughed as I headed to the bathroom to clean up, grabbing one of his soft, white shirts on the way. Even in this ridiculous situation, which made no sense whatsoever, he made me smile and laugh. The sink had been cleaned up, I guess the cleaner came back after all, and my gaze drifted up to the large mirror, embedded in the oversized, slate grey tiles.

The mirror lit up as I waved my hand over the sensor for the LED lights; my eyes bypassed my face and bruises and focused on the wings behind me. I'd naturally tucked them in as I walked through the doorway, so I did have some control, but they made me nervous, suspicious. I guess there was no denying now that the tales from Barke and Anwir were true – either that or I'd had a total breakdown and now resided in some fantasy world within my own mind.

Tentatively, I reached behind me to stroke the feathers, they were softer than anything I'd ever touched, the nearest sensation I could relate it to was having someone stroke my hair as I fell asleep. That hadn't happened since I was a child, but I recalled the memories warmly, and a sadness bloomed in me as I wished Anwir could be the one to do that for me now.

I went to lift the T-shirt over my head and froze, realising it wasn't going to fit and I still had no idea how to get the wings to retract; the science of how this all worked was beyond my comprehension. I willed them away, rolled my shoulders forwards and backwards, pushed them together and apart, but nothing happened.

With a sickness in my gut, I remembered what Barke had done and tried to shove them away, but I couldn't bend my arms to the necessary angle and get the force he'd had. That awful strength he'd had.

Tears pricked at my eyes once more; I just wanted this whole situation to melt away. A matter of weeks ago I'd been busy with my job, living a simple life, and now nothing made sense at all. I lived in fear and confusion, unsure what or who I was. Yet if I was offered the choice to go back, live oblivious to all this, I knew I wouldn't – because that would mean no Anwir, no love, and I knew I wouldn't ever feel alive again without him.

I rubbed the tears from my exhausted eyes on a hand towel, shuddering deeply as I sobbed. The shudder had a knock-on effect and my wings extended, crashing painfully into the shower screen and the door. A sharp scream escaped my lips as the impact ran through me, shook me.

"Amber?" I heard Anwir's footsteps heavy and fast as he headed towards me. He tried to push the bathroom door open, but it caught on my wing.

"I'm stuck," I sobbed, as I pushed at the damned things again.

"How are you stuck?" he asked, peering through the small gap in the doorway, taking in my extended wings in the small ensuite. "Oh..." His eyes were full of empathy as he reached a hand through, seeking mine.

I gratefully grasped his fingers. "I don't know how to control them. Do you know?"

"Squeeze your shoulders back, as tight as you can, squeeze them together," he said kindly.

I let go of his fingers and did so, with a deep, nervy breath. The wings tucked in again, arched elegantly against my back, allowing space for the door to open. Anwir burst in, his chest bare above his dark, denim jeans, and wrapped his arms around me.

"I'm so sorry, I didn't realise you didn't know, of course

you don't know. Amber..." his voice trailed off as he kissed my head repeatedly. He pulled back, rubbing his thumb across each of my cheekbones in turn to wipe the tears away. "Close your eyes," he said. "Try this with me."

His lips grazed mine as he took hold of my hands, pulling my naked body against him. "Your subconscious knows what to do, you just need to let your mind relax." His teeth pressed against my bottom lip for a moment, his breath hot on my face as mere millimetres separated us. "Remember when we first made love?"

My heart sped up, a slow smile etched itself upon me as I remembered, vividly. My lips brushed his as I spoke. "Yes."

"I could tell how nervous you were, but you were amazing. It was like with each deep, lungful of oxygen you absorbed, you moulded yourself underneath me. I've never felt anything that complete in my life."

I murmured incoherent words as the memories washed over me, as his breath flowed into me, and it was as though I was living it all over again, every exquisite moment of pleasure. I pressed my lips to his, not moving as they stuck here and there, rippling against each other through breath and speech.

"You can do that now, just breathe and trust me. Let them go, absorb them..." His words faded out as his tongue flicked against mine and then I was lost again, lost in this moment as with his touch, he made me feel safe, as if nothing mattered, nothing could hurt me.

After a minute he pulled back, with a long sigh and a smile. "All done."

"Wait, how?" I exclaimed, pivoting round to look in the mirror, relieved to see my normal shoulders. I twirled around a couple more times before pressing a soft kiss to his lips. "Thank you." I relished the blush that burst onto his normally stoic cheeks.

"Are they sore?" he asked, his eyes soft with concern.

I nodded and he held me close, my head cradled in the nook of his neck as he rubbed along my shoulder blades. I pressed my mouth to him as he nurtured the tender skin, like a parent would soothe the inflamed gums of an infant.

"That helps, it's good."

"I just like touching you," he smirked. "It's a purely selfish act."

"Don't put yourself down, you're not selfish."

"Every time I touch you, I'm torn. Part of me wants to tie you to my bed and never let you go, the other part of me just wants to worship you, treat you with utter reverence, touch you so softly you shiver."

His words set off tendrils of arousal within me. "Is it normal to want you constantly the way I do? I want to know everything about you. I want to see your home."

"I'm glad you'll never be able to, I wouldn't want you to witness my origins. Anyway, I hate myself for saying this," he said as he backed away with a sigh, "but you need to get dressed or else I'm going to have to introduce you to shower sex, and then we'll never get this talk."

"Maybe afterwards?" I said with a sly grin, as I stepped away.

"It's a date." He smiled and turned away.

"Do you have wings?" I blurted out clumsily.

Anwir nodded.

"Can I see them?"

A short laugh rippled out from deep within him. "Definitely not."

"Hmm," I said sulkily, as I pulled him back into the cramped space. "That's not fair."

He looked torn momentarily, before he dipped down to whisper in my ear. "How about I let you feel them? I haven't manifested them since I've been here, but I can..."

"Please," I said, as I ran my fingertips up his sides.

He waved his hand across the mirror again so that the LED lights blinked out, plunging the room into dimness once more. "Promise me you'll keep your eyes closed?"

"I promise, but you never have to hide from me."

He smiled and ran a finger over my eyelids, closing them before he pulled me tight against his chest. As soon as my lips sensed his skin within reach, I couldn't stop myself from kissing him, until a faint flurry of air passed over me as he took a sharp intake of breath.

"All yours..." he murmured, his body tensed.

I continued to kiss the warm skin of his chest, focusing above his heart as I heard its rhythmic thumping, powerful and quickening subtly with each glancing touch from my mouth. My hands moved to the bottom of his spine, and slowly I teased them upwards, gasping as I touched something familiar yet utterly unknown.

"They feel just like mine," I whispered, as I stroked along them, adoring each and every one, craving the sensation of them as much as I craved his smile, his breath, his touch. I stretched up onto my tiptoes, reaching past his upper arm to press a kiss to the feathers I could reach.

"Amber..." My name rumbled up from deep within his belly as he pulled back. My eyes remained closed, as promised. A noise rustled into my ears, as if delicate tissue paper had been folded in on itself, then his fingers stroked at my eyes again, encouraging them to open.

"Don't get trapped this time," he winked as he turned away, but I didn't miss the sadness that flashed over him. Was he thinking the same thoughts that I desperately tried to avoid? Was this the last time we'd be together?

Barke flashed through my mind, and I forced him immediately back out as I pulled the T-shirt over my head and tugged my pants up my legs before heading out to Anwir. I refused to let that monster invade my thoughts while I was here, with the most beautiful soul I'd ever known.

I padded barefoot down the hallway, pausing for a moment as I took in the sight of Anwir on the sofa cradling a mug, a matching one for me on the coffee table. I wished, with every ounce of me, that we were just a normal couple, clambering lazily out of bed in search of caffeine, but I knew we never would be.

I sat and tucked my legs up under me as I faced him, my knees touching his thigh and my hands gripping my hot drink.

"Jasmine tea?" I asked, with a smile.

He nodded. "What happened? Who did this to you?" He ran his finger over the bruises on my neck. His eyes looked as though his heart crumbled inside of him.

"Before we go into that..." I sighed, "why did you disappear on me? We had that amazing night, then I woke up and you were gone. I waited and waited for you, Anwir."

He drew his fingers down his face. "I love you more than anything I ever thought remotely possible. But how can I be with you without hurting you? You're an angel, you don't belong with someone like me. I thought it was better to just go, let you get on with your life."

"What if I want my life to be with you?" I asked, my eyes holding his defiantly.

"I will never again feel like I'm home unless I'm with you. But there is nowhere we can be together, nowhere. I feel like it's killing me." His voice was thick with emotion as he spoke. "So, I figured that all I could do was walk away, and let you go home, because you can have a home and be happy, and I'm not selfish enough to stop that based on my own needs."

I pulled his hand gently down and wrapped mine around it. "I don't have a home without you in it."

Anwir smiled sadly, leaning his head back against the sofa

as he closed his eyes, but not before I saw a well of tears build up in them. "They'd come for us. They wouldn't let this be."

"I think you're right." I squeaked, without meaning to, as fear gripped me.

"Tell me what happened. Everything, I need to know."

We played with each other's fingers as I began to explain, our skin warm from the mugs of tea. "Ben had been worried about me; nobody knew where I was. I agreed to go on a picnic with him, just as friends. It didn't seem like it would do any harm. He brought strawberries and I couldn't eat them." I bit my lip as an embarrassed warmth flooded my face. Anwir laughed, a sound I adored, happiness radiated from him, he needed to laugh more, and I wanted so badly to be the one who made him do that. "And then..." I paused, he pulled me closer to him, and his touch reassured me.

"You can tell me anything, I won't judge you."

"He was talking about Barke and Mireille, and I was so confused. I felt heartbroken about you. He asked to kiss me, and said that things would make sense, it would help my memories. I hoped those memories might give me some clue about how to find you, I never would've kissed him otherwise, never." My voice broke as I confessed my indiscretion, but Anwir just pressed his lips to my ear, soothed me with a scrape of his lips and the feel of his breath.

"Carry on."

"Then he held me, locked me down somehow, I couldn't move. He whispered, horribly, about how it had to be today. I don't know what he did, I couldn't see, but it felt like he had burning hot blades. As though he cut me, so my wings would come out. He forced them out."

"Amber..." Anwir sounded like he would cry for me as he spoke my name.

"It was excruciating. I tried to speak, but he..." I closed my eyes against the memory. "He pressed on my neck until I passed out. Said he hadn't given me permission to speak."

Anwir's body stiffened next to me, his fingers fisted up and I wrapped them around mine again before I continued. "While I was unconscious, I got my memories back, I remembered Mireille. But she wasn't happy on the angelic plane, with him. Barke..." I sighed, "he's an absolute monster, he beat her, he kept her isolated, he controlled her. They were bound together when she was very young, and he destroyed everything that was alive and vivid about her. Now he wants her back... I don't want to go back."

I slid onto Anwir's knee, curled up like a child as he wrapped his arms tight around me, kissing the top of my head over and over. I felt his tears mingle into my hair as his breath shuddered in his chest. "We'll find a way, Amber. You aren't going back, no matter what it takes. I won't let anyone hurt you."

"I don't want him to hurt *you*, I couldn't live with myself if you were hurt because of me. He knew about us, somehow."

"He has no idea what he's unleashed." Anwir scowled as I uncurled his fingers from angry fists once again. "How did you end up at the bar, though? I know I was drunk, but he wasn't there with you, was he?"

"He told me I could say goodbye to you, on one condition."

"What condition?" he asked, his eyebrows drawn tightly together. "Who the fuck is he to set conditions anyway, as if he owns you."

I shrugged. "He does think he owns me, some weird angelic binding contract."

"Over my dead body..."

"Please," I begged. "Please don't say that. Anwir, don't say that." I buried my head back into his chest and felt it deflate as he let out a long sigh.

"What's this condition, then?"

"That you tell me the reason you're here on this plane. I don't want to pander to his demands but... I have this feeling, that I need to know, Anwir."

I looked up at him, pleading behind my eyes as he slid me back onto the sofa, his face somehow full of regret.

"We need a proper drink for this," he said, as he headed towards the kitchen. A trickle of dread, that I couldn't quite place, dripped heavily down my spine.

TWENTY-FIVE

AMBER

A nwir handed me a crystal glass, beautifully designed with a long, elegant stem. Ruby red wine sloshed inside it, the aroma diffusing into the air around me, full of temptation.

"Is this the same wine I tried on the roof?"

"Yes, I'm not trying to corrupt you. You liked the taste, right?"

"I did, I could smell the oranges in it. I've always loved citrus smells. I know now that it's because I lived in a citrus orchard... with him."

Quick as a flash, Anwir threw both glasses against the window, turning to me with a wide, devilish grin as I blanched at the drips of wine that ran down the glass, amongst shards of broken crystal.

"In that case, fuck oranges," he yelled, gleefully. "Screw lemons and as for limes, who eats them anyway? If it was up to me, I'd burn every citrus grove to ash. Vitamin C is overrated; who needs that shit?" He pressed a deep kiss to my lips and strode to the kitchen with purpose. My mouth was still agape at his actions, but a laugh curled up at its edges. How could this man turn a bad memory into a moment of joy for me?

"Instead…" he shouted from the kitchen, amidst banging doors and clinking glasses, "you need to try something more decadent. Something distinctly unhealthy."

He crashed two heavy, glass tumblers down onto the table. Ice cubes clinked together within them as thick, beige liquid, marbled with brown settled into the spaces between the ice.

"You're crazy," I giggled as I reached for my drink. He pressed his glass to mine, looking into my eyes.

"Only for you," he said. "I'd do anything to put that smile on your face."

"Anwir…" I let out a happy sigh.

"Cheers, Amber Carmichael. The past, the future, it may hold more pain than we know, but I don't care. The short time we've had together here, it's worth a millennium of torture. I'd still remember the smile on your face, and I would never, ever stop loving you. To us."

I began to well up again, and Anwir shot me a feisty glance. "Drink, like there's no tomorrow. Be the angel they all wish they could be."

Following his lead, I downed the drink, closing my eyes to savour the delicious tang of caramel and coffee that coated my mouth as the creamy liquid popped every tastebud wide open. It burned as it ran down into my chest, but I enjoyed it.

"I could get used to that." Anwir leaned forward and kissed me, pressing his tongue to mine as I tasted the drink all over again on his mouth. He pulled away promptly, falling back onto the sofa cushions, seemingly drained from the last few minutes of excitement.

"I travelled here to finish a job that my father messed up," he said quietly, pressing his thumbs to the ends of his fingers in turn.

"You mentioned that," I said, eyeing him with caution. "Was it something to do with the war?"

"No, there was some ridiculous prophecy, ancient thing, that he believed in. He thought he'd found the person the prophecy talked about."

"So, he was trying to recruit them?"

"I told you that demons can't travel to the angelic plane, right?"

I nodded. "Was this person an angel?"

"She was. My father waited until she travelled to the human plane, his intention was to kill her."

"Your father, the demon?" My voice trembled, as a bitter coldness seeped within me.

His head barely moved, but I saw the subtle nod as he looked down at the floor.

"What was the angel's name?"

"If I've pieced it all together correctly, which I think I have, her name was... Mireille."

The silence became a deafening roar in my ear as I let the confession sink into me. My teeth tore at my gum as I tried to reconcile this knowledge with the vague memories of that day I'd lived through.

"Anwir, that's not your fault. I don't blame you for what your father did. In a way, he saved me from going home to Barke, at least." I reached for his hand, but he flinched, pulled it away. His eyes flashed upwards to mine, full of heat and passion.

"Think about it. I came here to finish what he'd failed at. Now, do you see?"

"You were going to kill me?" I stuttered, wringing my hands together.

"Yes, I spent years getting ready for it. I was looking forward to it if we're being honest." He stood, running his hands through his hair until it stuck up erratically as he paced up and down, to and from the kitchen.

"How did you know it was me? From bumping into me at the coffee shop? Was I that obvious?"

He laughed, but I could see it was an act as he attempted to hide what he truly felt behind bravado and masculinity. "The coffee shop was staged; I'd been following you for weeks. Learning all about you, your job, your home. I had to be one hundred per cent sure it was you, so I befriended you. Did you never feel uneasy looking out of your window at night?"

"Anwir, why weren't you just honest with me, then?"

"Excuse me," he mimed, dramatically. "I'm so sorry I spilt your tea; can I just check if your touch poisons me before I stab you through the heart?" He growled out an enraged cry as he kicked one of the kitchen units, cracking the wood, the splintering sound too loud for this space.

"You stalked me, to get close to me, to kill me?" I asked.

"Yes. Now do you see why I deserve my name?" He came back from the kitchen with a bottle of French vodka, guzzling from it as he flopped down onto the sofa.

"When did you decide not to kill me?"

"I think I always would have struggled, because there was something about you from the first moment I laid eyes on you. But the pivotal point was when I discovered you could touch me. I realised that maybe all I'd been told about angels was a lie, and I knew I had to stop denying what the warmness in my chest was, what the ache in my body was. It was unstoppable, undeniable love."

"How old were you when your father attacked Mireille?" I asked, my forehead settling into determined lines; I would never accept that she and I were one.

"I wasn't born until after."

"But I thought she killed him? Did I kill him? Anwir..." I gasped. "Did I kill your father?"

He shook his head as it rested in his hands, then dropped

towards his knees. "Amber, my lovely, lovely girl. How can you be so fucking good, that after learning those despicable facts, you worry that *you* have somehow wronged *me*?"

"I know I'm new to these random lifespans, but I don't understand the timeline here. If Mireille killed your father, how were you born later? And where have I been? Because I'm only twenty-five."

He shuffled along the sofa until he was next to me, but not touching.

"Mireille stabbed him with one of her feathers, he'd injured her wing."

"I remember," I sobbed, as the trauma and violation flooded into me, every sting and sensation burning into my mind.

"The blood on her feather poisoned him, but it was a tiny amount, so it took weeks to actually kill him. I was conceived during those weeks. Typical of my father, by all accounts, to chase women even on the way to his deathbed."

"You were created by a demon who had angel blood in his veins, albeit a tiny amount. Mireille's blood, my blood. That's why I can touch you. Some protection, or immunity, must have passed to you."

Anwir's eyes met mine, the tiniest glimmer of hope sparkled at the edges.

"But it doesn't negate what I tried to do to you, I was going to kill you, that's unforgiveable. That's why Barke let you come here with that condition; he knew you'd hate me once you learned the truth."

"Fuck Barke," I shouted out, as a relieved smile flashed over Anwir's face. "That just proves he's never really loved a person, if he thinks true love can be turned to hate so easily."

"You're sexy as hell when you say bad words, you know?" He smiled and slid his hand around my waist. "I honestly thought that revelation would be it for us."

"I'm not happy that you were lurking in shady corners with an intent to murder me. Not really a story for the grand-kids, is it? But... nothing about this is normal, and at least we solved a part of the mystery, we know why I can touch you, and Anwir, I fucking love touching you," I teased.

"Stop doing that," he groaned. "I'm trying to think of ways to save us, and all you make me think about is your body under mine."

"How long do you think we have?"

"I don't know, but it could be a million years and it wouldn't be enough." He rested his forehead against mine and despite my best efforts, a tear splashed down my cheek, landing on his T-shirt. "I'm homesick for a place I've never been and can never know – your home. I'll never be able to go there, and you'll never be able to come to mine. We have no place to be together other than this mortal realm, and we aren't safe here. We'll be targets for both sides."

"Then we'll fight them, every single time, until they stop."

"Amber, how much blood are you willing to have on your hands? Every time they come for us, humans will die. You've never seen a planar battle. We'd be sentencing thousands of people to death. There was a time I would have shrugged that off, but you've taught me how precious life is."

"There's too much darkness. I'd die before I'd go back there, I'd—"

"Don't you dare think it, don't say it. No, Amber." He pulled me to his chest as he spoke and as much as his arms reassured me, his heartbeat was fast and erratic and I could feel the stress pound throughout him.

"Do you have a copy of this prophecy?" I asked, bolting upright with excitement. "Maybe there's something in there that will help us?"

"I do." He paused, a look of utter contentment on his face as he leaned forward and kissed me, soft and slow. "You are beyond anything I could have imagined. All you've learned tonight and still, all you want to do is fight for us. What did I do to deserve you in my life?"

"You're everything to me," I smiled as I stroked his cheek. "I'm the lucky one here."

"Give me five minutes," he said. "It's buried in the stuff I brought with me."

Anwir headed down the hallway towards the bedroom, shouting back over his shoulder. "I love you! See how good I am at saying that now."

I grinned as I stood, stretching my arms out above me. "Hurry up so we can fuck. See how good I am at saying *that* now." I stuck my tongue out as he walked out of sight, laughing.

What a night this had been. Some parts of what I'd learned made me hugely uncomfortable, but wasn't that a part of love? Accepting the bad with the good, knowing that people had dubious pasts and loving them regardless, trusting them?

I grabbed a dustpan and brush from the cupboard under the kitchen sink and set about sweeping up the broken glass; the wine that had dripped down the walls lay on the floor now, resembling a crime scene.

"Ow!" I exclaimed, as a slither of sharp glass sliced into my finger. I raised it to my mouth, sucking the blood as I tossed the offending shard into the dustpan. I couldn't help but laugh at the thought of Anwir burning all the orange trees, just so I wouldn't have to smell them.

All at once, disorientation surrounded me as a brilliant white flash hit. My ears exploded into an agonising cacophony of ringing and buzzing as I raised my hands to them in pain. Then I fell, backwards, from the beautiful penthouse apartment. My arms outstretched as I looked up at the stars above me, knowing I had mere seconds before I would hit the ground. Seconds to love him, seconds to mourn the short time we had together, seconds to pray I would find him again, seconds to beg for another chance...

TWENTY-SIX

ANWIR

The shield that had protected us combusted; fragments of magical essence rained down over the building like splintered ice. I was knocked to the floor as an explosion rocked the apartment.

I staggered towards the living room calling Amber's name, but an entire pane of glass had been blown out and the wind whipped wickedly around the room, picking up any light objects and scattering them toward the sky.

A blind panic overtook me as I ran to the window, clinging onto the frame without a care for the raw shards of glass that plunged into my flesh. Screams sounded out from the road below and I was vaguely aware of my own joining in as I bellowed her name, desperation plaguing me.

I turned and ran for the staircase with no thought about my naked chest or feet, just a desperate need to find her, save her. An image of her twisted and broken at the foot of the building invaded my mind as I ran, jumped, clawed my way down the seemingly never-ending flights of stairs, begging gravity to get me closer to her.

Bursting out of the lobby doors, my heart froze mid-beat

as my eyes focused in on a figure, prostrate on the ground. Passers-by were standing next to a blood soaked body, as a woman placed a blanket over it, the same type as the one from the lobby that we'd snuggled under together.

Unable to move, rooted to the spot, I remained in place. Not wanting another second to pass in case it meant an awful truth, a possibility my mind couldn't handle. Blood seeped through the blanket and I was mesmerised, as though my brain was caught on a rusty nail, unable to move past the pattern of the ichor as it spilled. Please don't let it be her... I tore my eyes away, looking up to the stars above us as I prayed to anyone or anything that might exist.

Two tell-tale flares went off to the east. A dark green, strong, and powerful, followed by the briefest glimpse of orange, weak, almost hidden, but I would have recognised it anywhere. As my senses flooded back to life, I glimpsed down at the ground – the injured person was a man, not Amber. A large shard of glass had plummeted through his leg, an inno-cent bystander in this unavoidable fight, that I now knew I had to see through. A shooting pain plunged into my brain, our fight had spilled out already, hurting those who didn't need to be involved. But that hadn't been my doing. I had one focus: Amber.

There was no need to disguise myself now I realised, both angels and demons were caught up in this and it would only be a short time before more descended. I blurred myself from human eyes as my wings extended and my journey to her began. Clambering up buildings, jumping from rooftop to rooftop, grabbing at every thread of power I could to hasten my journey, I sped towards the flares of power that had lit up the horizon.

Initially they moved at the same speed as me, before stop-ping, quietening. I had to focus to find the colours, which slowed my journey, but also gave me time to prepare. The faint orange drifted away like mist, and I forced myself to imagine her somewhere safe, away from this horror.

I crept along the rooftop of a tall office building that took up a large corner plot at a busy crossroads in the city centre. Dusk had recently fallen, and the streets below heaved with people and traffic, bustling noise, flashing road signs, the strobes of car headlights as they passed by at speed. So much life below me, oblivious to the carnage that would soon be unleashed.

I looked across to the building diagonally opposite me. An old church, reimagined into a lively bar, holding fifty times as many people right now as it would have done in its previous incarnation. Atop its roof, staring directly at me, was a taller, uglier, winged caricature of Ben – this had to be Barke, and there was no sign of Amber.

He hovered above the ground, as the full width of his snow-white wings quivered silently in the air. It was a display of his power, his masculinity, his strength, and I sniggered at the very sight of it. A deep furrow appeared between his eyebrows as my response reached him, and, as the air thickened between us, the sounds of the human lives below us grew muffled.

I spoke the words quietly, sending them over to him on shards of cold air with a flick of my wrist. "You can twirl those wings around all day, Barke, be a little ballerina for all I care. We know the truth, though, don't we, you, and me? For only a coward would be entrusted with the beautiful soul that you were, only to beat her, hurt her, keep her bowed down. Why were you afraid to let her shine? Scared to let the world see how worthless you were without her?"

He tucked his wings in, the points of them low behind his legs as he cranked his neck from side to side. His hand jerked momentarily in my direction, and I cursed as pinpricks of fire crashed into me, carrying his message. "You dared to touch what was not yours. You defiled the body of an angel. For this, the entire demonic plane will pay."

He looked down with a self-satisfied smile as the sounds of crumpling metal drifted up, accompanied by rage filled screams and shouts. On the ground below, a riot hurtled into existence. Cars had careered into buildings on both sides of the crossroads, doors slammed as drivers exited, obscenities being flung carelessly at each other. A few individuals hurried from the scene, worriedly clutching loved ones and children, but most seemed to be feeling the animosity that trickled down from the rooftop, from us, as the hatred boiled over and leaked into their minds, feeding every dark, violent impulse that lay dormant within them.

Humans had no idea how many of their darkest points of history had actually come to pass through angelic and demonic scuffles, this busy realm that lay between ours had paid in blood over and over for its position, through no fault of its own. To us, it had simply been a gateway, a place to antagonise each other, but as I looked down now, I saw the devastation we had wrought on it over and over. How many people were losing their loved ones, themselves, right now, because of us?

"Barke!" I stepped forwards onto the thickened air that now bridged the space between the buildings, my own wings having extended to their full width as adrenaline pricked them to attention. "They don't need to pay for a battle that is between us." I motioned towards the ground, my eyes boring into his, as he took a matching step toward me.

"Why would I care about them?" he snarled.

"Do you care about Mireille? Because she cares about them, she cares about you."

"Don't you dare say her name!" he screamed, contemptuously, as he flew towards me, landing inches from my face. I heard the sickening noise of fighting below, screams of pain and anguish, the crack of bone snapping, the ripping of flesh as the event spiralled out of control.

As hard as it was, I had to stay calm. Mere weeks ago, I would have torn into him, but everything had changed, there was someone who mattered more, and I needed to keep her in the forefront of my mind. He knew I couldn't touch him, but neither would he want to touch me; angels thought themselves ruined if they touched the flesh of a demon. I could see no weapon on him, and I was wary of how this was going to play out.

"Where is she?" I asked, sucking in a deep breath, trying to bring some calm to the chaos below me.

"Gone." He smirked, his face contorted and ugly. "You think she'd be allowed back home after being with you? You wrote her death sentence the moment you tricked her into your bed."

Try as I might, my blood boiled within me, threatening to spill out, erupt and turn the whole world to ash with a vile combination of rage, guilt, grief, and pure, pure hatred.

I howled, a feral cry full of desperation, as I flew at him. My shoulder hit his chest bone, taking him by surprise as it pushed him backwards. I let my wings propel me, using the momentum to keep pushing as his arms flailed, looking for something to grab hold of, something that wasn't me.

It felt like a hundred miles passed that way, before his back crashed into the old stone of the church he'd been stood atop. Pieces of it fell with splintering cracks into the crowd below who were still baying for blood, trying their best to tear each other apart. I stepped back, breathing heavily, the ominous tingling becoming apparent in my shoulder where I'd been in physical contact with him.

"You know you can't touch me," he spat. "I can stay here for as long as I need to, while her body rots. Keep me here, watch that riot spread, until the city burns, until the country burns, until the whole world is destroyed. Do it, let history blame a failed, piss-poor excuse of a demon for the desecration of the middle plane."

"Your mistake, Barke," I spat his name with disdain, revelling in the flash of panic he failed to hide as my breath hit his face, "is that you took away the one thing I had to live for. So, what's to stop me from touching you? What's to stop me from teaching you my lessons, the way you taught Mireille yours? Beating you senseless, choking the breath from your throat, forcing myself on you. What's to stop me?"

"The fact that you'd fail. You'd fail like your pathetic excuse of a father did. I'll destroy you and I'll scatter your body in every corner of this realm, make sure that not one atom touches her ever again."

I lowered my hands to my sides, wafting them through the larger feathers that brushed against my lower back, grasping one in each hand as I leant forward. My voice was low as I whispered, "The only failure here is you, to have a woman like her and not surround her with your love. I may have had mere days with her, but they were worth a thousand lifetimes. Nothing you do or say can ever lessen what we had. You're powerless, impotent, and now..." I paused briefly, readying myself, "tainted by this failure of a demon."

I licked him roughly up his cheek as flustered panic bubbled up and out of his throat. He raised his hands to me, as I'd hoped he would, and, as quick as the lightning that had played out for Amber and me, I tore two feathers from myself and plunged them into the joints at the top of his wings, blocking their movement.

He screamed, an inhuman sound of absolute rage, accompanied by explosions and the stench of burning bodies from the ground below us. His hands grasped the sides of my face, melting into me like acid as he twisted around, pushing me onto the rooftop.

He'd taken her, and the longer I dragged this out, the more human lives would be extinguished in our names, and that was something I couldn't allow. I lay on the rooftop, smiling inside as he levelled blow after blow to my face and body. For slowly, but surely, my feathers leaked into him, the pure white of his own growing mottled, as if poison ivy leached across them. Ugly veins of angry maroon spread from each section as the prominent, perfect ends withered and died.

I closed my eyes to the world, to every world, as my mind began to shut down, echoing my body, defeated and pained. Yet her face remained. She persevered; her smile imprinted upon my soul. Every cell in me would remember her touch, her love; I didn't regret a moment, for I was dying with a blazing inferno of love inside me, that nobody could ever take away.

All that was left for me to do now, was to burn.

Twenty-Seven

Mireille

A tendril of panic bloomed within me as I struggled to open my eyes, realising that I couldn't. Something glued them together as the darkness infringed upon me, menacing and unnatural.

Was this death? I had no idea. I recalled a long fall and then this, this... nothingness. With trepidation I pressed my hands below me, grasping and hoping to feel something recognisable. A cold, hard surface met me, it could have been anywhere, the feel of it held no clue as to my predicament or my health.

Thankfully, my hands were not restrained and I raised them to my eyes in expectation of a blindfold or mask but found no such barrier. My eyelashes felt as if they'd been in the ocean, for weeks, months even. They were crusted closed, a salted seal which I picked and clawed at, feeling no concern as I scratched at my skin.

Slowly and painfully, light began to filter through and I grimaced against its harshness, allowing myself time to adjust as I turned my head. My vision was blurred, unclear, my mind ached and a bubble of panic grew in intensity, my breaths ragged as I tried to put the pieces together. Where could I be?

I inhaled and then the terror imprisoned me. A scent so loved by many wound itself into my nose, crashed into my brain and paralysed me. Oranges. All I could smell was oranges.

I crawled backwards, still blind other than the strips of light which flashed periodically, desperate to escape but knowing I was powerless. My back hit a stone wall, cold and damp, and effortlessly I released my wings, wrapped them around myself in a vague attempt to hide, wrapped like a foetus within an umbilical sac.

"Mireille," a voice hissed, a voice I couldn't place. I stayed as still as a statue within the cocoon of my wings, too scared to move, to flinch. "Please, my darling, it's been so long. You're wasting away."

The voice was kind, I didn't sense any threat, but that smell overpowered me, and I had no choice but to unlock my wings from around me as I vomited onto the cold, hard floor. A hand stroked my hair causing me to flinch away, then a shriek escaped my lips as I tried to burrow further back but found myself in a tight corner.

"Darling, please. It's Amani. Let me in, listen to me. You're fading away, please Mireille, please." I heard sobs overtake the words and slowly I blinked, looking up towards the sound.

"Amani?" I whispered, croakily.

Her face crumbled with emotion as she smiled down at me, lovingly. "Yes," she beamed, beautiful, wise lines of age forming into familiar creases all over her face.

"Where am I?"

"You're at my house."

"Why?" I asked, my voice pained.

"Come with me," she said, her voice full of affection as she held my hand and led me through a doorway. My vision was still diminished but I was aware of the concrete floor giving way to lush grass and relief flooded into me as I sucked fresh air into my lungs.

Amani settled me into an outside chair and wrapped a cream shawl around me before she pressed a ceramic cup into my hands. I gripped it tightly, inhaling the smell of honey as I raised it to my lips, allowing the warm liquid to soothe my throat and return some strength to my voice.

"Why am I here?" I repeated.

"It's a mystery to me," she replied, a frown settling into her forehead. "You always looked after me, though, fetched my herbs, worried about my cough." She tapped herself on the chest with a brave smile. "I knew I had to look after you too, there was no question."

"Why does my heart hurt?" I asked pitifully as I placed the empty cup down and clutched at my chest. "Who is Amber? Her voice is inside of me, I can't stand it."

"You were attacked by a demon. Do you remember? A long, long time ago now."

I nodded, clutching my head. "I remember."

"Barke was incensed. Everyone commented on how forlorn he was without you. I knew though, Mireille. I was the only one who lived close enough to you to know. I used to hear your screams, his anger. He wasn't heartbroken, he was just annoyed that you'd been hidden away, to heal."

She topped my cup up from a large ceramic jug before she continued. "This place wasn't the same without you, it was as though all the joy had been taken. Almost two hundred long years and then he spread the word that the elders had given him permission to go get you, awaken you and bring you home."

She tucked the shawl tighter around me as I shivered. "Moons came and went, rumours flew around like wildfire, none of us knew what had happened, but neither you nor Barke returned. Then, one night, the most unnatural, sinister storm broke."

I looked up at her as I wiped tears from my eyes once more. "A storm?"

"Like a hurricane," she continued. "It felt as though the entire realm would be torn asunder. Hours and hours it lasted. Your villa had been deserted for so long, I was looking out of my bedroom window to check how many trees had fallen when I saw... something... crash through your roof.

"I'll never forgive myself," she continued. "But I was too weak to battle the storm. I had to wait until the next day, an eerie calm had settled, too calm to be trusted. I headed over to see what had hit your villa."

"What was it, Amani?" I asked, as my breath shuddered within me.

"I think... I think it was you, my darling. You were lying on the floor, your chest barely moved. I assumed he'd attacked you again, but he was nowhere to be seen. I wished I'd braved the storm, you were like ice, almost blue as you lay there."

I winced as a memory of falling from a tall building shuddered into me. Surely not a memory, though, I didn't know any such place.

"You wouldn't speak to me, but I couldn't leave you there, the roof was destroyed. I brought you here, settled you in my bed, warmed you up with drinks and tinctures until a tiny bit of life blossomed in your cheeks again. The next morning when I woke, you were gone. I couldn't find you and I was worried sick. I searched so hard my lungs ached, and when I sat down for a rest, I heard it."

"Heard what?" I asked, as anxiety threatened to suffocate me.

"I heard crying, heartbroken sobs. I followed the noise and you'd dragged yourself down to the cellar. You'd cried for so long that your eyes were clogged with tears. I led you back up, cleaned them with warm water and got you back into bed. But every day, every single day, you go back down there and lie on the concrete floor, cry as you repeat the same word over and over. It's been almost two moons now, it's torture, as if I watch you die inside each day. This is the first time you've seemed lucid."

"What word?"

She looked at me, her pale blue eyes scrunched up in confusion.

"Amani, what word do I say?"

"Anwir," she replied. "I don't know what it means, but you call it over and over."

My insides tightened but I couldn't comprehend why. "Can we move away from the trees? Inside?" I asked, as the citrus smell washed over me again in the breeze and I gagged in revulsion. The evening was drawing in with speed, and the darkening sky worried me.

"Of course."

"What's that?" I pointed up at a sparkling point of light in the sky as a familiar yet unpleasant aura settled inside my mind.

"That's Arcturus. It's just a star. Come with me." She led me inside, pointing towards a bedroom. "This is where you've been sleeping, at least until you wander. Do you want a few minutes to compose yourself?" She wiped my cheeks and I realised tears poured from me once again. "I never thought an angel could cry themselves to death. But you, Mireille, I fear that's your fate."

She closed the door behind us and I slumped down onto the feather-soft bed. New tears already formed and descended onto the embroidered blanket below me. My soul was barren, my heart empty, my body defeated, but I couldn't fathom what had caused it all.

A framed piece of cross-stitch hung on the wall, and I focused in on it through my blur. Tattered around the edges, the material was almost threadbare. I wondered how many hundreds, if not thousands of years ago, angelic fingers had stitched the words in fine, black thread.

A feather torn asunder
Will call out, through misted skies
Fragmented in his terror
Truth reflected in her eyes

Threads entangled by melody
She will slumber in his domain
Then consent her own demise
Never to see her hallow again

The liar
Will survey his miracle
As the darkness
Kisses the light

All will wane to grey...
All will fade away...

"The liar..." I whispered to myself, frowning as I paced up and down the room. I remembered a fall, but not from where. I was home, back amongst my hallow, but nothing felt right. The only relief right now was that Barke seemed to have disappeared; a red rage rose within me as I sent a wish out to the universe that he wouldn't ever be seen again.

A soft knock sounded out and I opened the door, smiling

at Amani, as kindness shone out of her every pore. "What's the poem?" I asked, motioning to the embroidery on the wall.

"My grandmother's work." Her chest puffed up with pride as she glanced over it. "She was insistent that my mother keep it and pass it to her daughter. She wanted the tradition to carry on but as you know, I was never bound, and I never had a child."

I reached out and stroked her arm. "I wish I'd never been bound."

"You're like a daughter to me. I was so scared for you when I heard about the attack, but I knew you were strong. You had to be, to live with him." Her mouth curled up at the corner with disgust.

"Has there been no sign of Barke at all?" I asked.

"Not one, good riddance. Come with me."

She led me to her kitchen; herbs and seedlings grew in different coloured clay pots, there were spices in a pestle, and jars of different concoctions littered every wooden surface.

"The maternal line in my hallow have always had a special talent, did I ever tell you?" she asked as we sat at her sturdy, wooden table.

I shook my head. "What talent?"

"We can glimpse a version of the past and let it teach us a lesson about our future. Supposedly, that's what my grand-mother did when she wrote that poem. I don't want to bring back bad memories; I think that every vile deed I heard him rain down on you was likely not even half of what actually occurred. But, Mireille, you seem lost. This might give you some direction."

"It's like I'm broken, but I don't know how," I whispered, scraping my fingers along the wooden grooves of the table as I fought back yet more tears. The delicate skin around my eyes ached with the constant friction.

"Shall we try?" Her hand rubbed mine gently, soothingly,

as she shuffled closer. She held her arms out to me as a mother would to her child and I buried my face into her, sobbing until it felt as though my heart would shatter with the agony. An agony I couldn't place.

"It's not a precise art, my darling. But let's try. Close your eyes, let yourself drift."

I felt a warmness buzz into the air of the kitchen as her fingers rubbed soft, slow circles over my temples. She hummed a tune, a haunting melody. I tried to place it, but my mind was worn down and sinking into this feeling seemed like such a lovely plan.

"Amber?"

A deep voice called my name, I jumped up from the sofa, tugging a white T-shirt lower down my thighs as I bounded excitedly towards the door.

"You better have the almond croissants, I'm starved," I called, as I peeped into the hallway, frowning when I found it empty. "Where are you?"

"Right here." I jumped, before his arms wrapped around my middle, my heart hastened at his touch. I twisted around, looping my arms around his neck as I pulled him close for a kiss.

"I missed you," I whispered into his mouth.

"I've been gone twenty minutes. And it was you who insisted on croissants from one particular bakery." He brushed my hair out of my eyes and rubbed his lips tenderly over mine.

"It was a long twenty minutes." I smiled, saturated with the love that lived within his deep, honey-brown eyes.

"I live for Saturday mornings," he moaned, as he pushed me against the wall with gentle yet firm hands, the bag of croissants forgotten as he set a fire of lust raging within me.

"What would we have done if we hadn't found each other?" I asked while he kissed my neck, nudging my head to the side.

My eyes fluttered, watching the storm that began to swirl outside.

"We were always meant to find each other. My dark needed to kiss your light. We only found freedom when everything else faded away. You and I were the grey."

"How did everything fade away? I don't remember."

"Remember me, Amber. Remember me..."

He grasped my cheeks between his palms, his eyes begged me as reality blurred into a dizzy swirl of memory and pain. Leaving my parents, being beaten by Barke, plunging my feather into a demon, hiding on the human realm in body after body until I was Amber. Round and round it went, nauseating me; it all felt horrifically wrong.

In one split second it stopped. I opened my eyes, and he held me. The wind chapped my skin as we stood atop the skyscraper. Our eyes were locked on each other, his pupils wide with fear. They advanced on us, and we had no way out, nobody understood the love between us, but I knew, with absolute clarity, that there was no future ahead of me, not without Anwir.

The air raced past us, bursting against my eardrums like explosives bombarding a fortress.

"Then we'll fall together."

I gasped, stricken, as I bolted upright, my chest heaved as I struggled to catch a breath that couldn't fit inside of me between the sobs and the misery. Tears fell like rain down my cheeks as Amani rocked me backwards and forwards, stroking my hair and shushing me until many long minutes later, and the panic attack subsided.

"He's dead, Amani. Barke killed him, I know he did. I can feel it. He killed him." I dissolved into crushed whimpers as Amani placed a hot cup of tea into my hands.

"I'm sorry, sometimes it shows good, sometimes bad, I

have no control over that. You found the angel you truly loved? And Barke took him away? Was that your vision?"

"Not quite. Amani..." I paused, "I love a man with all my heart, he's kind and brave, selfless and loyal. His very presence eases my soul, his smile is the most beautiful sight my eyes will ever see. I'd forsake a thousand of my lifetimes for one day with him."

"I'm so sorry he was taken from you."

"Would you still be sorry if I told you he was a demon?" I asked, the defiant streak in me asserting itself.

"Love is love, Mireille. When you get to my age you realise the truth of what really matters. I don't judge you for who you love."

"Thank you," I stammered at her unexpected but welcome reaction.

"When did he die?"

"It's all so blurry, I'm not sure. I remember falling and you said I landed here. I think it must have been Barke who pushed me back to this plane, so I assume he attacked afterwards." I tasted blood on my lip as I pulled my teeth back and a shuddering sigh of grief filled the room. "I don't want to live without him." I moaned into my hands. My whole body itched as though the grief burrowed under my skin, an absolute torture that I could never rid myself of, the ache of which would be with me forever.

"I saw Amber, while you were under the power."

"What did you see? Did you see Anwir?" I gasped.

She smiled, genuine and warm. "So that's his name, that's why you kept repeating it. No, I didn't see him. I saw Amber help people in their final moments, comfort and draw pain away from them and their families. Day after day."

I looked up to the ceiling as I remembered how she, I, had loved that job. A true calling that I'd been drawn to and was adamant I wanted to pursue.

"I don't have long left in this place; I grow weaker every day. You know how long this illness has been progressing."

"Amani, I'm sorry. You shouldn't have been looking after me, you should have been resting."

"Pfft," she scolded. "You brought hope back to me. I want to help. I need you to agree."

I sipped at the herbal tea, cocking my head to one side as I surveyed her. I could see how thin she was under her clothes, in the silence the rasp of her struggling lungs was like an alarm, alerting me to how frail she was. I placed the now empty cup down and took her tiny wrist in my hand, letting her slow pulse flow into my fingers as I counted and checked the colour of her skin, the laborious rise and fall of her chest.

"You aren't getting enough oxygen," I frowned. On the human plane I'd have equipment to help her.

"You've been here for two moons," she said, ignoring my concern. "I have two moons left in me, at the most. That can't be a coincidence."

"Don't give up, I'll make you some medicine, and I'll find help."

"Shh, Mireille, or shall we stick to Amber?" Her eyes glimmered with mischief. "I want you to take my time."

"Amani, no!"

"Take the two moons of life left within me. Go back, back to when you were last with Anwir, right the wrongs. Save your demon."

"I will not sentence you to death over my own grief, stop this," I implored her.

"Do you know how long I've lived? I want to pass; I want to see what's next. You, my darling, you are so young, and you suffered so much at the hands of that brute..." Her fingers clenched in scarcely hidden anger.

"I can't..." I whispered.

"You must."

We eyed each other for what felt like an eternity, letting our souls and secrets spill into each other with abandon. I saw her truth, the absolute pure intention she had to do this for me. I felt how tired she was, how ready to move on from the pain and the struggle for each breath. In return I let her experience every ounce of love I had for Anwir, the way he made me feel, the softness with which his soul reached for mine. When I regained focus, the skies outside had darkened as dusk began to close in, lifting that orange blossom scent onto the breeze, toward me.

"I'll see you again, I know I will. Go to him," she whispered.

Every ounce of air was sucked wholly out of the room as I choked on the nothingness that surrounded me. My hands grasped and clawed, trying to find something to hold on to, something to anchor me. Then, the blackness took me as its own, once more.

Twenty-Eight

Amber

I'd been trapped in a vortex, wrung out over and over until all the pieces of me unravelled like threads. I reached forwards in search of something to steady myself on and felt smooth ceramic under my palms.

Terror thrummed within me as I tentatively opened my eyes, blinking into the large mirror, lit by LEDs. A laugh of pure, heartfelt relief surged from me as I waved my hand over the sensor that Anwir found so amusing, turning the lights on and off.

My wings were out, one touching the shower screen whilst the other pushed against the bathroom door at an awkward angle. I was back at the point I'd got stuck and Anwir had rushed to help me; I recalled the memory with unrivalled glee.

I pressed my forehead to my reflection in the mirror. "Thank you, Amani. I won't waste this chance, and I will never, ever forget you." A spark of warmth flared in my peripheral vision, a lavender hue which faded calmly out of the room.

With a simple thought my wings retracted; I could feel confidence and strength expand within me. Amani's voice was firm and guiding - love is love. I ran with abandon down the hallway and into the kitchen, still pulling the T-shirt on as I barrelled into Anwir, my mouth erupting into a wide smile.

"I missed you," I cried out as I wrapped my arms tightly around him, smothering kisses all over his face and neck, not wanting to ever stop.

"Amber," he laughed, as he cupped my face and placed a single, soft kiss to my lips. "It's been about... four minutes. But I missed you, too." He pulled me over to the sofa, slumping down, a look of defeat heavy on his shoulders. I swung my legs up and over so they lay over his own, as I tangled my fingers around his. "I guess we need to talk, then," he began.

"Nope," I replied, grinning giddily, unable to tear my eyes away from him as my love pulsated like an out-of-control force that was about to burst.

He frowned, and a bemused sound escaped his lips. "You wanted to know why I was here. It's important."

"Anwir," I raised his hand to my lips and pressed kisses along his knuckles. "We found each other, we're together. I don't care about anything you did before this day, none of it matters. The lives we both had before this... they were meaningless. This is where we begin, I want to let the rest go. Forget you were the man who couldn't love or be loved. Forget I was the victim, the weak one." I swung one leg around, twisting so I straddled his knees. Taking his face in my hands, I laughed gleefully at his confused expression. "We begin now. Amber and Anwir, Anwir and Amber. Screw the past, their planes, their laws, their pathetic little wars. Me and you... we'll rule them all. We begin now."

His lips were on me in an instant, his breath raspy as his words interspersed heavy kisses. "What... happened to you... in that...bathroom?"

He moaned as I bit at the fleshy point where his neck

sloped into his shoulder magnificently. "My liar showed me the truth..." I licked my tongue back up to his ear before I whispered. "Please take me back to bed now."

We careered from wall to wall as we stumbled towards the bedroom, an entangled mess. His T-shirt was torn from my body within seconds as I fumbled at his belt, desperate to feel every inch of his skin. For him it may have been minutes since we were together, but for me it had felt like a lifetime. As he kicked the bedroom door closed behind us, my wings sprang out proud and alert.

"Oh, we're doing wings now, are we? My confident angel," he smirked as he pulled me to him, gripping my waist whilst stepping me backwards toward the bed.

"Show me." I stroked a finger down his spine as I felt him stiffen.

"I don't—"

"You are my entire world," I interrupted. "Never, ever feel an ounce of shame for who you are. You are everything to me and I embrace and adore every single thing about you. So just let me see you, before I go insane with longing." He gulped and I could sense how much he wanted to do this, yet the little boy who'd never been loved remained within him, that last barrier that tottered weakly between us. "I'll close my eyes," I volunteered as I kissed him, falling back against the door as his body pressed upon me, my arms tight around his middle.

He ran his hands up my thighs, gripping me as I leapt up to wrap my legs around his hips while his hands cradled me. "I love you so fucking much it burns me alive," he growled into my ear as I felt him press against me, hard and absolutely perfect.

"Then we'll burn together..."

He pushed all the way into me with one deep action, and as he did so, I felt the silk of his feathers brush over my arms. As promised, my eyes remained closed, but I let my fingers travel through his wings, stroking and caressing as he moved rapidly inside me. He craned his neck to reach further, his mouth kissing the downy feathers that were in reach just over my shoulder.

"You don't have to keep your eyes closed," he moaned to me, as he lowered his mouth to my chest. "If you don't want to."

A tight pull expanded in my lower stomach as I let my eyes open, languid, and lustful. His head was bowed as he kissed down my breastbone, which allowed me a dazzling view of his wings. Whereas mine were uniform and white, his were a stunning kaleidoscope.

Grey, mocha, slate, walnut, bronze, chocolate brown, the colours rippled and pulsed in a pattern as they moved above his muscles. Like a living mosaic, every single one was different. Some plain, some mottled, some striped, spotted, my eyes darted between them all, so unique and beautiful. They took my breath away.

"You're exquisite," I said, as he raised his mouth back to mine, our lips clinging together like glue.

He pushed me harder against the door, his arms hooked underneath mine, forcing my shoulders down as he strained to get as deep inside me as possible. His wings bumped against my own with each thrust and it only added an extra dimension to my pleasure as I pressed my face into his neck, gasping for breath, my whole body trembling under his touch before I succumbed to the absolute ecstasy and bliss that he wove into me.

Anwir carried me to the bed, pressing doting kisses all over my face as I struggled to come back down from the moment, my breaths still quivering against him. It had been absolutely hot and urgent and this time all that demand had come from me.

"I'm sorry," he whispered as he lay me down, stroking my hair.

My face screwed up in confusion. "Sorry for what?"

"It's all new to you and I kind of, lost myself there, I didn't mean to be so rough."

I ran a finger up his thigh, feeling the dampness from both the exertion and my arousal, before he shivered as my finger met his tip. "Anwir, did I say 'strawberry'?"

A lopsided smile graced his mouth as I let my finger glide up and down him. "No," he whispered, and his eyelids fluttered for a moment.

"So, that means it wasn't too rough. It was bliss."

"You seem different..."

"I think..." I pressed my cheek to his as I tried to explain, "I found some strength I didn't know was within me, I saw a future I don't want to live. I'm not going to let Barke hurt you, or me, ever again. We need to be together."

I whispered the truths I'd learned about Barke and his abuse, holding my finger over Anwir's mouth to still his reply, ending with a promise to not speak of it again this night.

Anwir's wings rippled as I shifted around on the bed until I was flush to his back. I buried my face in the sanctuary of his feathers as my legs snaked around him possessively.

"This one," I whispered, as I stroked a feather between my fingers, "looks like a lightning flash, it will always remind me of the first night we spent together." My hand meandered around his side, my fingers traced patterns on his stomach. "And this one is mesmerising; the grey in it is so deep, it's like your strength."

I heard him gulp before I moved on. "Whereas this one... is the exact colour I like my tea, which you make perfectly." As I leant forwards his feathers tickled my naked chest; I bit on his earlobe. "Want me to stop?"

"No..." he said, his voice deep and gravelly. I knew he

hadn't found his release when I did, as, to be fair, for me it had been weeks since we made love, for him it had been about twenty minutes. I intended to remedy this situation.

My palm clenched around him as I began to stroke up and down, all the while selecting another feather. "I love this one. The way the five circles are placed they could be fingerprints. I want your fingerprints all over me." I kissed the feather before moving on, my right hand continuing to pleasure him. "This one is the same colour as your eyes, those eyes that I fall deeper into every time I look at you."

He rolled his head to one side and sighed and I took the opportunity to trail my lips along his neck until another feather caught my eye.

"The colour has barely grazed this one, it just skimmed across it, the way your lips skim across my stomach. There's one that's pure white, it's hidden quite far back, you might not have ever seen it. It's just like mine, I told you we weren't that different. It's here, as if I was meant to come home to you."

"Your hands feel so good on them. Nobody has ever touched them this way, the way that you do," he murmured.

"How did they touch them?" I asked, as I rubbed at the smaller feathers which grew on the underside, my other hand consistent with its motion upon him.

"Nobody ever wanted to touch them, it was always just by accident, or in a fight or something, you know?" An image flashed through my mind of Barke, bending my feathers as punishment for some long-forgotten error. I shook it away with a shiver. "You're the only one I've ever trusted..."

"I love them, and I want to touch and know every single last one. I'd pluck each one of my own out right now and let you sleep underneath them, if I thought they'd grow back as beautiful as yours."

He moaned deeply as my hand grew firmer and faster, my

naked chest pressed tightly against his back, his wings, as I kissed his neck and shoulders, a fire burning inside of me.

I purred into his ear, "I'm obsessed with you, I want your wings, your mind, your body, your lips, you. I just want you, constantly." I felt him shudder silently, my hand cupped him and relished his essence as it spilled through my fingers.

Neither of us moved. The only sound was our breath as it mingled and joined together in the air. Anwir kissed me as he stood, smiling, his posture relaxed as he walked to the bathroom. His head popped back around momentarily as he tossed a hot, damp face towel to me. "Give me one minute, don't go anywhere."

I lay back on the bed after cleaning myself up, a frown cemented itself on me as I puzzled over our predicament. As Anwir left the bathroom I saw his wings were away, and I mirrored it, still unsure of the correct way to behave with these feathery appendages.

He reclined next to me, his fingers laced through mine as always.

"I've been thinking about this prophecy," I said.

"What about it?" he asked, his voice piqued with interest.

"It's us."

A small laugh burst from his lips. "It's not about anybody, it's not real. Let me find it, I'll show you."

"I've seen it, I know it."

He swiped his hair back from his face as his gaze flickered towards the window.

"We need to talk. I—"

"Anwir, stop." I pressed a finger to his lips. "I'll explain later, there isn't time now. You came here to kill me, I know, don't worry about it."

He paled. "How do you..."

"It doesn't matter for now," I reiterated. "A feather torn asunder, that could be the one I stabbed him with, right?"

He nodded. A dimple appeared in his cheek as he sucked on the inside of his gum. "But, how do you know the prophecy?"

"I wasn't sure I did, but you just confirmed it. I promise I'll explain, but right now we're short of time. Fragmented in his terror – that's what you call your family, right?"

He nodded, a glimmer of something I couldn't place passed over his eyes. "Threads entangled by melody," he said. "Since I met you, the threads of power I use, they're different."

"She will slumber in his domain," I grinned and motioned down to his bed. "And I know I'll never see my hallow again. I'm one hundred percent fine with that. Mireille was an ancient word for miracle – the Liar will survey his miracle. It's me and you. It was always me and you."

"But you're not Mireille anymore. And it talks of your demise, of fading away. They're not options I'm willing to consider."

"I've been back to the angel plane. I've been Mireille and I'm never doing it again. I choose to be Amber, I choose to be yours, but I carry the strength of both Mireille and another angel, Amani, inside of me now."

"When did you go there?" Anwir sat bolt upright. "Did he take you?"

"It was while I was in the bathroom." My heart melted as I took in how adorable the wrinkles of confusion atop his nose were. "I promise I'll explain but not now, he'll be here soon. If we do nothing, he will take me and throw me back into the angel realm. He'll tell you I'm dead, then he will kill you. I refuse that future."

"Your bruises are gone," he marvelled as he stroked my neck, peering closely at the skin. "I believe you; I trust you. That's possibly even harder to say than I love you, after I spent my life in mistrust of every other person."

"It's ironic, this prophecy. Your father tried to kill me to stop it happening, not knowing it was his future son who I was destined to love." I stood and gathered my clothes. "Get dressed, quick. I'll let him think I'm defeated, just go with it. Fight him with all that you have and trust me, when it comes to the end, trust me."

As he tugged his jeans up and straightened his T-shirt, he smiled, looking me up and down in the yellow dress – it felt like several lifetimes had passed since I'd put it on for the picnic. He held his arms out wide and I sank into him, inhaling him into my lungs like medicine that kept me alive. I needed him to get me through this final test.

"Forever, Amber," he whispered, as he pressed his lips to the top of my head.

"Forever, Anwir," I replied, closing my eyes as the white flash hit us, and the cycle of events began once again.

Twenty-Nine

Anwir

I ducked down as a blinding, white light flashed and burned into me. Splintered sounds crashed around, as if icicles dropped and smashed against the floor. My heart sank as I understood that those crashes were caused by my protection shield being blown inwards. We were now visible to any angels and demons who may be looking for us on this plane.

My arms wrapped tightly around Amber. She'd asked me to trust her, there seemed to be a plan in that beautiful mind of hers, but every protective instinct in me screamed to keep hold of her, keep her away from him.

"Demon... She doesn't belong to you. Let her go or be responsible for what happens next." His face barely moved yet I saw evil that cavorted behind his eyes; he reeked of it. I couldn't imagine any smile on his lips ever being honest. The very sight of him drove me to the edge of fury as every muscle in me tensed, ready to strike, begging to hurt him for everything he had put her through. I slowed my breath as Amber's fingers stroked my back, calming me, reassuring me.

"Barke..." My lip curled up in disgust as I shifted, sheltering Amber as much as I could behind my body.

He held his palm up with an absolute disregard for my voice, and as much as I shouldn't have cared, it triggered something within me. I'd lived on the demon plane, if it could be called living, always been looked down on, despised, the butt of jokes thanks to my father's actions. Yet this woman in my arms had noticed me, seen me, shown me what I could be, what I could achieve. No longer would I be cowed by people who thought themselves better than me.

"You could just leave me here, Barke," Amber said, looking towards him, her hand remaining within the cradle of my own. "Return home, tell them I died, there wouldn't be any shame."

"I was nice enough to let you say goodbye, wasn't I? Don't be an ungrateful little bitch, Mireille." He let his wings loose at this point, in some ridiculous show of dominance that did little to impress me. For the first time in my life, I felt brave enough to show my own to someone other than a demon. The truth was, they no longer felt ugly, Amber had made them feel... exquisite – hadn't that been her word?

I extended them; the stretch felt magnificent after the last few weeks of being tucked away like a dirty secret. He couldn't hide the surprise that flicked between his narrowed eyes. I saw the smile that rose on Amber's face as she looked up at me with pride. I placed a kiss on her forehead before I stepped closer to Barke.

"You dare to touch her in front of me?" he growled. "Exactly how stupid are you?"

"Don't worry, I'd never touch her the way that you do. I'd never hit her." I stepped forwards with each affirmation. "I'd never push her down, degrade her, scare her, treat her like my property. Only you are man enough to do that, right?" I could see him bristle with anger, unable to tear his eyes away from mine. The closer I got, the more I understood why people would fear him. He was tall and strongly built, power seemed to emanate from him, but I knew it was all posture, because a truly powerful man wouldn't treat someone he loved like a stray dog he could kick to the kerb.

"Mireille, come here," he commanded.

"What's wrong, am I a little close for comfort?" I taunted him. "Worried I'll taint you? That they won't let you back into your little angel domain?"

"You think I'd give you a second thought? You're obviously not even a whole demon, just some outcast. Otherwise, how did you fuck her without it killing you? You're nothing. Also, about the fucking... she'll pay for that for a thousand years."

I slammed into him, unable to take anymore. A dark noise exploded, a cross between laughter, hysteria and rage which exploded from him as I forced him back against the wall. Plaster crumbled down around us, sticking in those ridiculous blonde curls. We weren't skin-to-skin yet still I could feel the burn against me. He was old, powerful, and I knew he easily had the upper hand, all he had to do was touch me enough to destroy me. It would be at the cost of his own reputation and esteem, but right now I could see he was blinded to that.

A piece of me withered inside as I heard screams and crashes from below, every human in this building would be tearing into each other by now as our anger leached into them, and for the first time ever, I hated that I was part of it.

Tiny, silver threads of power fell around me, forming a protective sheath, and as I smelt honey and vanilla encase me once more, I realised it was Amber who protected me. I hadn't known her use power before, I guess she really had learned a lot from whatever the hell happened when I left her in the bathroom. I'd never seen tendrils of power that looked like this before, and more interesting was that Barke seemed oblivious to them as he focused his gaze upon me, like a pig-headed child in a staring match across the schoolyard.

"Mireille," he continued with his glare of intimidation as he spoke to her. "I'll let him live if you come with me, now. Otherwise, he'll die, and I'll make you relive it over and over, that will be your punishment every time you let me down."

I wanted to bite his fucking throat out, but Amber had asked me to trust her, and I did. She had a plan, I just had to have faith that she knew him well enough for whatever it was to work.

As animosity bulged and rippled in the space between us, forming a dense wedge that air couldn't pass through, I heard her footsteps pad over and I gulped down the bile that threatened to fill my throat. What if I let her go now and the plan failed? What if I never saw her again?

Amber stood between us, one hand flat on my chest and one on his, and even this connection to me seemed to pale his tanned face.

"Anwir," she said. "It's fine, he's right. I have to go, I'm bound to him, I can't ignore that." She smiled sadly as she spoke, but I could see she still had hope in her eyes. "Go home, be happy."

My eyes moved wildly between the two of them as he pulled her, and she staggered into his arms. Every fibre within my body implored me to stop this, but in this instant, I had to invest every scrap of trust in her.

Barke locked her in a tight grasp, and it felt as though I was being torn apart from the inside as my muscles strained to strike him down. "You're unbelievably stupid," he spat at her before he leapt upwards. I felt him call upon threads of power as the two of them crashed through the ceiling; debris and dust cascaded down in their wake.

Thanks to Amber's shield it rolled off me like rain and crashed to the ground. I didn't hesitate in taking chase as I pursued them to the rooftop. The buzz of electrical wires hummed in my ear like a vicious swarm as I zoomed by, sparks began to ignite and fall into the penthouse I'd begun to call home.

My ears were assaulted with the sounds of brawling and looting below, as shop windows were smashed, cars were jacked and subsequently crashed. The people tore into each other for no reason other than our emotions spreading out like a vile, poison cloud that would consume them. But it all silenced as the scene in front of me embedded itself deep into my amygdala.

Barke hammered blows upon Amber as she curled up on the ground, trying to protect herself, but she stood no chance as he moved with inhuman speed and ferocity. "You think I could ever let you go home after the disgrace you've brought upon us? You've destroyed us." His face was snarled up in anger as I ran to her, placing myself between her fragile body and his brutal fists.

Barke and I tumbled to the side as I dragged him as far away as possible, desperate to allow her time to recover, escape, hide. I became the focus of his fury as he blew venomously against me, punch after punch, kick after kick. The shield she'd given me stopped his toxicity from spreading internally, but he still stung like acid on my skin with each touch. He was bigger than me, twice as strong, and had the advantage of my weakness to his angel blood. There was one thing he didn't have, though: Amber's love. That was all mine and it empowered me.

As I finally pinned him down, I crawled onto him, my legs around his chest as my own blows pummelled down. He was reviled by my touch, and it just added fuel to my fire. I scraped my nails across his skin, sank my teeth into his hand as he raised it to push me away.

Amber's voice travelled into my mind, like a melody on a

breeze. I could see her shamble towards us from the corner of my eye, and I begged her to stay away, to be safe. "Taint his wings. You've done it before, do it again. A feather torn asunder."

I tried to comprehend her words as he fought back with everything he had. His frame was colossal, and it crushed me to think of how tiny Mireille must have seemed as he unleashed his hell upon her. Before I knew what was happening, he flipped me onto my back, his grin leered over me as he celebrated his tiny victory. His lips moved but I didn't take in a word as I thought back on Amber's words.

A feather torn asunder... Mireille had defeated my father with one feather. Was she suggesting I do the same? Taint his wings... I grimaced as he punched me in the mouth, and I felt blood spatter to the side and spray the ground.

I could barely think as the assault continued. He was ultimately cocky as he called her over, making her struggle painfully to him as he forced her to look at me. She acted – at least I prayed it was acting – coyly, nodding and agreeing to whatever he said, I couldn't hear through the buzz in my ears and as he relaxed, she mouthed one word to me with a wide smile: "Strawberry."

I laughed, blood spilled from my mouth, as my perfectly positioned hands yanked two large feathers from the outer edges of my wings and embedded them into the skin of his shoulders.

He shrieked, a sound contrived of agony and disgust as he fell backwards, clawing at himself as he attempted to dislodge them. Amber stamped down on one arm and my love swelled with pride for this amazing woman.

He writhed and screamed on the floor as the scent of burning reached my nose. I thought at first it was him, but as I looked up, I saw the raft of inferno-ridden buildings on the skyline. Police helicopters circled, the city was in a state of emergency as riots spread and deaths multiplied.

Barke dropped to the floor, tearing wildly at his feathers; I watched in amazement as the pure, snow-white he'd been so proud to display, began to shrivel and wane. As they withered, deep red veins appeared, spreading like a plague, marking him as the evil soul he undoubtedly was.

"One day, Mireille, you'll pay for this." His voice echoed around the skies before the heavens flashed jet black, reminiscent of a reverse lightning strike as Barke crumpled to the floor.

I moved to Amber as swiftly as my injuries allowed, dragging broken limbs, and ignoring the sharp stabs of pain across my body. She bled from multiple wounds, and I knew her entire body would be black and blue tomorrow, but he was gone; I could look after her now.

Amber wrapped me in her arms and through my swollen eye, I saw the angry, heated lick of flames flicker up from the hole in the floor. We were trapped and the whole city seemed to be in uproar as I heard sirens, screams, gunshots, desperate cries, even the roar of a water canon being deployed.

"Thank you for trusting me," she whispered through sobs. "You know I never would have gone with him."

"Anything for you," I wheezed, wiping blood from her cheek. I coughed and her eyes widened as a pool of dark blood spread from my mouth.

"You need help," she cried, as she looked around, her eyes wild and desperate.

"I'll be OK, as long as you're with me."

The fire had now spread to the artificial grass that was layered on the ground of the roof terrace. The flames ripped through as the plastic fed it, releasing an acrid stench. "Try and move with me," she urged as she held me, supporting me as best she could as we shuffled away from the flames and towards the edge of the rooftop. She pushed me up onto the wide ledge and clambered up immediately after.

"These are fine for a flutter," she said, jerking her head towards her perfectly pure wings. "But they're not strong enough to fly us out of here."

"Mine might be," I croaked through jagged coughs. "But I'm pretty sure one's broken. I can't feel it, it's numb."

Amber pressed her forehead to mine, and her hands stroked my cheeks before she dropped them and bundled them up inside my own. "You know what my favourite fantasy is?"

"This isn't the time to get sexy," I teased, as she pressed a soft kiss to my lips.

"I imagine that we just met, like boys and girls do every day in this world. In a bar or a coffee shop. We fell in love, met each other's families. Had one of those weddings with drunk aunties and bad seafood platters. We grew up, got boring jobs, had babies, and saw our faces form wrinkles. Life seemed hard and we fought about silly things, we felt like we wouldn't get through it, but we did. We always did. Life passed by in the happiest blur, seventy years together gone in the snap of a finger, until we were saying final goodbyes, but knowing we'd lived every possible moment together. That's all I want, Anwir. That's all I'll ever want."

She somehow held it together, although I felt her pain career around me as she barely restrained her power. My own eyes streamed with tears as I choked on a mixture of sobs and blood. "I've never, for a moment, regretted meeting you, Amber Carmichael. I can't believe we've only been together for a few days."

She smiled softly. "Me neither, it feels like forever, but at the same time mere seconds. Let me help you with your wings. You're beautiful when you're soppy, you know?" She leaned in and pulled them gently around us, whispering as she did so.

"You're my only love, a thousand lifetimes in a thousand worlds and there'd only be you."

She wrapped my wings around us, like a concertinaed wind break that blocked out the world and cast us in shadow. Then her own wrapped around us too, as her legs and arms sought mine out. Our noses were pressed against each other, and I could see her vibrant blue eyes in the dim, heavenly cocoon we'd created between us.

"Did we just kill an angel?" she asked, her voice quiet in our sacred space.

I nodded, my forehead pushing against hers. "I think so. They'll be here any minute, both sides."

Our lips met, slow and careful, before more coughs overtook me and I saw droplets of blood hit her white wings, sullying their perfection.

"I can't let you go," she whispered, her eyes dropping.

I lifted her chin up, forcing a smile, just for her, onto my pained lips. Then, my blood froze in fear at the tremble of the roof as multiple sets of feet touched down, and even from within our darkness the heavy rustle of wings was a bell that tolled to signal the end. "I'd die for you, a million times. I would die for you, my angel."

Her eyes flashed, mirroring my dread as she pressed her lips to my ear, pulling me tightly against her.

"You already did, my beautiful demon."

She pushed us away from the edge.

We fell. A tumble that seemed to go on for an eternity, lost in the agony as we were wrenched apart.

We fell together, the only way we knew.

Thirty

Amber

"He can't keep his eyes off you," Ellie said, grinning as she nudged me with her elbow, pointing out the dark-haired guy at the end of the bar. My stomach exploded into tingles as he headed towards me, sucked me into his eyes which were reminiscent of honeycomb laced chocolate.

"Hi, I'm Anwir. Blame my mother for the odd name," he smiled. "Can I buy you a drink?"

In my peripheral vision I saw Ellie slink away, her thumbs upraised as she smiled widely.

"Sure," I replied confidently. "I'm Amber."

"Why are you still crying? Stop crying... Please..."

"I know it's only been a few months," he said, his cheeks pinked up as he knelt in front of me. "But I am adamant, there is *nobody else in any universe, in any life, that I am meant to be with. Amber Carmichael, will you marry me?"*

"Please, stop crying. I'm begging you..."

"Twins? Seriously? Twins?" He grabbed me in the middle of the doctor's office, twirling me round and round in his arms, before showering me with kisses.

"What have you done to me?" I smiled, as I stroked my stomach. I was already utterly besotted and in love with the babies that grew inside me. Our babies...

"Amber... Mireille... Just look at me, look at me..."

"I'm sorry it was such a rough shift," he said, as he cast my socks aside and rubbed my aching feet. "I don't know how you do it. How about I order your favourite Kung Pao chicken and look after you for the night?"

"I love you, Anwir." I smiled, pulling him to me for a kiss. There was something I'd like much more than Kung Pao chicken, but just as I was about to whisper my idea into his ear, I heard the shrill scream of a toddler from upstairs.

"Nightmares..." Anwir sighed, heading upstairs to soothe our little girl.

"This can't be how it ends, it can't. I'm begging you, Amber... Stop crying, wake up to me."

. . .

"I know, OK?! I know I work ridiculous hours, but have you noticed how much teenagers eat? How much they cost? I'd love to be here this weekend, but that's not going to pay the bills, is it?" He raised his voice and immediately looked regretful.

"I just miss you," I mumbled. "I miss that guy who seduced me at the bar."

"I'm still that guy..."

"Just squeeze my fingers, show me. Come on, baby. For us..."

"Surprise," he whispered, wrapping his arms around my stomach from behind. I shrugged away from him and saw a flash of disappointment in his eyes. "Sweetheart, I've told you a thousand times, I love your stomach. It's where our babies grew. Don't shrug me away."

I glanced around at the room, he'd set up a fake bar, the same drinks on it from the night we met. The same soundtrack played through the speakers. It was adorable and I hated myself for ruining the moment.

"I just feel ugly and old."

"You are perfect and beautiful," he whispered, as he pressed his lips to mine. "Happy anniversary."

"You taught me how to love, don't leave me. Don't leave me..."

I stood in the centre of the empty room and sobbed as though my heart would fall out of me. His arms, so strong, snaked around me, holding me close to his chest as I listened to his familiar heart thud its rhythm against my ear.

"They'll be fine," he reassured me. "They need to explore the world, live, find their true loves, like we did. They'll be home in twelve months."

"Our babies. Where did the time go?" I sobbed.

He shook his head as he pulled me to him. "I have no idea."

"I'll do anything, whatever it takes. I know you're in there, you're still crying. Why? Why do you cry?"

"This is unbelievable," he whispered, his mouth breaking into the widest smile as his eyes crinkled. I looked at the grey which overtook his hair day by day - mine was delayed thanks to a very good hairdresser – then let my eyes fall to his, still as beautiful and all-encompassing as the day we met.

"Twins for our twin," I said quietly, not wanting to wake the sleepy baby girl in my arms, identical to her sister in Anwir's arms. "How can we be grandparents?" I asked.

"I have no idea. But we'll be the coolest. They'll have sleep overs, all the sweets, and double pocket money!"

My heart melted at the sparkle in his eyes, his youth recaptured.

"I need you to stop, I need you to wake up. We can't stay here much longer. Wake up, Amber..."

"What do you mean? A blockage?" The blood had frozen within my veins.

"The doctor said there's furring in my artery, fatty deposits. They need to operate; the chest pains have been... a warning."

He was trying to look brave, but I could see he was petrified, as was I.

"When?"

"Three weeks," he replied.

"But... we were twenty-five, it feels like six months ago. I'm scared."

"I'm here, I'm right here. You don't need to weep for us. Just open your eyes and you'll see. I'm here..."

"He lived a good, happy life."

"Beautiful service, Amber. He'd have been proud."

"Call if you need us, promise?"

They all had a similar, vague phrase as they filed out of our house. Our house – was it now just my house?

People didn't know what to say to grief, and I couldn't blame them. It was best kept at arm's length, who would willingly invite it in? Who would ever, ever want to live through this?

The kids had arranged to pick me up at twelve tomorrow. They filled my calendar with picnics and Sunday lunches, shopping trips and school plays, as if leaving me to sit with the grief might kill me, too. I knew they did it out of love, but I just wanted to lie down, alone. Drink some wine, fade away into the memory of his eyes, his smile. The bed still smelled of him, why did they keep making me get out of bed?

"I'm going to count to three, Amber. Count to three and then you'll open your eyes. You have to open them, for me, for us…"

THIRTY-ONE

AMBER

"I'm too tired to count," I muttered, annoyed at whoever this was for expecting me to figure out numbers when all I wanted to do was go back to sleep. I was so very warm as I rolled over to reach for a pillow but instead found my fingers brushing over something else, something soft, yet with a hard centre.

My eyes burst open to find darkness. A shot of panic fired off within me as warm breath whispered over my lips. Stretching my fingers out, a snug and toasty environment welcomed me, a wriggle of my toes connected to the same sensation.

As my pupils drank in each scarce drop of light available, I began to focus and that brought me to a face pressed very close to my own. The eyes flickered open, slowly, and a power from within those gaping, exposed pupils infused itself into me.

"Amber..." He exhaled a sigh of pure relief as his hands grasped me tight. "You're awake."

The fight, the fall, it all shot into my mind in an anguished burn. I flinched and he pressed those soft lips of his to mine, barely moving, simply soothing.

"Are we dead? Is this merely a dream? I was already dreaming, though, that you had heart surgery. So how can I have a dream within a dream?"

"I've definitely never had heart surgery," he said. "I don't think that's a thing where I come from."

"We fell..." I grasped for words, scared to learn what was actually happening to us.

Anwir nodded, rotating his shoulders slightly which caused the darkened cocoon we inhabited to ripple. "I'm confident that in *that* world, we are no more. I don't know what 'this' is, but you're here. You're here." His voice faltered, and I squeezed his body even harder to mine. "I've been trying to wake you; you were crying in your sleep."

"Falling off a building will do that to you." I rubbed my nose side to side against his. "All those people, Anwir."

"I know, I wish there'd been another way." he sighed.

"Have you looked around?"

"No. I tried to peek, but we seem to have a little wing tangle situation."

I laughed in spite of the apparent hopelessness of this situation. "I'm rubbish with these things, aren't I?"

"Kiss me..." He shuddered as he made the request, a request I was eternally unable to deny; my lips lived for his touch. He was so close to me that all I needed to do was twist my head and we connected. I ran my fingers up his chest, let them rest on his shoulders as I slowly smoothed my mouth over his, each touch between our lips sending a fizz of connection, a deepening of love directly into my soul. His tongue flicked at mine unhurriedly as I ran mine over his bottom lip, and desire spiralled inside me regardless of whatever peril we may have been in.

Without breaking the kiss for a moment, he lifted his arms above my head, gently stroking amongst the feathers, as if teasing tangles out of lengths of hair. Every so often he'd come to an obstruction, yet his fingers never hurt me as he reached the outer edges, where his own feathers had become intertwined in a muddle with mine.

"I told you we were a collision." His words were breathy against me as I raised my own arms and began to unravel in the same way, learning from him.

"I wouldn't have it any other way," I gasped, as his fingers circled around the base of my wing bone, sending shivers of pleasure throughout my body. "What are you doing?"

"Showing you that I love you," he whispered as he pressed kisses down my jaw, grazing my neck. "When we open these wings, I don't know where we'll be. It could all end, I... If there's any chance that these are our last moments together, then we're blessed to have them. I want to show you that you are my every world, my every life."

He lifted himself awkwardly in the cramped space as I tugged his jeans down, hearing the rip of my yellow dress and not caring as I stretched my aching limbs and shuffled onto his hips. I held tightly onto his back, so as not to tumble and as I did so, I circled my fingers across every feather I could reach, slowly, delicately, letting them fall through my grasp, rubbing the softness as I envisaged them thriving under my touch.

"When you touch them..." he sighed against me, "it's the best feeling."

His hardness twitched against me as my fingers continued their dance across his feathers and I had to have more of him. I lowered myself onto him, my hands never stopping, as his tongue pressed down on mine, and I felt every ounce of his lust spill into me like fire.

All thoughts of wing tangles and our uncertain situation fell into a void as we melted into a crashing frenzy, desperately pulling at each other as I breathlessly pressed against him. His muscles were taut as he held us in place whilst spilling himself into me with a force I'd never known, while he repeated my name over and over into my ear, like a melodic lullaby – to soothe which of us, though, I didn't know.

I kissed tears from his cheeks as shudders still ran through us, only then realising they merged and flowed with my own. "It doesn't matter what's out there," I said quietly. "We've still had more love in this short time than most souls experience in a hundred lives."

He sucked a long, deep breath into his lungs as his fingers dropped from my feathers, the last knot between his and mine released.

"I know, but it will never stop me longing for more. I never meant to take your life away from you, your job, your friends..."

"I know, I know you didn't. *He* did though, he wanted to snatch it all away, make me his prisoner. You couldn't be more opposite. You showed me the life I could have, how empty my existence has been and how full it could be. You showed me everything." I softly kissed him as my words paused. "That life... my life... I'd leave it behind in a heartbeat. One week with you or eighty years of that. No contest, Anwir."

He held me tight, breathing me in, letting his love seep into my soul. Dead or alive, it didn't matter as long as he held me.

"It's just occurred to me that we might be in the middle of a coffee shop, putting on an X-rated display." I laughed, my lips landing against his neck.

"I think someone would've stopped us." His hand wandered to the nape of my neck, stroking the fine hairs. "Shall we open our wings together?"

"I'm scared..."

"Me too."

I rested my cheek against the pulse in his neck, allowing the feel and rhythm of his heartbeat absorb into me. "After three?" I asked, choking back a sob.

"One, two..." he stopped and pressed a kiss to the top of my head. "Three."

Fear rose within me, threatening to explode out in panic, but Anwir caught my eyes in his gaze and held my focus. We both blinked against the light as our safe cocoon burst open. I could see landscape in my peripheral vision, but something else drew all my attention.

"Your wings..." I gasped as I stepped behind him, a painful cramp ran through my legs as they bore my weight after so long. The sight was magnificent. They were his, evolved. The patterns had been random before, but they'd shifted.

The large feathers on the leading edge were now pure white, purer than mine had surely ever been. The primaries beside them were spotted with the most beautiful lilac-grey colour, as if I'd dipped my fingers into rich ink and painted each one with my touch. The secondary feathers and the wingtips began pure white at the base, and then marbled out to a deep, rich mulberry-violet. I'd never witnessed a more stunning display.

"Wait," he said, as he twisted round, turned me with him so he could examine mine. "Your wings, they're completely changed. They're still white at the top but—"

"Patterned with circles like fingerprints underneath?"

"Yes. In a beautiful heather colour."

I smiled as I turned and wrapped my arms around him giddily. "Please say they're marbled at the bottom, white which fades to a deeper purple?"

He looked into my eyes; his mouth widened into a grin. "Are we twinning?" he asked with a mischievous sparkle.

"I think so. Wow..." I murmured, still trying to process how stunning the feathers were, never mind contemplating that mine might be as beautiful.

Our clothes were tattered and torn but as we wiped blood and soot from each other, it became apparent we had not a single wound on our bodies. I wiped away a nasty looking patch on Anwir's arm, but the blood fell away in dried flakes.

"Your wounds are healed." I marvelled as I continued to rub at his body, finding clean skin under my touch.

"Yours too," he added, as he licked his thumb and rubbed a streak of dirt from my collarbone. "Think the dress might be a little beyond saving."

I rested my head on his shoulder and linked our fingers together as I looked around. "Where are we?"

We stood in the middle of a meadow, dusk waned, and an array of stars wakened from their sleep as the sky turned inky black. The scent of pollen hovered against me in the breeze as I spotted a stone path meandering down a gentle slope, into an orchard of deep and dark trees.

As we walked cautiously under them Anwir grasped a leaf, rubbing it between his fingers. "I know these, we had them at home, purple-leaf plum trees."

"Do you think we're in the demon realm?" I asked, an involuntary shiver shaming me as it ran down my spine.

"No, I don't. The air would never smell so sweet there."

I blinked and saw a faint light glow ahead of us, illuminated as if through glass. "This way, I guess," I said, as I motioned towards it.

We gripped our hands together as we approached an idyllic log cabin. A plume of smoke rose from the chimney and the light from inside gave of an aura of warmth in the darkened sky. I scanned the horizon, a frown settled upon my forehead.

"I can't see any other lights or buildings nearby."

Anwir reached forward and knocked on the door. "Me neither. Have you seen what's growing, though?"

Large bushes framed the front door and as I peered close, I saw that they burst with strawberries, many ready to pick, others tiny green buds just beginning to grow. "Do you think they're safe to eat?" I asked, as my stomach rumbled at the thought.

"We just plummeted from the roof of a building, I wouldn't worry about the fruit," smiled Anwir, as he placed a deep, red berry into my mouth. My tongue slid lightly over his fingers as he did so.

His lips were drawn into his mouth as he listened for any sign of life within the building, given that no answer had sounded out to his knock.

I pushed on the door; my heart hastened in my chest as it slid open.

"Hello?" I called, tightening my grip on Anwir's hand as we headed into a large, open plan room. One half contained a rustic, wooden kitchen, centred around a large log burner which crackled as it threw out a glorious warmth. The other half contained a loveseat, facing out of a large window with a view down the hillside, over a blossoming forest. It all seemed familiar, but I couldn't quite place it.

In between the two sections of the cabin was an oval table. I did a double take, and my breath caught in my throat as a figure rose.

"I knew you could do it." Her voice shook as she raised her arms to me.

"Amani!" I cried, almost tugging Anwir over before I dropped my death grip on his hand and ran to her. I smothered my face against her as she embraced me. "How? How are you here?" I gasped as I pulled back. "We're dead, aren't we? That's why you're here."

"Before I tell you anything, I demand an introduction to the man who claimed your heart." She smiled kindly, raising her eyebrows in Anwir's direction.

"Amani, this is Anwir," I stated proudly.

She looked him up and down appraisingly, pursing her lips

in appreciation as she took him in. "Your demon?" she asked, her eyes focused on me.

"My everything," I replied, as his thumb brushed over my knuckles.

"You two have started quite the chain reaction. Sit."

We lowered ourselves onto a wooden bench, accepting mugs of hot soup from Amani; the heat seemed to heal me within. "My grandmother was insistent that the prophecy be passed on to each daughter, and when I wasn't blessed with a bond or a child, I feared I'd let her down." She reached forwards and rubbed my hand. "Then I met you, and I loved you as if you were my daughter. The way you cared for me, even though you had your own struggles every single day."

She turned to Anwir; lines imprinted themselves between her eyebrows. "You seem like a good, good man, and I can see the love between you two. If you ever mistreat her, though..." she warned.

"I never would, I never could," he reassured her, as he tucked my hair behind my ear. "We had the same prophecy in the demon realm."

"Interesting. Maybe you two weren't the first misplaced hearts to fall in love. Maybe demon and angel romances have come and gone, but never reached their happy ending, until now."

My eyes shot up to hers. "A happy ending? We're not even alive, are we?"

"Hold my hands..." She laid her palms flat on the table, I took one and Anwir took the other. His face was focused, I could see him struggle to trust another angel, worry about touching her. I squeezed his spare hand with my own, then closed my eyes.

We fell in slow motion; I could see the panic and fear on my scrunched-up face as I pressed it against Anwir's stricken expression. We were bundled up as tight as could be, in a winged cocoon of love, love that wouldn't ever be allowed to exist.

As we hurtled to the floor, I saw the volatile expressions of the humans, as spittle flew from their mouths alongside their curses and punches. They hadn't noticed us fall from the roof, so preoccupied in their venom for each other which was caused by the fight we'd just undertaken.

We hit the ground and it was as if an atomic bomb went off, of the planar variety. Our powers had already begun to change as we connected on deeper, complex levels. As the force of that combined power hit the earth, a piece of each of the three realms fissured away, splintered, and spread part of its magic outwards.

A mystical, magical, nuclear winter swirled and pooled overhead as Anwir tried to wake me within our winged cocoon. I saw his tears flow out of our haven, mixed with my unconscious ones. The scene stuttered to our lovemaking, thankfully sparing my blushes, as it zoomed out to the world around us, which was caught in some kind of reverse tornado, whilst land twisted, water flowed and clouds raced around the skies, seeking their positions. Then, as Anwir and I ceased our motion with a smile and a soft kiss, the world settled.

Amani was behind us as the vision ceased, one hand on Anwir's wings and one on mine. My eyes flicked to him, unsure how he would take to this, but his face was relaxed, mellow. "They really are incredible. I've never seen anything like them."

"How are you still here, Amani?" I asked. "You gave up the last of your time for me."

"That left a piece of my soul inside you, Amber." I swelled

with happiness as she used my chosen name, and she nodded subtly, knowingly. "When you two... exploded, for want of a better word, it threw me into this plane with you."

"Which plane are we on?" Anwir asked, his fingers playing with mine, giving away his anxiety.

"It's yours," said Amani, nodding as if this was common knowledge. "The love between you two, the tangle of different powers, the fall, the magical explosion – it created this place. That's what the prophecy was trying to tell us."

I turned to Anwir, my eyes wide, emotions threatening to spill as they bubbled up internally. "A brand-new plane..." I whispered, as his hand ran down the side of my face.

Amani pressed a kiss to the top of Anwir's head and then to mine. "I know why Amber doesn't hurt me when she touches me, but why don't you?" he asked.

"Because you're not a demon anymore, and my beautiful girl here isn't an angel. You're both new, evolved, in this untouched plane. I can't stay for much longer; my soul truly is on its last gasp. You two can create the world you want here, it's all in your hands. There'll always be a piece of me with you, Amber, I love you, my darling."

Then she faded away, a smile on her face as the familiar lavender mist that I'd seen in Anwir's bathroom, blew out of the cabin, on a warm, contented breeze.

"A fourth plane?" Anwir asked, I could feel his pulse hammer away through his wrist as my fingers rested there.

"Home," I smiled. "We thought there was nowhere we could ever call home, but we're here. This is so much to take in. Today, we died, set off a magic nuke, and created a new plane..." I shook my head in disbelief.

"I'm exhausted." Anwir's tired eyes crinkled as he smiled and hugged me close.

"Me, too," I whispered, as I stood, taking his hand, and led him to the bedroom. I knew now why this place was familiar;

it was almost identical to Amani's house, as if pulled from my mind as the plane formed.

The minutes of the night ticked by, not that there was any way or need to know the time here. We'd made the sweetest, slowest love imaginable, both absolutely entranced by the fact we got to stay together, when we'd been so sure that we'd reached the end too soon.

Anwir's breaths were slow and contented as I lay against his chest, listening to the familiar beat of his heart, the sound that my soul needed. I meant what I'd said - that a few days with him would have been worth all of this, even if that was all we ever got, but the fact we got a new lifetime here, together, filled me with joyous anticipation.

Moonlight streamed in through the window. I had no idea where this plane lay in the grand scheme of things, but the fact this was the same moon that shone on my old life, back with Ellie, the hospice, the town I knew so well, was inconceivable. My eyes wandered around the walls. As exhausted as I was, sleep evaded me, and my mind was on overdrive as I tried to absorb all that had happened this day.

I noticed a frame, identical to that on Amani's walls, but the words in it were not the old prophecy. These words were fresh, the stitches tight, dark, and new. I smiled as I read them, kissing Anwir's chest above his heart as my eyelids finally fluttered close, and I slumbered for the first time in our new world.

A love born without boundary
Limitless, destined to burn
Aftershocks of essence flowed
No need for hearts to yearn

For the fall was sheer bliss

So warm amidst a dream
Of the glow that encompasses
All their wings could ever have been

Hearts bound with soul strings
Cradled within their forever
The mystery entombed within, now free
Written on every feather

May your love eternally soar

Thank you so much for taking the time to read Liar.
I hope you fell in love with our star crossed lovers.
If you have a few minutes spare to leave a star rating / brief
review on Amazon / Goodreads, that would mean the world
to an indie author who wants to write a sequel for Anwir &
Amber.

AFTERWORD

I appreciate every single person who takes the time to read my books, and I hope I allow you a little escape from the everyday mundane.

As an Indie author, reviews are hugely appreciated and help me to build my audience and work on more stories.

If you enjoyed Liar, any reviews on Amazon, Goodreads or social media would be hugely appreciated

ABOUT THE AUTHOR

Olivia Lockhart (Livvie to her friends) is an English author who can't quite decide if she wants to write contemporary romance or paranormal romance. Either way, it HAS to be romance.

She loves to write about the underdog, the one that got away, the bits of love stories we can all relate to.

When not writing, she can be found drinking wine, cuddling her beloved pooch, or with her head buried in a book.

Printed in Great Britain
by Amazon

23467471R00158